THE END
of the
WORLD

and Other Catastrophes

D1359617

THE END
of the
WORLD

and Other Catastrophes

edited by

MIKE ASHLEY

This collection first published in 2019 by
The British Library
96 Euston Road
London NW1 2DB

Introduction and notes © 2019 Mike Ashley

Cataloguing in Publication Data
A catalogue record for this publication is available from the British Library

ISBN 978 0 7123 5273 4
e-ISBN 978 0 7123 6472 0

Frontispiece illustration from the first publication of
The Last American by J.A. Mitchell, Frederick A. Stokes and Brother, 1889.

Cover artwork © David A Hardy / www.astroart.org
Cover design by Jason Anscomb
Text design and typesetting by Tetragon, London
Printed in England by CPI Group (UK) Ltd, Croydon, CRO 4YY

CONTENTS

INTRODUCTION

T.S. Eliot memorably wrote in his melancholic post-war poem "The Hollow Men", "This is the way the world ends, not with a bang but a whimper."

Eliot was thinking about the horrors of the Great War and the suffering both physical and psychological of the soldiers who met their deaths on the battlefields, and of the survivors who lived with disabled bodies and minds. There were those, including Sir Winston Churchill, who compared the Great War to Armageddon, the final battle forecast in the Bible's Book of Revelation, between good and evil.

Despite the millions of lives lost in the Great War, it was not the end of human life on Earth, or the end of the world, for all it must have seemed like it to many. Throughout the history of the Earth there have been cataclysms that came perilously close. 250 million years ago a major calamity or series of disasters brought about the extinction of over 95% of all life in the sea and over 70% of life on land. It is not fully known whether this was caused by a significant impact event, such as a giant asteroid, or by runaway volcanic action, but whatever the cause, it is a miracle that life survived at all. There were other such major catastrophes in the Earth's early years, the best known being 66 million years ago when the Earth collided with an asteroid resulting in the extinction of most of the dinosaurs.

There have been plenty of disasters during the period of human life on Earth, not least the end of the last Ice Age about 12,000 years ago which saw the rise of sea levels. This, of course, happened over generations but probably enough during certain lifetimes to become imprinted upon human consciousness. There may have been more sudden events, such as the deluge which rapidly expanded the Black Sea as a result of overflow from the Mediterranean. The dating of this is uncertain but could have happened as recently as 5600BC. This has led some to speculate that this might be the origin of the story of the Biblical Flood at the time of Noah, and there are plenty of ancient stories about a Deluge to suggest that rising sea levels caused floods across the globe, though not covering the whole surface of the Earth.

Humans will have witnessed some major cosmic impacts. One such collision about 3000BC created what is now called the Burckle Crater in the Indian Ocean which would have caused massive floods throughout the region. A probable meteor impact in China in AD 1490, known as the Ch'ing-yang event, is believed to have caused the deaths of over ten thousand people. Many major volcanic eruptions have devastated localities, such as that of Vesuvius in AD79 which destroyed Pompeii and Herculaneum in Italy. The massive eruptions of Mount Tambora in 1815 and Krakatoa in 1883, both in Indonesia, not only killed tens of thousands and left devastation locally but had a significant global impact.

Cosmic collisions, volcanos and floods were three major catastrophes humans experienced and feared, but they were not the only disasters. Plagues and epidemics were considerably more common and thus a more immediate threat. The Black Death of the mid fourteenth century is the one we all know from history, and is believed to have wiped out about a third of the population of Europe. An earlier plague in the sixth and seventh centuries is believed to have killed half the population of Europe. Other epidemics over the centuries include smallpox, malaria, typhus, cholera, measles and, of course, influenza. The pandemic of Spanish flu that followed the First World War in 1918 caused the deaths of over 75 million people worldwide.

In our present time the possibility of apocalyptic events has multiplied, with the threats of nuclear annihilation, climate change, new forms of plague and even economic or social collapse through cyber attacks or internet meltdown. We may all be apprehensive that we may experience a major catastrophe at any moment.

It has been said that this generation is the first to realize it can destroy the planet. But in fact, every generation has had its fears and that has been reflected in science fiction. The writers included in this anthology and discussed further below suspected we could destroy the world over a century ago.

This anthology brings together thirteen stories which consider a wide range of catastrophes, some global others more local—London being a particular target—showing the concerns of the public from the late nineteenth century into the twentieth. The threat of cosmic annihilation was matched by fears of pollution, plague, flood, fire and, with the conquest of the atom, nuclear devastation. Moreover, civilization itself is a threat, through over industrialization and meddling with the balance of nature. The planet may continue to exist for millions of years, but will humanity? The final two stories consider what may happen after a nuclear war.

To set these stories in context the following explores in more detail how our fears for our survival have inspired fiction over the last two centuries.

THE ENDS OF THE EARTH

Towards the end of *The Time Machine* (1895) H.G. Wells's Time Traveller ventures thirty million years into the future to witness a dying Earth. A bloated livid red sun covers a tenth of the sky, the atmosphere is thin, and the world seems lifeless apart from a black tentacled blob clinging to a rock. Such was his vision of the last days of Earth.

It's a memorable image, but not the first to depict a dying Earth. Almost eighty years before, in July 1816, Lord Byron published his poem "Darkness", which begins:

> I had a dream, which was not all a dream.
> The bright sun was extinguish'd, and the stars
> Did wander darkling in the eternal space,
> Rayless, and pathless, and the icy earth
> Swung blind and blackening in the moonless air…

And ends:

> The world was void,
> The populous and the powerful was a lump,
> Seasonless, herbless, treeless, manless, lifeless—
> A lump of death—a chaos of hard clay.
> The rivers, lakes and ocean all stood still,
> And nothing stirr'd within their silent depths;
> Ships sailorless lay rotting on the sea,
> And their masts fell down piecemeal: as they dropp'd
> They slept on the abyss without a surge—
> The waves were dead; the tides were in their grave,
> The moon, their mistress, had expir'd before;
> The winds were wither'd in the stagnant air,
> And the clouds perish'd; Darkness had no need
> Of aid from them—She was the Universe.

Byron was impelled to write this vision because 1816 was a bleak year, known as the Year without a Summer. It had been caused by the explosive eruption of Mount Tambora in Indonesia in April 1815. Its effect in Europe was devastating. The sun was obscured for most of the year. Rain was incessant, temperatures plummeted and crops failed, leading to the worst famine in Europe in living memory. An Italian astronomer from Bologna who had observed increased sun-spot activity predicted that the sun would go out on 18 July 1816 and this caused widespread panic with rioting and looting. One report told that on 11 July in Ghent a recently arrived regiment of cavalry sounded their trumpets that evening during a thunderstorm. The town's inhabitants rushed out of their homes and threw themselves on the ground believing this was the Last Trump and the Day of Judgement was at hand.

This may seem laughable today, but the weather and harvest had been so abominable that year that many believed Armageddon was imminent. This happened at the end of two appalling decades that had seen the worst atrocities of the French Revolution and the horrors of the Napoleonic Wars. Britain and Europe were at their lowest ebb. A few years earlier the author Anne Laetitia Barbauld had published a poem "Eighteen Hundred and Eleven" (1812) which forecast that the Napoleonic Wars would be the ruin of Britain. She wrote, in part:

> England, the seat of arts, be only known
> By the grey ruin and the mouldering stone;
> That Time may tear the garland from her brow,
> And Europe sit in dust, as Asia now.

Those of the gentry and aristocracy who had experienced the Grand Tour of Europe had witnessed the ruins of ancient Rome,

Greece and Egypt and knew that great empires could crumble and die. Percy Bysshe Shelley caught this mood brilliantly in his poem "Ozymandias", completed at the end of 1817. It talks of a traveller in a desert finding the ruined statue of the pharaoh Ozymandias. The poem quotes the inscription and ends:

> "My name is Ozymandias, King of Kings;
> Look on my Works, ye Mighty, and despair!"
> Nothing beside remains. Round the decay
> of that colossal Wreck, boundless and bare
> the lone and level sands stretch far away.

It became fashionable to paint images of Britain's public places in ruins, such as those by Joseph Gandy, comparing them to the grandeur of Rome and depicting the British Empire as the equal of any empire of antiquity. But it also planted in the minds of many the idea of future desolation and the ruin of greatness.

These visions of death and decay were further fuelled by the theory of population growth put forward by Thomas Malthus in his *Essay on the Principle of Population* in 1798. He believed that population growth would outstrip the production of food, although there were the inevitable checks on growth, notably plague, famine and war.

This mood of doom and despair at the start of the nineteenth century inevitably led to speculation in fiction. The one-time French priest Jean-Baptiste Cousin de Grainville turned his mind to the end of humanity in *Le Dernier Homme* (1805). It is told in both quasi-religious and quasi-scientific terms. In the far future the Earth has been ruined by mankind and humanity has become sterile. The last fertile man, Omegarus, is seeking the last fertile woman, Syderia, whom he discovers in Brazil. Returning to Europe they are met by the First Man, Adam, who has been kept alive by God to witness the decline of his progeny. Adam convinces Omegarus and Syderia not to bear children and with that all hope of mankind ends.

The book, which Cousin de Grainville had worked on since he was sixteen, was only a draft for a projected prose poem which he never completed. Early in 1805, already deeply depressed, he fell ill of a fever and drowned himself. It was left to others to publish the book which initially had extremely poor sales. It steadily gained a readership, especially in England where an anonymous but corrupt translation as *The Last Man* was published in 1806.

One work it inspired was the poem "The Last Man" by Thomas Campbell which, though written in 1806, was not published until 1823. When reprinted in 1825 the literary world suddenly discovered it and argued it was a plagiarism of Byron's "Darkness" even though Campbell claimed it was the other way round. The resulting furore led to a rash of poems, a satire of the concept by Thomas Hood, a story in *Blackwood's Magazine*, and a projected stage play, all in 1826. But more significant, and what cemented the genre in fiction, was a novel, *The Last Man*, by no less than Mary Shelley, the author of *Frankenstein*.

In the years since she completed *Frankenstein*, Mary had become increasingly despondent, grieving from the accumulated loss of her husband, her children and close friends. This poured from her in *The Last Man* where many of the characters are transparent portrayals of her acquaintances, including Percy Shelley and Lord Byron. It is set at the end of the twenty-first century when Britain has become a republic. Plague is raging across Europe and though Britain tries to isolate itself, it too falls prey. The plague motif accurately reflected the known peril of a cholera epidemic which had started in India in 1817 and spread throughout Asia and east Africa, halted, albeit temporarily, in 1824. The last few survivors try to reach Switzerland, believing the plague is less virulent there, but all but one are drowned in a storm. The Last Man, Lionel Verney, makes it to Rome and decides he will wander ceaselessly across Europe and Africa.

It's a depressing novel and was criticized mercilessly at the time but is now seen as a key book in the evolution of apocalyptic fiction. Brian Aldiss remarked that her description of the end of the human race was "striking", to the point of "alarming." The image of a lone survivor exploring the world in hope and despair has become a key image of the genre.

If the French Revolution, the climate, and the Asian cholera epidemic had inspired the emergence of apocalyptic fiction, the next factor came from the heavens. Comets had long been seen as portents of doom, such as the one portrayed in the Bayeux Tapestry just before the invasion of England by the Normans in 1066. Science was steadily getting to grips with the nature of comets, especially the realization that they orbited the Sun, like the planets, and thus returned periodically. Most famously Edmund Halley predicted that the comet now named after him would be seen again in 1758, and this proved to be true, though it was a few months later than Halley's calculations, believed to be because of the gravitational influences of the outer planets, notably Jupiter. Consequently, people realized that even though comet trajectories could be calculated, external influences could still mean the comet and Earth might collide.

The concern about comets grew in 1832 when it was realized that Biela's comet, which had a periodicity of 6.6 years, would pass through the same plane of orbit as the Earth in late October. Calculations showed that there was a gap of over sixty days between

the comet and the Earth but people had already speculated that
if Halley's comet could be late, so might Biela's. It wasn't just an
impact with the comet that concerned everyone but that passing
through the comet's tail might prove sufficiently injurious as to
"destroy all animal and vegetable life" as a reporter wrote in the *Bury
and Norwich Post*. The American poet and essayist Oliver Wendell
Holmes depicted a scene in his poem "The Comet" (1832) which,
whilst somewhat tongue-in-cheek, nevertheless conjured up such
frightening images as eyes popping, brains frying and animals
bursting into flames. In one stanza he wrote:

> And what would happen to the land,
> And how would look the sea,
> If in the bearded devil's path
> Our earth should chance to be?
> Full hot and high the sea would boil,
> Full red the forests gleam;

Other destructive qualities of a comet were considered by the enig-
matic S. Austin, Jr. in "The Comet" (1838) which includes a philo-
sophical discussion of whether God would allow the Earth to be
destroyed, all to no avail as the comet does indeed strike the Earth.
Similarly, in "The Conversation of Eiros and Charmion" (1839) Edgar
Allan Poe tells of a passing comet that sucks the nitrogen from the
Earth's atmosphere leaving pure oxygen, which ignites.

The comet became the doom of choice for many writers
throughout the nineteenth century and into the twentieth, though
increasingly authors sort ways to avoid the threat or to explore the
post-apocalyptic events. Astronomers observing Biela's comet in
1845 discovered it had split in two. It became harder to detect but

in 1872 it was believed that a spectacular meteor shower had been caused by debris from the comet. Many still believed that enough of the comet remained to prove a danger to Earth and some resurrected the old and long discredited theory of the Comte de Buffon that the solar system had been created when a comet grazed the Sun and disturbed masses of material. Perhaps the same might happen to the Earth, an idea developed by Jules Verne a few years later in one of his least satisfactory novels, *Hector Servadec* (serial, 1877). Here the comet, Gallia, crashes into the Earth and takes away with it a large fragment on which some thirty-or-so individuals try and survive until the comet returns them to Earth two years later.

An Austrian scientist, Rudolf Falb, predicted in 1892 that Tempel's comet, which had a short-term orbital period of five-and-a-half years, would collide with the Earth in 1895, a date he later revised to 13 November 1899 at 3.09. Since this coincided with the end of the millennium it caused considerable panic, mostly in Russia where it was believed the comet would strike.

George Griffith chose a more positive response to the comet threat. In "The Great Crellin Comet" he took the remarkable step of having a missile fired at the comet in order to destroy it before it struck the Earth. Griffith was the first to have a countdown for firing the missile. In "The Star", published the same month (both Christmas 1897), H.G. Wells has a rogue piece of space flotsam create tidal pressures and earthquakes destroying much of humanity, although the worst effects are alleviated by the Moon passing between the "star" and the Earth. Wells returned to this theme a decade later with *In the Days of the Comet* (1906) but this time the human race is affected only by the gases in the comet's tail which creates a euphoria leading to altruism. Despite both stories being very different in treatment, in each case Wells saw the effects of a comet or space flotsam being beneficial in the long-term. Sir Arthur Conan Doyle explored the same thoughts in *The Poison Belt* (1913) though here his scientist hero, Professor Challenger, is convinced the belt of gas the Earth will pass through in space is toxic and will destroy all of mankind. Although it has only a short-term effect, it allowed Doyle to portray a desolate London strewn with what look like the dead.

Richard Jefferies had taken a different course in *After London* (1885). This is set over a century after some unexplained disaster, possibly caused by a comet or asteroid, had cataclysmic effects upon the Earth, tilting the planet on its axis, changing the climate and having a deep psychological impact upon humanity. The result is an almost desolate, overgrown England, much altered, with a central lake and a deeply polluted area that was once London. Jefferies was one of a growing number who, horrified at the pollution inflicted upon England by factories and over-industrialization, looked back to more bucolic times.

Pollution had already been central to *The Doom of the Great City* (1880) by William Delisle Hay where the narrator looks back sixty years to the collapse of London in 1882 as a result of excessive smog. People have had enough and there is a massive exodus from the city leaving behind the corpses of those who have succumbed to the fumes.

These two books, with London as their focus, started a vogue in the popular magazines of the time, for stories portraying London as the epicentre of catastrophes of all kinds. Robert Barr started the trend in his magazine *The Idler* with "The Doom of London" (1892) which repeats Hay's idea of a London suffocating in the smog. Fred M. White wrote a six-part series under the generic title "The Doom of London" (1903) where London is threatened by climate change (extreme snow), bubonic plague, pollution, earthquakes as a result of the underground system, and financial ruin on the stock market. The consequences of climate change are included in other stories here whether arising naturally, in Cutcliffe Hyne's "London's Danger" (1896), or through a meddlesome scientist, in Herbert Ridout's "The Freezing of London" (1909).

The idea of a scientist holding the world to ransom with a new weapon of mass destruction dates back at least as far as "The Case of Summerfield" (1871) by William Henry Rhodes. Here a scientist claims he has a method of separating all the world's water into its constituent parts of hydrogen and oxygen which will then combust unless he is paid a million dollars. Jules Verne had introduced his super-scientist inventor known only by the name Captain Nemo in *Twenty Thousand Leagues Under the Sea* (serial, 1869-70) but Nemo is not intent on destroying the world. His later eccentric scientist Robur, in *Robur the Conqueror* (1886) and more particularly its sequel *Master of the World* (1904), does rise to the heights of megalomania in believing he can rule the world through his amazing flying machine.

The egotistical super-scientist or master criminal intent on world domination has since become such a stock item in science fiction that it is accepted as the norm, and features regularly in spy novels, such as Blofeld in the James Bond novel *Thunderball* (1961). One Victorian author who developed this theme was E. Douglas Fawcett. In *Hartmann the Anarchist; or the Doom of a Great City* (1893) the eponymous super-villain wreaks havoc on London which he destroys by his all-powerful airships.

Fawcett's novel was illustrated by Fred T. Jane, who later became a brand name with *Jane's Fighting Ships*. Jane also wrote novels and in *The Violet Flame* (1899) introduced perhaps the ultimate mad scientist and the ultimate catastrophe. Professor Mirzabeau, known as The

Beast, has discovered how to use the atomic power released from the hydrogen atom to create a disintegrator ray with which he controls the world. Just a few colleagues and friends are immune thanks to a disc Mirzabeau invents which negates the ray. By subterfuge Mirzabeau is killed and his machines destroyed, before everyone realizes that one of his machines was holding back a comet heading to Earth. The comet plunges into the Earth destroying all human, animal and plant life. Only two people who have the special discs survive and become the Adam and Eve of the new world.

Jane wasn't the first to consider atomic energy. Four years earlier, Robert Cromie had published *The Crack of Doom* (1895) in which another megalomaniac, Herbert Brande, believes not just the Earth but the whole solar system is corrupt and that it needs to be restored to its virgin state. He has perfected a method for releasing energy from the hydrogen and oxygen in water with devastating results. Although his plans are thwarted it is not before he destroys an entire island in a scene reminiscent of the detonation of the first atomic bomb. H.G. Wells took this to the logical conclusion in *The World Set Free* (1914) in which governments fight for control of the process for creating atomic bombs with the result that most of the Earth's major cities are destroyed. In *The Man Who Rocked the Earth* (serial 1914) by Arthur Train and Robert Williams Wood, which appeared a few months after Wells's novel, a megalomaniac succeeds in halting the Great War, demonstrating his power by creating a channel from the Mediterranean to the Sahara desert. When his demands aren't met he uses his awesome power to tilt the Earth on its axis. It transpires he has mastered atomic energy, derived from uranium, with which he can counteract gravity.

There were scores of mad scientist novels in the inter-war years, many involving the discovery of atomic power, such as *Green Fire*

(1928) by John Taine where the release of atomic energy not only threatens the Earth but the entire galaxy. A literary descendant of these stories is included here, with Warwick Deeping's "The Madness of Professor Pye" (1933) where we encounter both a mad scientist and an atomic death ray.

While some writers were exploring how scientists could create ever greater weapons to destroy the world, others still considered how the Earth itself could be its greatest enemy. In *The Purple Cloud* (1901) M.P. Shiel wipes out most of mankind by a toxic hydrocyanic acid gas released following volcanic action. The narrator, Jeffson, was the only survivor of an expedition to the North Pole, where the gas had not reached, and he returns to civilization to find everywhere deserted. He explores Britain and Europe looking for others but grows despondent and his sanity is tested. He starts to destroy all the cities. After seventeen years alone, he is amazed to discover a woman in Constantinople. By now his mental state is such that he tries to kill her but she survives and eventually they reconcile. It will be no surprise that Jeffson's first name is Adam. Leaving aside Jeffson's misogyny, many regard this as Shiel's best novel and, according to critic E.F. Bleiler, the best last-man novel.

Jack London was almost as cynical as Shiel in *The Scarlet Plague* (serial 1912) where near the end of the twenty-first century a disease, which kills in a few hours, sweeps across the world. There are only a handful of survivors all returning to primitivism. London has the story told by a grandfather to his grandchildren, but the children, who are illiterate, find it hard to believe his description of the civilized world and the old man holds out little hope.

Many of the stories written either side of the First World War were cynical about the future. In *The Last Generation* (1908) James

Elroy Flecker, best known for his stage play *Hassan*, has the narrator whisked through different stages of the future by the Wind of Time. Society becomes obsessed by death, with suicide clubs and a ban on childbirth. Eventually mankind destroys itself but the narrator witnesses a group of apes seeking to control fire. *The Lord of the World* (1907) by R.H. Benson describes a religious apocalypse when God intervenes and destroys the world after a secular world government, ruled by the Anti-Christ, has banned all religion and where wars have already destroyed most of civilization. In *The Second Deluge* (1912) by Garrett P. Serviss few believe a scientist who claims a spiral nebula consisting of water will engulf the Earth and, as with Noah, when Versal builds his ark, he is mocked. The nebula strikes and the world is drowned but a few who had taken notice of Versal had prepared and survive though the population is drastically reduced.

In *Darkness and Dawn* (1915) by George Allan England some unexplained disaster, possibly an asteroid grazing the Earth, has left a huge chasm on the North American continent and released a gas that killed most of mankind. Our hero survives through suspended animation and awakes to discover a world that has reverted to savagery. Likewise, in *The People of the Ruins* (1920), written within months of the end of the War, Edward Shanks sees considerable social strife and predicts a General Strike for 1924 (he was just two years out). The Strike leads to economic and social collapse so that in little more than a century civilization clings on by the slightest thread with every possibility of a reversion to barbarism which is finally provoked by an outbreak of war.

In *The Torch* (serial 1920) by Jack Bechdolt a radioactive comet destroys most of mankind and the few survivors split into two factions with a form of medieval aristocracy living in skyscrapers and the feudal serfs living in underground tunnels. The "torch" of the title is the Torch of the Statue of Liberty which was destroyed but a new one is created and becomes the symbol of freedom. J.J. Connington, better known for his detective novels, portrayed an especially ruthless future in *Nordenholt's Million* (1923). An accident releases a virulent new bacterium that attacks all plant life and before long the world will have no food. Nordenholt, a millionaire, creates an enclave in Scotland to escape the bacterium and horde food. Meanwhile there is organized genocide throughout the rest of Britain to protect the enclave. It is later discovered that a few other enclaves survived elsewhere but it is only as the bacterium itself fails and with the discovery of atomic energy that the world starts to recover, with few lessons learned. In *Deluge* (1928) and its sequel *Dawn* (1929), S. Fowler Wright was less concerned with the catastrophe itself—where upheavals in the Earth's crust led to much of the land sinking beneath the oceans but elsewhere parts rising, making England a series of islands—but with the aftermath and how the survivors rebuild society. Wright explores the various factions that emerge and shows, with evident despondency, how difficult it will be to have any form of decent society. The upheaval of the Earth becomes an allegory for the upheaval of humanity and how society itself becomes a series of islands that have little in common.

Throughout the 1920s and 1930s there was a growing belief that the power of the atom would be released to devastating effect. Even the best-selling writer of occult romances, Marie Corelli, considered the problem in *The Secret Power* (1921) where a physicist manages to create atomic bombs that could be carried in a suitcase. When they are accidentally detonated they cause chaos. Fred MacIsaac was intriguingly prescient in "World Brigands" (serial, 1928) where in 1940 a war is threatened by Europe against the

United States. The American government claims it has a devastating secret weapon (which it doesn't) but a private organization does develop an atomic bomb and when tested in the Nevada desert brings an end to the potential hostilities. The weapon in *The Last Man* (1940) by Alfred Noyes, is not described in much detail but is effectively a death ray which stops the heart from any distance. Rapidly all the nations of the world arm themselves with this weapon but, as Noyes notes:

> The result was that all the combatants, in all parts of the world, possessed a secret weapon so formidable that, to do them justice, most of them would have shrunk with horror from using it, except—and this was the fatal reservation—*except in the last resort.*

Unfortunately, a megalomaniac does use it and the resulting retaliation wipes out most of mankind. Were it not for the fanatic the world would have held an uneasy peace. Noyes had predicted the nuclear stalemate which is what has existed since the first atom bombs were used in 1945.

No one, apart from a few scientists and science-fiction writers, had understood the devastation that a nuclear bomb could unleash and it has become the Sword of Damocles hanging over all our heads. Since 1945 there have been hundreds of novels depicting a post-nuclear world, far too many to cover here. They include *The Long Loud Silence* (1952) by Wilson Tucker where a nuclear attack was made worse by bacteriological warfare resulting in quarantine for the survivors; *Alas, Babylon* (1959) by Pat Frank where events following the downing of a Soviet spy plane spiral out of control and nuclear war erupts with few survivors; *On the Beach* (1957) by Nevil Shute where an all-out nuclear war destroys all life in the northern hemisphere and where the southern hemisphere will eventually succumb as the global weather patterns carries the radiation to the rest of the world; and *Red Alert* (1958; also as *Two Hours to Doom*) by Peter George where a nuclear war is only narrowly avoided after a paranoid general despatches a nuclear attack on the Soviet Union. This book inspired the film *Dr. Strangelove* (1964). In the real world the Cuban missile crisis of October 1962 brought us as close to the possibility of nuclear war as we ever want to be.

The fact that civilization fails to learn any lessons and that any post-apocalyptic society will have difficult surviving continues in fiction to this day. One of the classics of science-fiction is *Earth Abides* (1949) by George R. Stewart where a disease wipes out most of humanity, and despite every effort by the main character and his son, the future of human life seems doomed. David Brin was more positive in *The Postman* (1985), which has close similarities to *Earth Abides*, with its lead character travelling through a United States devastated by bio-engineered plagues. He hints that given time a decent society might eventually emerge, but it would be far from easy.

It should be no surprise that during the 1950s a significant number of British science-fiction novels brought the nation and the world under threat of destruction. Britain had survived the Second World War but was left with its scars not just in the physical destruction from bombs and air raids, but the mental cost of the returning soldiers who had lived through the horrors of war, and of the British at home, in constant fear of invasion. Brian W. Aldiss dubbed these novels "cosy" catastrophes. He did not mean that the catastrophe itself was not formidable, but that the narrator of the events somehow seemed to escape the worst of the disaster. Aldiss wrote his own cosy catastrophe in *Greybeard* (1964) which took T.S.

Eliot's "not with a bang but a whimper" almost literally. As a result of nuclear bomb tests, the entire human race is rendered infertile meaning that the current generation is the last.

The best known of the doom merchants of the 1950s were John Wyndham and John Christopher. Wyndham's horrors usually originated from outer space, notably in *The Day of the Triffids* (1951) and *The Kraken Wakes* (1953) whilst Christopher's were closer to home. His best known work, *The Death of Grass* (1956), in which a virus affects all grains and grasses leading to famine and a breakdown in society, still has resonance today. During the 1950s and 1960s society is threatened by snow in *White August* (1955) by John Boland, plague in *A Scent of New-Mown Hay* (1958) by John Blackburn, global deluge in *The Drowned World* (1962) by J.G. Ballard and a Biblical plague of insects in *The Furies* (1966) by Keith Roberts. In two of Charles Eric Maine's novels nuclear tests have dire results. In *The Tide Went Out* (1958) the tests crack open the Earth's crust so that all the seas drain away. In *The Darkest of Nights* (1962) the tests cause viruses to mutate into an incurable plague.

Whilst many disaster stories are set in the present or near future some consider the end of the world on a more cosmic time scale. In *La fin du monde* (serial 1893), translated as *Omega: The Last Days of the World* (1894), the French astronomer Camille Flammarion has the Earth almost destroyed by a giant comet. Despite a kaleidoscopic meteor-shower and global storm most of humanity survives, except new-born children. Flammarion uses the comet as a portent to explore how life on Earth develops but then declines till only a few humans remain. The Earth cools, water dissipates and Earth dies, but... life on Jupiter is just beginning.

Flammarion's long-term vision of a dying Earth inspired others. His fellow countryman and Professor of Philosophy, Gabriel de

Tarde, considered a future World State faced with the cooling of the Sun in "Fragment d'histoire future" (1896), later translated as *Underground Man* (1905). After much of the Earth's surface freezes the survivors build a new world underground, utilizing the heat of the Earth. J.-H. Rosny *ainé*, seen by many as the successor to Jules Verne, created a bleak far-future in his novella "La mort de la terre" (1910) where both human exploitation and geological upheavals result in a dry almost uninhabitable landscape. Humans are becoming extinct and are being replaced by a totally new form of life, based on iron, the "ferromagnetics", which can draw upon the iron in human blood. An even more dramatic far-future vision is *The Night Land* (1912) by William Hope Hodgson. Set millions of years in the future when the sun has been extinguished, what is left of humanity exists in two Redoubts. The rest of the world is uninhabitable by humans but is the domain of many bizarre creatures which one of the inhabitants must face as he tries to rescue the last survivor from the smaller Redoubt.

The grand visionary of the future was Olaf Stapledon. In *Last and First Men* (1930), which covers a mere two billion years, and *Star Maker* (1937), which covers a hundred billion years, Stapledon follows the future history and evolution not just of mankind but of our solar system and the universe as it was then imagined. The ultimate revelation that the Creator—the Star Maker itself, or Cosmic Mind—is still experimenting to master the art of creating universes and improvements still need to be made.

These visions of a far future, and the imagery of a world where the sun has gone or will soon die, is haunting and addictive. As we saw in *The Time Machine*, Wells saw the last days of the sun ten million years in the future. In "The Last Days of Earth" (1901), George C. Wallis has the Earth freeze and the last two humans leave the planet thirteen million years in the future. The teenage prodigy G. Peyton Wertenbaker explored the end in "The Coming of the Ice" (1926) in which the world's only immortal man watches the changes in mankind and the world for millions of years until the sun grows cold and the world freezes. The same mood is evoked by John W. Campbell, Jr., the editor of *Astounding SF* (later *Analog*), in "Twilight" (1934) and its sequel "Night" (1935) where, seven million years in the future, humanity is all but extinct and fully automated cities continue to function and, indeed, supersede mankind. It is ten billion years in the future in *Against the Fall of Night* (1948) by Arthur C. Clarke when what remains of humanity survives in domed cities, not unlike in *The Night Land*, unaware of each other's existence. As the novel develops survivors discover that forebears had created a being of pure mentality, but it was insane and had almost destroyed the galaxy. That idea had been used by Donald Wandrei in "The Red Brain" (1927) where almost all planets in the Universe have crumbled into dust and only one world survives, Antares, which is enclosed in a glass shell. The world is becoming overwhelmed by the cosmic dust and the few surviving giant brains try to find how to rid the universe of the dust. They place their reliance in the Red Brain, a being of unbelievable powers but, alas, the Red Brain is insane.

And so we end as we began with a universe of darkness. But perhaps the universe itself is cyclical, an idea that was once held to be consistent with the Big Bang theory, meaning that if the universe is expanding, it might reach an ultimate limit and then begin to contract to a singularity, called the Big Crunch, from which there is a new Big Bang. Of all the stories and novels using this theme, the one that stands out is *Tau Zero* (1970) by Poul Anderson. A spaceship, designed to reach speeds approaching that of light, malfunctions and the crew cannot slow it down. They travel farther and farther into the future at such a speed that whilst time is normal to them, billions of years pass outside the ship. In the end they pass through the contraction of the universe, the Big Crunch and the next Big Bang and enter a new universe to find what might be a new Earth.

Perhaps there is no end after all...

MIKE ASHLEY

THE END OF THE WORLD

Helen Sutherland

This story gets us off to a rousing start by covering just about every catastrophe that can afflict mankind in a little over fifteen hundred words. I have been unable to determine whether or not it was by the patron of the arts Helen Christian Sutherland (1881–1965). Whilst it seems unlikely, Sutherland was such a maverick that this may just represent her view of our future!

I HAVE DREAMED A DREAM, AND THE MANNER OF MY DREAMING was thus. I stood on a high place, overlooking the nations of the world. I beheld them arise from the chaos occasioned by the third World War, and saw that they strove yet once again to build up a world peace. And I saw in my dream that the populations of the world had undergone a change. I saw women in offices; women in factories; women in workshops, in greater numbers than had ever before been known. The vehicles that whirled up and down the roadways of town and country, the trains and the various aircraft that winged their ways across the face of the sky—were all in the power of women. I saw men grown arrogant, by reason of their exceeding scarcity. Like Sultans they strode about among a mass of womenkind—issuing orders, exacting homage, expecting and receiving obedience and devotion wherever they went. They married and had children, but of those families it was the female sex that predominated—daughters, aunts, sisters, mothers, grandmothers—all these increased and multiplied mightily, but of sons, uncles, brothers, fathers, and grandfathers there was a very great falling-off.

The seasons came and went, and lo! it was winter, and I saw a winged Blackness appear over the rim of the world. So black was the apparition that the sun and the moon were darkened, and so mighty were its pinions that in a little space they had borne the Blackness over all the nations of the earth. Now this winged horror was Plague, and I saw in my dream that the peoples of every nation were stricken down in their hundreds and in their thousands—but when, after a time, the darkness cleared from off the face of the earth—lo, it was the males of every nation that had succumbed!

Then in my dream I looked down into the bowels of the earth, into the coal mines, the ore mines, and into the secret places where precious gems lie hid—and there were women there! I looked upon the swift ships as they sped here and there over the waters of the world; and down below the waters where fair pearls are to be found—and lo, there were women there also. In the fields and the vineyards, and upon the hillsides where grazed the herds and the flocks, there women were also.

Then in my dream did all the great nations of the earth make a decree, that every man, from every city, town or village, should meet in one place and discuss, with the wisest and most learned in the land, how they might avert the approaching disaster that threatened the world, in the declining of its male populations. It was determined, therefore, that the meeting-place for this immense convocation should be a certain island in the mid-Pacific, as being the spot most convenient for every nation. From all parts of the earth they came, and it was a great marvel to see so many men gathered together at one time, in one place. The sky above the island was dark with aircraft of every description, and the women therein gazed down with eager, marvelling eyes, at a sight so exceeding strange. And I saw in my dream that a great storm arose and blew across the ocean, lashing its waters to white-foamed fury, and wrecking very many of the aircraft that kept their vigil over the island. And a great earthquake shook the island to its foundations. Buildings fell with the noise of thunder, the earth heaved and cracked, and the vast halls in which was gathered the flower of the world's manhood tottered and crashed to utter ruin. Then did I perceive that there was great consternation among the women of the world, and the sound of their wailing rose on the wind. For now there were scarce a hundred thousand men left on the earth. Nor did the rising generations bring any comfort into the desolate hearts of that vast population of women, since, for every fifty children born to them, one only was a boy.

Then were laws passed whereby a man should have wives in great number, and the mother of sons was honoured above all women. From being as Sultans and Lords of the earth, men, so I saw in my dream, became household treasures—cherished specimens. So overwhelmed did they become by the great forces of the opposite sex, that when a man met a man he scarce knew what to say or how to conduct himself towards his fellow male. Nor was any male allowed to go forth without a bodyguard of women, and every precaution that desperate brains could devise was taken in order to preserve the steadily decreasing male element throughout the world.

The seasons came and went, and I looked once more upon the earth. Then in my dream I beheld women in the Law Courts and in the robes of judges, magistrates, and all other dignitaries of the law. Women I beheld in the pulpits of the world, and in all offices of the Church, high or low. I turned to Governments and Parliaments of the nations. Here, too, my eyes beheld nought but women. Women sat on the chairs of presidents, on the seats of dictators, nay, on the very thrones of kings! And even as I looked, the male element of the human world dwindled and decreased. Further laws were passed whereby a man child, on the completion of his third year, became the property of the State. Large sums were paid from the countries' coffers to the parents of the young male, and his education and subsequent career were thereafter entirely in the hands of the State. Societies were formed, researches made, and experiments undertaken by the greatest scientists to discover the means of preserving and increasing mankind.

Then in my dream I became aware that no more men children were being born into the world. So great was the atmosphere of feminism, and so all-pervading was the female element, that it seemed as if no male being could survive therein. The existing men grew old, and one by one death claimed them. At length, so it appeared to me in my dream, a man child was born. Beacons flamed the good tidings from every hill. Bells rang out from a thousand steeples. Aircraft wrote the happy news in letters of fire and smoke across the skies. Upon the mother of the child, whose husband had died at the age of sixty-nine in the preceding month, were bestowed the highest orders, the most honourable titles that the nations of the world could give.

The child was reared with infinite care—protected by every means that Science could offer from the ills of babyhood, boyhood, and adolescence. In so great esteem was he held, and so marvellous was this man accounted in a world of women, that women from far and near flocked in endless pilgrimage to behold him. At the earliest possible age he was married, and in the following years vast palaces were built to house his retinue of wives. But as I watched I saw that no male issue blessed these unions.

The seasons came and went, and I beheld once more, in my dream, the nations of the earth—and lo, there arose a great cry of mourning through the lands, for the Last Man was lying desperately ill in one of the world's most, famous hospitals. Without the gates of the hospital I perceived an immense crowd of women. Like a great sea troubled by storm and tempest it heaved to and fro in the throes of anxiety and apprehension. Some women prayed, throwing up their arms in a frenzy of expectation; others beat upon the mammoth doors of the hospital's wide outer court; others waited in stony silence, their great eyes staring unseeingly at the balcony on the upper part of the vast building, inside which the Last Man, whitened with the snows of age, was lying.

Then did I see in my dream that doctors and surgeons of the highest skill and learning had been summoned from near and far, yea from the very ends of the earth, in order that the life of the Last Man might be prolonged. At length, so I saw, it was decided, after earnest discussion among these wise and skilful women, that only an operation of the most delicate and ingenious sort could save the patient. When it became known to the multitudes without a great silence fell over them—and in all the world was there no sound, only a vast apprehensive silence.

Then I beheld in my dream a woman, clothed in white, step out on to the balcony that overlooked that great crowd. Every eye was fixed on the famous surgeon—every ear strained to hear the result of the operation. Then did the words of the woman in white resound like the blast of trumpets, north and south and east and west—

"IT IS THE END OF THE WORLD."

The Three Dooms
of London

LONDON'S DANGER

C.J. Cutcliffe Hyne

It seems hard to imagine now but at the end of the 1890s Cutcliffe Hyne created a character who once rivalled Sherlock Holmes in popularity. This was Captain Kettle, or Red Kettle as he was often called, partly because of his red hair and beard but also because of his temper. He was fiery, fiercely independent and belligerent. A merchant seaman, who was essentially a "boat for hire" by whoever paid enough, Kettle first appeared as a secondary character in Honour of Thieves *(1895) but he proved so popular that* Pearson's Magazine *commissioned Hyne to make him a central character in a series of stories, which continued for the next forty years.*

    Charles John Cutcliffe Hyne (1866–1944) was something of a model for Kettle. He was an adventurer, serving on board ship and travelling around much of the globe. He started writing soon after leaving Cambridge University in 1887 and earned enough money to fulfil his ambition to explore the world. But the popularity of Captain Kettle made his work much in demand and though he still travelled, he was increasingly desk-bound. He has over sixty books to his credit, including ones under the pen-names Weatherby Chesney and Nicholson West. A fair proportion of his output qualifies as science fiction or fantastic adventure. The best known is The Lost Continent *(serial, 1899), itself a disaster novel as it deals with the destruction of Atlantis. Other titles include* Beneath Your Very Boots *(1889) about a lost world under England, and* Empire of the World *(1910) where a scientist has created a ray that can destroy iron and uses this to ensure peace in the world. The following story, published in 1896, shows how climate change could seriously affect Britain's standing in the world at the time when the British Empire was at its greatest extent.*

THE FIRST-CLASS CARRIAGE WE WERE IN WAS HEATED BY steam, we had each abundance of coats and rugs, our feet were on a fresh foot-warmer, but the draught of the hurricane crept in by a score of chinks, and the vehemence of the cold made us ache. At Doncaster we moved across to the Pullman car, and found that a trifle more endurable; but still I noted that Gerard's moustache continued to glisten with icicles.

At Grantham we had still further evidence (if such a thing were needed) of the lowness of the temperature. The express, which is timed to stop there only three minutes at the outside, made a wait that seemed interminable. The conductor, I saw, was getting uneasy. At length he buttoned his coat and went out into the freezing gale on the platform. In a minute he returned, purple-cheeked and blowing his fingers. He came to us with the tidings. Both driver and stoker of our engine were, it seemed, half perished with the exposure to that bitter cold; it was with difficulty they had brought the express to a standstill in the station; and they were utterly unfit to proceed further. It was doubtful, the conductor said, whether one of them, but I forgot which it was, would recover; and meanwhile the railway authorities were seeking substitutes to take us on to London. He said, too, that news had been brought down of a colossal fire in Hammersmith, but could add no details.

"Nice weather this for getting married in," said I; "if we'd had warning of this blizzard beforehand, I should either have shirked being your best man, or suggested having the affair postponed."

"If tomorrow's like this," said Gerard, "the wedding can't take place till the weather changes. It would be brutal to drag any woman out into such a nipping cold."

We saw men filling the engine with buckets from a well outside the station, because the ordinary water supply was frozen solid; and then the train began to move again, and slid out of Grantham into the open country. The south-westerly hurricane beat upon it till the flanges of the lee wheels grated upon the rails with a roar of sound; and in some of the heavier squalls I thought we should have been upset. A queer, lurid light hung in the sky. But with dogged slowness we crawled on, and drew up under the shelter of King's Cross station.

It was four o'clock, and we were three hours late. There was a bellow of life from the departure side of the station. I don't think I ever heard such a noise of trains and passengers; but where we were, the place seemed deserted. Half the roof was off, and there was not a porter to be seen. The platform was littered with dirty, trodden snow.

We got out, and I noticed that there were only two other passengers in the train. The conductor of the Pullman put out our luggage, and Gerard told him to order a hansom. There was only one on the rank—a thing that had never been known before since King's Cross station was built.

We got into that lonely cab, and told the muffled driver to take us to Queen's Gate, in Kensington. As the glass door was clattering down, a boy came out of some sheltered corner, and thrust in a paper.

"Evening paper, sir?" he cried. "There's half Chelsea on fire."

"Give him a penny, Methuen," said Gerard.

"No, sir," said the boy. "Five bob or nothing. I've only two papers left, and there's ten firemen killed. They say half London will be burnt."

I fumbled out two half-crowns, and the window closed down with a clash, and the cab drove off. Then I bent my head over the fluttering sheet and scanned the headlines: *"Disastrous fire." "Fanned by the furious gale." "All hydrants frozen!" "Every drop of water in London solid ice." "Nothing to check the flames." "Metropolis in terrible danger." "Suicide of the Chief of the Fire Brigade."*

The sky above us was full of driving blackness, but a strange yellow glare hung beneath it, and the print stood out clearly:

"The fire in Hammersmith, which we reported in our last edition," I read, "has since assumed gigantic proportions. The united fire brigades of London are helpless to cope with it. The unprecedented severity of the frost, and the fury of the hurricane, which is now upon us, have set at derision all our vaunted precautions.

"It is with water alone that our fire-extinguishing services have been hitherto armed to fight devouring flames; and now in this moment of our desperate need even a trickle of water is denied them. They are as helpless as the lay citizens.

"The fire in its awful majesty has beat down all resistance. Hammersmith is a burnt-out rubbish heap. West Kensington is a furnace. Amongst the dwellers in South Kensington and Chelsea there is more panic than an invading army could produce. So far as human eye can see, nothing but a change of wind or an act of God can save the greatest city ever built by man from being in the next few hours changed to twisted, smoking ruins."

Gerard dropped the paper with a cry of horror, and thrust up the hatch. "A fiver if you keep your horse at a gallop," he shouted to the cabman. "My God, Methuen," he said to me, "what an awful thing this is."

"The newspaper has made the worst of it for the sake of the sensation," I answered. "London is not built of wood; it is an impossible thing for the whole of it to burn."

"I'm thinking of Queen's Gate, and my little girl there. She'll have expected me three hours ago, and I'm here now."

The cab stopped with a jar against the curb. I scraped the frost rime from a window, and peered out. Five great dray-loads of household goods were coming thundering past us, with the horses at a gallop. We got beyond them, and entered Piccadilly. The street was one solid block of every imaginable kind of vehicle, bearing salvage and fugitives eastwards. With infinite trouble, our cabman wormed his way across the struggling mass, and tried to take us on our road by the smaller streets to southward; but these were one and all brim-filled by the traffic, or blocked by broken-down vehicles.

Gerard's impatience grew too great to be held in check any longer. He sprang from the cab, gave the man a ten-pound note, with orders to follow as best he could and started off through the hurrying crowds on foot.

Then for the first time we began fully to realize the fright which had bitten into five millions of people. The most orderly city on earth had turned into a seething nest of anarchy. Even the police made no effort to quell the terror or curb its lashings: they had their own houses and their own lives to think about. And as we went on, with the gale beating in our faces, we ourselves became smitten with the prevailing spirit.

We jostled and thrust at everyone that came in our way; we climbed over broken-down loads of rarities which lay in the roadways as though they had been so much coal. Three times I saw bodies lying motionless in my path, and the passers-by cursed as they stumbled against them, but no one stopped to help.

And once I saw a woman of elegant dress, who was driving a landau filled with trunks and boxes, drop the reins when a heavy dray cut off one of her wheels, and pull out a pistol and kill herself before a thousand lookers-on. But no one gave her more than a cursory glance. Each one looked ahead on his own path, and hurried away about his business, wrestling and thrusting amongst the others. And every minute the crush thickened, and every by-street vomited people.

The air grew warmer as we pressed on westwards. There was no glimpse of flame apparent yet; nothing but fat, black rolls of smoke could be seen overhead, with an underlining of yellow reflected from the distant blaze. And everywhere hung icicles, and the lines of the bursted water-mains glistened in the roadways. We were in an Arctic city more like St. Petersburg than the London we had known before.

There was the taint of burning in every breath we drew, and from the inky sky above fell a constant patter of charred embers. As we drew on, these embers grew bright, and by the time we were through Brompton (and seven had clanged out from some clock in the neighbourhood), live sparks were falling on the seething mobs in the streets, and the air grew sour with the smell of singeing cloth.

But by the time we got abreast of the South Kensington Museum, the glow of the flames was beginning to smear more lurid yellows against the amorphous black of the driving smoke clouds; and soon the thunder of the blaze and the crash of the trundling masonry came to us in a dim roar above the booming and swishing of the gale. The great warren of dwelling-houses to westward of us yielded up its thousand emigrants every minute. The fugitives had started out of home hugging their dearest possessions; but the din of that awful enemy which was sacking the city at their heels thrust terror into their hearts; and they had it taught them that to each one naked life is dearer than all else the world contains. So the streets were paved with the cream of the household goods, and we smashed with our feet a Jew's ransom with every mile we went.

The fire was advancing whole streets by the hour. Earl's Court was already half burnt out; the houses in a line with Cornwall Gardens and Emperor's Gate were beginning to yield up trickles of fire through their windows. The bright scoriæ from the volcano of fire fell around and on us more thickly as we pressed on. The mob thinned as we drew towards the seat of the blaze, and when we turned up Queen's Gate, the street, though half filled by furniture and *débris*, was almost deserted by human beings. The population had fled already. The gale was sending the flames horizontally, like the jet from a blow-pipe, across the house-tops.

Gerard by this time was nearly beside himself with anxiety and foreboding. But at last we reached the house, and Gerard dashed up the steps. The girl whom that morning he had thought to make his bride within the next thirty hours stood waiting for him in the doorway.

"Oh, my love," I heard her say, as she leant on his shoulder, "I am here alone. They have all gone. But you said you would come for me; and I knew you would if you were alive; and if you were not, I did not wish to live either."

But meanwhile the heat was growing upon us, and whilst I stood and watched, I saw flames beginning to spout from the upper windows of a house near the Cromwell Road.

A swirl of smoke came up and stung my eyes like nettles. "Look," I said, "we must go. This house will be burning in another ten minutes"; and at the word Miss Vivian picked up a jewel-case from a table in the hall, and came with Gerard down the steps. We were walking quickly northwards, and as we were passing Queen's Gate-terrace a man joined us whom I knew. His name is an old and an honoured one, but I omit it here for the sake of others who have borne the title.

"Oh!" he cried, "I am beggared! Fifty-five and beggared! What is that you have?" said he. "Jewels?" He snatched the morocco box from Miss Vivian's hands. "I must have something," he cried. "I refuse to starve." And he ran off howling.

A van stood in the roadway, with horses trembling and snorting. "The law is dead," I said. "Every man takes what he wants now. Jump in."

My friend and his promised wife got under the tilt of the van, away from the fiery shower which was raining on us, and I mounted the box. The horses sprang away at a gallop. At the end of the road was a tangled block. The furniture of two houses had been pitched out helter-skelter, and lay there in wild confusion. A hansom had tried to cross it, and the horse had broken a leg, and lay deserted, and moving feebly. But it was no time for hesitation. I charged my team at the barrier, and with a crash and a bang and a rattle we were over.

We crossed the Knightsbridge-road; and entered Kensington Gardens by the Queen's Gate. A water main had burst in the middle of the roadway, and thrust up an ice-fountain twenty feet in height. I headed across for the Marble Arch, intending to get to one of the railway stations, where we could run away north out of this horrible city of fire and terror.

But before we were half-way across the parks the scent of fire came to us anew, and the horses began to snort with fresh terror. Bayswater was blazing, Paddington was on fire, and soon the fingers of the flames would be seizing Oxford Street in their awful grip. There seemed no chance of a respite. The gale raged more furiously than ever. I turned and made for Hyde Park Corner, and as we drove I saw no fewer than ten huge trees crash down before the straining of the wind.

But past Hyde Park Corner I could get the van no farther. The roadways were piled up to the doors of the houses on either side with a mass of vehicles, and alive with madly plunging horses. Never was known such a scene since the world began. And there they were doomed to wait, in that inextricable tangle, till the flames swept up and ground them into smoke.

We deserted our van, and hand-in-hand we skirted that awful block. We rounded Buckingham Palace Gardens, and got down to Victoria Street; but that was impassable, and we were forced to make our way through unconsidered bye-paths where the crowds were less densely wedged.

Only once was our slow struggle onward interrupted. Of a sudden the air was split by a terrific roar; another followed; and another. The pavement beneath us shook, and the tall houses on either side shed dust. The gale for a moment stopped; then hit us with a fresh blast which there was no standing against; and then a tornado of dust and fragments swept down so thick that we could barely catch a breath. They were blowing up a line of houses along the forefront of the fire, in the desperate hope that the flames would not leap the gap.

The crowd realized what had happened, and began to surge onward again. We fought our way along in its eddies. The exertion was something fearful, and for long enough I struggled on like a man in a dream, with one hand dragging at Miss Vivian, and the other wrestling with the people who thronged us. By a sort of dull instinct I was heading for the eastward. Hours must have passed—though they seemed like years—and when my weariness had grown so great that it seemed I could not drag myself a yard further, I became dimly conscious that we were in Northumberland Avenue.

By a sort of natural impulse, and without a word being said, we turned into the Metropole. The hall of the hotel was filled with a rabble which would have done credit to the Ratcliffe Highway, and I duly wondered what they were doing there. But then I caught a glimpse of my own self in a mirror. My clothes were burnt full of holes; with the smoke and the falling soot I was black as a man who had worked a week in coal; I looked a greater outcast than any of them.

It seemed useless to ask for a room; in fact, there were no officials visible; each bedroom was overflowing, and in the corridors the grimy tenants made a human carpet. At length, up in the attics (where fewer of the crowd had dared to go through dread of the fire) we found a tiny room with only half a dozen occupants. Miss Vivian shared the bed with two other women, and Gerard and I threw ourselves on the floor and huddled against the others for warmth.

Sour-mouthed from want of sleep, I woke to the tune of splintering glass. Once more the fire was upon us. The gap of blown-up houses had done nothing to check its march. We roused the sleepers, and rushed to the stairways. Gleaming ice lay everywhere in the track of the bursted water pipes. The wind shook the great building as we ran towards the entrance, and the roar of the advancing fire re-echoed in the passages. A torrent of humanity was pouring out into Northumberland Avenue.

But I had no wish that we should be driven further eastward in that frightened sheep-pack before the wolves of flame. Retreat to the north was barred; we must get to the Surrey side; we must run somehow from this horrible city, where each in his blind terror was trampling down his neighbour.

We thrust our way through the crowds into Charing Cross Station, but the press was so great that the lines were blocked with writhing humanity, and no train could get in across the bridge. Then a thought occurred to me: The river was frozen, and we could make passage across the ice. We struggled back again, getting to the Embankment by Villiers-street, and feeling the breath of the advancing flames hot upon our faces. We went down the steps by Cleopatra's Needle, and got on the frozen surface without so much as a shoe wet. Under that intense frost even the tide of the Thames could not keep a patch of open water.

There were thousands of other people with us on the ice, and with them we made our way across to the southern bank. The buildings there had escaped the conflagration, and stood out in cold black silhouette against the windy sky. Men were standing on the white roofs to keep any flying embers from finding a lodgment. But of the other side, which we had left, who could put in mere words the grandeur and awfulness of the sight which it presented then? It seemed as though the great city had been first gripped by a polar winter, and was now being snatched back again by the powers of hell. And against that raid, human resistance was a puny derision.

Chelsea yielded now only a thin smoke; the Houses of Parliament and Westminster were skeletons outlined in flame. The Clock Tower was a great torch, lighting heaven. Whitehall was a furnace, where yellows and reds struggled for the mastery, and no trace of building could be seen. The great hotels of Northumberland Avenue, and the National Gallery beyond, were oozing reek and fire. And the drift of burning fragments drove over the icy roofs in front of the fire, and lit two score new streets every hour.

We watched on as the blaze drove eastwards, and saw it bite the end of the Strand, and then from the great shelter of Charing Cross Station there came a stream of shrieks which made us shudder. That, too, had been ravished by the flames, and of the thousands within it, all who could not escape were being baked alive or crushed by the falling roof.

But meanwhile the freezing gale sweeping down the reaches of the river was nipping us with a more real kind of chill, and I saw that Miss Vivian was almost fainting with the exposure. Gerard said we must try and find some shelter, so we got ashore through a merchant's yard, and made our way to the Waterloo-road. This, too, was crammed with fugitives, but the terrifying scent of the fire was farther away, and the retreat was more orderly. We found a cab, and had nearly chartered it when two other men came up and bid against us. But we had the more gold, and the ride was ours. We were driven away to Dulwich, where Gerard had friends.

And that is the last I saw of the actual burning of London. We were bruised, all three of us, from face to foot; we were badly scorched in many places; we were bone-weary; and once a hospitable door closed behind us, our limbs stiffened, and we were incapable of further struggle. For five awful days the fire strode on and gutted the whole of the City and almost all North London; and the glare of it was seen on the Cheviot Hills.

It turned into crumbling ruins the Bank of England and the Tower; it blasted out of existence the slums which lie between Wapping High Street and the Mile End Road. It burnt the shipping and the warehouses, the shops, and the offices, the private dwellings, and the wooden pavement of the streets; and by one means and another it had caused the death of five hundred thousand of the population.

Yes; half a million human beings perished in that awful tornado of flame, or died of the subsequent exposure and want; three thousand thousand were changed from house-holders into homeless outcasts; but figures will give no idea of the vast amount of property that was blotted out of existence. Not only was solid, visible wealth wafted away in smoke, but that mysterious asset, paper money, shrank from milliards into nothingness. The national credit was blasted, and the bourses of the outside world were smitten to their foundations. Civilization has received no such shock since old Atlantis sank beneath the ocean waves.

And now we are face to face with the result. The awe-struck outer world had recovered its self-possession; we are still paralysed. The starving hordes of London have spread over the whole face of the fair land, and our towns bristle with riot. The other nations, forgetting their momentary pity, remember only their old hate. Shameful treaties are thrust upon us. Our colonies are being invaded. Trade has been reft from us. We are a nation with a glorious history, but no future.

New Chicago arose like a phœnix from the ashes of the old. But our London was no flimsy place of wooden joists and weatherboarding. It was a monument of centuries, and the nation is too heart-sick to begin again to build it on the old scale. The Government sits at Manchester, and the world mocks at it.

In the hour of our pride we boasted that no nation on earth could lay us low. But the elements were set to war against our might, and they have humbled the British Empire even unto the ground.

THE FREEZING OF LONDON

Herbert C. Ridout

Forgotten today, Herbert Currington Ridout (1881–1948) was in his later years a popular radio broadcaster on the BBC, compiling and introducing programmes of popular music to which he narrated the story of the recording artists. Before joining the BBC in 1938 he had worked for Columbia Records and is credited with introducing sleeve notes for records. The son of a butler, Ridout became a journalist at the turn of the century and moved into editing trade magazines. He had a gift for promotion and soon became the editor of Advertising. *He even promoted the subject in a short story, "The Great Scourge" (1908) where advertising is used to reduce the calamity arising when it is discovered the certain foods have been contaminated. The following, published a year later, provides another warning about meddling with nature. Perhaps most astonishing about this story is that although purportedly set in around 2022, looking back to 1972, it does not recognize any scientific progress.*

T HERE WAS ONLY ONE MAN WHO CAME THROUGH THE TER-
rible visitation of London by the intense cold of 1972, and he
barely lived to tell the complete story. I happened to be one of the
party who met the survivor upon his dramatic arrival here, so that
I can tell the story almost as he told it himself.

I can give, too, the secret of how the extraordinary affair came
about. For though I am an old man, and the last of the six men who
heard the story from the lips of the survivor himself, my memory is
as clear as if it were yesterday that I listened to it instead of nearly
fifty years ago. Indeed, the event was such that one could hardly
forget.

As I write, the scene is vividly stretched out before me—the
blank road with the blinding dust whirling hither and thither; a dark
object in the distance rapidly approaching, assuming the form of
a low-lying motor-vehicle as it drew near; a crash, a form hurled
through the air, and silence. How we all rushed to the spot—But I am
forgetting! This is all riddles to you. I must begin at the beginning.

I have by me a few copies of the newspapers of that day with the
paragraphs which first suggested something to be wrong marked
in blue pencil. This was the first intimation of all, taken from the
"Irlingham Chronicle," where it appeared in the Stop-Press column:

"Telegraphic and telephonic communication with London is
suspended. Fears are entertained that local meteorological disturbances have affected the whole of the wiring in the metropolis."

That was all we knew for an hour or two. Then a special edition
told us that a series of alarming railway accidents were reported,

each with a terrifying list of fatalities, on the outskirts of London. At first seven such were reported, but a little later came news of several others. It was stated that each of these disasters, by a remarkable coincidence, occurred at a distance of about fifteen miles from London, and every line into London was blocked by train wreckage.

As this grave intelligence filtered out and became public property, the streets of Irlingham, in the vicinity of the newspaper offices, became congested with people, and arrangements were made to post large bulletin-boards with later items of news as they came to hand.

I stood there among the crowd and shuddered as the rapidly changed notices on the huge white boards told of disaster after disaster, all on the outskirts of the metropolis, fifteen and seventeen miles from London. And I remember to this day some of the more terrible of the announcements.

One of them was:

"Regt. 115th Highldrs., 1,500 men meet death at Watford. Cause unknown. None escaped."

They were all in that abbreviated form, yet they were sufficient to convey to the multitude a sense of appalling tragedy. Very soon every man who stood there had bared his head, while women were sobbing without attempting to disguise the fact.

Irlingham is, as all the world knows, a little over a hundred miles from London, and only about two hours' journey. It was, therefore, amazing to find that nothing definite as to what was actually happening in the great city had reached us.

Thinking that, perhaps, all save the bare facts were being withheld by the newspaper people for use in their papers, I forced my way quietly out of the crowd and hurried as quickly as was possible through the knots of people gathered all along the streets, towards my club, the Athenian. This, as any Irlingham man will tell you, is almost in the suburbs of the town, an unusual site for so important an institution, but selected by members' votes when the old building got too small for us.

The tram services seemed to be suspended, the cars lying idle in a long line stretching from the edge of the crowd for about a quarter of a mile. So I had to walk, and I stepped out briskly, for I was anxious to see whether any more detailed information was reaching the club over the tape. As we had tape machines connected with Orthampton and Lanchester, there seemed a probability that we should learn all that was to be known.

I will not dwell upon the curious sights I witnessed as I strode along; police-stations apparently empty, shops deserted, children playing in the streets while their elders were pressing forward to the spot I had just left. Suffice it to say that when I reached the Athenian, it seemed as though that was deserted, too.

I passed into the smoking-room without meeting a soul, to find the Orthampton tape working and surrounded by half a dozen members. As I joined them, one was reading aloud the message being ticked out. No one took the slightest notice of me:

"... no word from London. Communications destroyed. Calamity feared, but no explanations possible. Windsor, nearest point of connection with London available, reports intense cold. Traffic by road or rail paralysed by wrecked vehicles and trains. Loss of life incalculable. Efforts being made at Windsor to establish communications with Buckingham Palace. The King in Scotland has been informed..."

Then there was a break, and we waited in breathless silence for a continuance of the message. I was about to speak when the instrument began to tick out again:

"... Telegram from Tilbury, Thames estuary, received via Chelmsford and Colchester, as no wires open through London, states that H.M.S. 'Fortune,' 750 men on board, sailing up river, exploded and sunk. Supposed boilers burst through intense cold which prevails. Grave anxiety experienced at silence of London; mystery growing as telegraphists say all wires apparently uninjured. No response can be obtained. SPECIAL: small motor-car, painted grey, running high speed, covered dust as though long journey, just passed through, man driving, on Irlingham Road. Car long and thin, not any standard pattern. Supposed from London. Attempt made to stop it, but without success. Heading for Irlingham direct. Stop or warn all along road. Orthampton Chief Constable instructs..."

It broke off again, and the reader dropped the strip of paper and shouted:

"Upstairs, you chaps! That car must be stopped. Chuck everything you see out in the road; make a heap!"

How we flew! Soon we had a great pile of the club furniture stretching across the road, a barrier sufficient to stop a dozen motorcars. Almost as we finished someone shouted:

"Here he comes!"

In the distance we saw a cloud of dust, a dark speck just ahead of it, flying along towards us. Nobody spoke. All eyes were fixed on the object now coming quickly into view. In less time than it takes to write, we saw it to be a long, boat-shaped car, built close to the ground. At the rate it was coming, the vehicle and its occupant, if it had one, would be smashed into a thousand pieces when it struck our barricade, and, as this thought came, something happened. A swerve, ever so slight, but into the side of the road, and into a friendly hedge. The car went up on end, stood erect for the fraction of a second, and turned turtle with a crash. As it did so a heavy form flashed into the air and fell several yards away from the wreck.

Men never moved quicker than did we to reach the spot, though we feared our task would be but a grim one. We tenderly raised the silent body and hurried it into the building.

In the billiard-room—the only one handy, with tables left standing—we laid the form down, and one or two of us, myself among them, rushed into the kitchens to find brandy and restoratives.

When I got back, the others had removed a heavy coat and exposed a dark-visaged man of about forty-five, warmly clad. He had a keen-cut face, pale, of course, and a forehead that suggested at a glance rare strength of purpose. An ugly bruise over his right eye showed how heavily he had fallen. As I stared at him, I forgot to be surprised that there was any face to look at after such a fall. When this struck me, I looked round to see what could have protected him, and my eyes fell upon a long garment thrown across a chair. There were already five fellows busy administering restoratives, chafing the hands and feet of the stranger, and I saw that I could do nothing to help, so I examined the coat rather closely. It was curiously shaped—a cloak with a headpiece and legs all in one, full protection for its wearer. Its thickness and weight surprised me, and, looking closer, I found it to be divided into squares by the process known to our womenfolk as "quilting," and feeling as if it was made of flexible tubing. I mention this here, for I never saw the garment after; I think one of the fellows must have taken a fancy to it.

I suppose it was about half an hour before there was any sign of returning life, and then we heard a distinct groan. Our efforts were redoubled, and soon we had the satisfaction of seeing our patient seated erect, propped against a heap of coats and cloths.

He stared at us all somewhat unseeingly for a time, and then, after a gulp of brandy, he spoke his first words:

"What place is this?"

"Irlingham—Athenian Club, Irlingham," said one of the fellows, Ronaldson, I think.

"Irlingham—that's over a hundred miles away then," was his next remark. And when he said that we knew he had come from London. Now we should hear something, I thought, but I never had a suspicion of the amazing things he was going to tell us.

We waited until he had recovered somewhat, and then Ronaldson put a question to him.

"What's wrong in London?"

The man's eyes opened wide, and he trembled perceptibly. It looked for the moment as though he would collapse again, until Ronaldson gave him a drink, and said:

"You are all right now, and among friends, so don't hesitate to speak freely. Something has happened to London and the people there; what is it?"

The man looked at each of us in turn, then, almost sullenly I should have said, but for his palpable weakness, muttered slowly:

"London—is frozen—to death!"

This amazing reply set my brain spinning, while exclamations of dismay from the others, and the looks of horror on their faces, clearly showed the impression it had made upon them. In his agitation, Ronaldson shook the poor fellow.

We were dumbfounded for several minutes, and only a liberal dose of brandy pulled me straight. Then Ronaldson said sharply:

"London frozen—in the height of summer as it is—you must be crazy, or think we are, to believe such a story. Tell us what you know, and don't keep us waiting. When did you leave London?"

The man weakly raised his head and looked round at us all again. As his head dropped back upon the improvised pillow he said:

"Don't hurry me—let me take my own time, and—I'll tell you what I know." He paused, and a shudder passed through his frame. Then he added, as if to himself: "Awful sights—frozen stark—millions!"

Ronaldson frowned, and one or two of the fellows in the background tapped their foreheads significantly. But they were wrong. The man was sane enough.

At last we got him started on the story that all the world knows so well in its main issues, but of which few know so little in its details. To give it as we heard it would only mean a halting narrative full of repetitions and interspersed with many colloquialisms, so I set it down in plain, ungarnished language.

Three days before, it seems—June 5th, to be exact—Londoners awoke to find a hoarfrost covering everything. This occasioned great surprise, as the previous day had been unbearably hot. Surprise grew into amazement, for the cold gradually grew more intense as the day wore on, the evening finding everybody snugly ensconced in their houses around big fires. The open-air amusement gardens were absolutely deserted, and when London went to bed that night, the ornamental waters bore thin sheets of ice.

By the next morning, strange to say, the cold had increased to such an extent that but few people possessed the courage to venture out to their places of business, and those who did so had many unpleasant experiences where misguided local authorities had during the night flushed the roads from the deeply laid street mains.

Colder and colder it grew, until by midday work which necessitated the use of the naked hands became impossible, and large numbers of people were forced to seek the warmth and shelter of their homes. Work by the riverside was absolutely suspended, shipping being held in a steely grip of ice—a grip which in many cases threatened to crush the resisting timbers, and later actually did so.

Piteous scenes, upon which I am loth to dwell, were witnessed in the East and other poor districts of London. Without fuel, and without the means to get it, a number of poor creatures in these parts had turned out into the streets to find warmth in movement. But, alas, they never found it!

The newspapers made their appearance, of course, though their distribution was precarious and their volume less than usual. The extreme cold was the chief topic of news, and many theories, fantastic and weird, were advanced to explain the extraordinary weather. If you read one, you were assured most convincingly that the Gulf Stream had unaccountably been diverted out of its course. According to another, the earth's crust was growing colder; while a third declared that this vast globe had shifted on its axis farther away from the sun.

One thing that all the papers noted with surprise is worth mentioning. In most of the leading articles it was pointed out that the wintry condition was peculiar to London. All other places beyond the suburbs seemed unaffected. Indeed, most were revelling in glorious sunshine, and even complaining of the heat. This knowledge caused many thousands of people to leave London during the day, scores of extra trains being run to accommodate the heavy traffic thus occasioned.

But the greater part of London simply endured the discomfort in the belief that another sunrise would assuredly bring weather more in keeping with the calendar.

Coals were now in sudden demand, and the price jumped from 19s. to 30s. in the day, and telegrams were pouring in calling for immediate supplies. Flowers and plants were shrivelled as they stood, and the trees shed their leaves continuously as the cold nipped them. Birds fell from on high like stones. The icy grip had fallen like a blight.

Each hour the change became more noticeable. The pavements were already deserted, and hastily written notices on theatre-doors announced that most of these places of amusement would be closed, to open again as soon as the weather permitted. Street traffic, goods-vans, and public conveyances grew perceptibly less, and by six o'clock the streets were empty of all but a few homeless wayfarers, and some whom business necessity had compelled to brave the unseasonable elements.

The evening newspapers in their late editions told of destruction all over the county of London: the famous Observatory, at Greenwich, had its delicate instruments rendered useless, so that records of the precise degree of cold were unobtainable. Two of the river bridges were in danger of collapse owing to extensive damage by huge bergs of ice which crashed and crunched against them with the tidal action of the river.

One feature threatened to impose great hardship even upon those who were snug in the security of well-warmed houses. And that was a shortage of water. Until the early evening of the second day, the water supply had not been affected, the main pipes being deep in the ground, and those near the surface being well protected. But now they had yielded to the abnormal fall in temperature, and no water was to be had. Fortunately, the hour was one at which the day's necessities had practically been satisfied, and no great inconvenience was felt, especially as what small quantities were required could be drawn from the house cisterns.

That night was the greatest in the world's history—the reader knows why. And the moon rose on a city of perfect quiet, a scene that none looked upon, and a picture that no man can paint. The imagination staggers at the idea of London without a soul in its streets. Yet that is how the night of June 6th found it—a city bereft of outdoor life.

Amazing to relate, the morning of June 7th broke upon a balmy summer day. The transformation was remarkable. Those who happened to be awake at the time, stated that the change occurred about 2 a.m., when their heated rooms became insufferably oppressive.

London was delighted, and the streets at an early hour were thronged with people, all talking of the astounding trick the weather had played. An early edition of an evening paper (published at 9.30 a.m.) described the sudden change with an almost amusing picturesqueness of detail. Indeed, it made the utmost of that subject, with the result that nobody paid the slightest attention to a three-line paragraph printed elsewhere, stating that a Cabinet Council had been called for that morning at the unusually early hour of ten o'clock. Even the newspaper, apparently, had not troubled to investigate this hastily summoned meeting, thinking, no doubt, that the news-value of the "unparalleled meteorological conditions," as the "Daily Telephone" put it, was greater at the moment than any political event.

The significance of this Cabinet Council was, therefore, never understood, and though historians have attributed it to being for the purpose of discussing, perhaps, the disastrous effect of the two days' cold upon the country's trade and commerce, that view was quite a mistaken one.

The revelations of the man who told the story, as he sat erect upon the billiard-table in the Irlington Athenian Club, enabled me to say that the Premier and his Ministers were assembled to discuss, not the effect, but *the cause of the great frost*.

I merely allude to this in passing to show that the strictures passed by some latter-day writers upon the Government of that time for its inactivity, were unmerited.

To the general public on this glorious day, it seemed almost a fitting opportunity to make holiday, and by 10.30 the streets and parks and open spaces were full of men, women, and children intent upon making up for the discomforts attendant upon the inexplicable cold of the preceding forty-eight hours.

To the ordinary observer, otherwise, all things were going on much as usual, for the equilibrium of the Englishman is not easily disturbed. The only noticeable difference on this memorable day was, as I say, a lightness of spirit, a tendency to "maffick"—an early century term for general street enjoyment, so-called from the outburst of popular feeling after an incident in the South African War, concluded a few years before—harmless, but very contagious good fellowship.

A more unsuspecting people at this time it would be impossible to find, and when we come to think how soon the tragedy was to commence, the pathos of this great city in playful mood becomes very real. Not one—stay, only one!—dreamed of impending disaster.

A quarter to eleven—ten minutes—five minutes to the hour—and then Big Ben chimed out eleven o'clock.

Eleven o'clock on June 7th, 1972.

The solemn boom of the eleventh stroke had scarcely died away when suddenly it was noticed to be growing chill. People looked surprised, and that was all.

Without a moment's warning, the tragedy occurred.

A heavy mist passed between the sun and the earth, resembling a white sheet suspended in mid-air. Then it dropped like a shroud.

No one can describe the diabolical workings of the vapour as it insidiously permeated every living and inanimate thing. But the effect was tragic—the word seems mild to describe it all.

Imagine, if you can, a group of everyday folk in the hands of a mesmerist who poses them in the most natural positions, and leaves them standing so. Imagine, if you can, not one group, but twelve millions of people so posed, and imagine them, not mesmerized, but mercilessly frozen in those attitudes.

Such is what had happened. The vapour was a freezing agent of such intensity that its operation was instantaneous and all-powerful. In whatever position a man stood when that mist touched him, so he remained, rigid and stark.

My own words fail me at this point. If I continue at all, I must do so in the words of our informant, even at the risk of the narrative appearing disjointed.

"… the vapour fell. Its action closed upon all like a vice, extracting the humidity that is in everything, and solidifying it in icy shapes. The ground yielded up its dampness, and an icy surface was instantly created—a surface that held tight everything that rested upon it. The moisture of living bodies, of clothing and footwear, was irresistibly drawn out, and then a heavy coating of ice left over all. The effect was that when the moisture of the footwear and of the ground hardened into solid ice, figures, a moment before moving along, were held immovable by the vapour's relentless action.

"It riveted every living soul to the spot on which he stood. Vehicles in the street simply stopped dead, for the horses were frozen in the shafts—frozen hard to the ground. The men upon the carts, in the cabs, or other conveyances, still sat erect, but in death. The vapour was effective upon the motor carriages and omnibuses, for it solidified the watery elements of the oil used as the motive-power, and in the working parts, and rendered them immovable. Weird, terrible sights! Conductors of stage carriages frozen with hands outstretched inviting patronage; passengers in the act of entering or alighting, transformed into icy columns.

"On the buildings the vapour worked great destruction. Windows crashed at its touch and hundreds of tons of glass hurtled into the streets. In many jerry-built houses, the mortar simply crumbled to dust and blew away, so that the walls, left to bear their own weight without any cohesive substance, tumbled pell-mell to the ground. Even in main and important thoroughfares like Fleet Street, Holborn, and Oxford Street, where buildings were thought to be above such suspicion, whole houses had melted into piles of débris.

"Indoors, of course, the same terrible results had been wrought. Workpeople were still seemingly engaged in their work; railway signalmen still held their hands upon the levers: telegraphists their fingers upon the keys: writers their pens to paper—and so on, a hideous nightmare of a living death!

"Every living soul in that vapour zone succumbed. Steam-engines, where employed, burst at the touch of the vapour, wrecking many buildings. On the railways, the explosions of the locomotive boilers caused a series of deafening thunder-claps. Machinery fell to pieces as if shattered by some giant hand. Yet nothing bore a sign, beyond its stillness and rigidity, of anything but life. London still stands as it did at eleven o'clock this morning; it will stand so for two days, and anyone who enters the area of the vapour will—"

Here the speaker broke off, and a clock chimed six. Seven hours before London had met its awful doom!

Ronaldson, I remember, gave him more brandy. I felt a nausea stealing over me, and clutched at the table. Some of the others were sobbing bitterly. The wretched man went on:

"... I escaped. I had invented a car propelled by liquid air, and wore clothes padded with tubes containing a preparation of which liquid air formed part. Liquid air* is not affected by extreme cold as other things, so that I was protected... I was in my car at eleven o'clock, and when I found myself alone I grew afraid... and tried to leave the city... four hours getting from Whitehall to Willesden... hideous sights... picking my way through streets crowded with ghastly objects... The silence was terrifying... nothing moved... my senses were leaving me... I kept on... out... out... out. Reached Watford, dashed suddenly into body of men... soldiers... hundreds... dead... Outside Watford... green country... lovely trees, flowers, birds... life... nothing more..."

Ronaldson groaned heavily, and gently stirred the man from his lethargy.

"How do you explain it? What is the reason?" he asked.

The man raised himself slowly, and we shuddered as we saw in his eyes a great and growing terror. The sights he had witnessed were enough to turn any brain. Then we heard what I, as the only survivor of the little party who stood in that club, alone in this world know—we heard the story of how this thing came about:

"The reason... ah! the reason... an inventor... nobody took him seriously... harebrained they said... said *then*... offered the British Government... a freezing agent... for use in war... more subtle than fighting... release vapour... annihilation... idea poohpoohed... offered demonstrations... Government fell back on Berne Convention as excuse... laughed at it... yes, laughed at it... He warned them once... twice... then gave London sample... two

---

* This indeed is true as recent scientific demonstrations have shown. Liquid air placed on ice, boiled, and when placed over a flame became solid ice.—H.C.R.

days cold... they laughed again... called it a coincidence... could not entertain proposals... final... inventor maddened with rage... this morning... eleven o'clock... set free, two gallons... the vapour... effective radius fifteen miles... annihilation... millions... frozen..."

His voice broke into disconnected syllables. We looked at each other, incredulous, dazed, terrorized at what we had heard. Ronaldson recovered his composure first, and, turning to the man said, almost roughly:

"How do you know this? What grounds have you for making such an awful accusation?"

The lengthy story had proved too much for the man and his head had fallen back, but his lips moved.

We leaned forward expectantly, and these words framed themselves in a whisper:

"I... am... the... man!"

His head dropped.

A master-criminal was dead.

The secret is out, and now all speculation is set at rest.

The mystery of the terrible event of 1972 is explained at last.

There is no need for me to tell of the days of grief that followed for the nation; I need not set forth how London became repeopled in a magical manner by the incursion of six or seven millions from all parts of the world. This is not news to anybody now.

But I shall rest easier in my mind now that I have parted with my secret.

DAYS OF DARKNESS

Owen Oliver

Owen Oliver was the pseudonym of Joshua Albert Flynn (1863–1933) who was a leading civil servant. He had entered the Admiralty in 1884 and was soon transferred to the War Office. He became financial adviser to Lord Kitchener during the Boer War and thereafter served in a financial capacity until his retirement in 1920. He was knighted in 1919. It is surprising that he found as much time to write as he did as he was a prolific contributor to the popular magazines. A fair proportion of his output can be classified as science fiction starting with "The Black Shadow" (1903) where it appears a life force of the lunar civilization still survives on the Moon and is able to take possession of humans. Several stories deal with either an invasion by alien life forms, as in "The Plague of Lights" (1904) or a cosmic disaster. "The Long Night" (1906) has a comet affect the Earth's rotation so that the nights grow longer. The following story, written after his retirement, considers in more detail how Londoners cope when an inexplicable darkness descends upon the capital.

Thank God for Light

I FORESEE THAT THIS CUSTOMARY PREFIX TO ALL LETTERS AND documents will come to be written as a mere formality, unless future generations realize the privations and terrors from which they are delivered by the blessing of light. I therefore make this personal record in the hope of bringing them home to my son's children, if he has any. At present—November, 1965—he is only four and a half days old.

In July, 1963, when the Days of Darkness came upon us, I was twenty-eight, a bachelor, and deputy manager of the Export Department of Bilton & Brash. I was returning home to my flat in Vauxhall Bridge Road (now Daylight Avenue) at about 5.20 by one of the motor-buses, since practically superseded by the Underground Non-Stop Platforms, and had reached the Strand (now Sun Street). It had been a fine day, without any warning of atmospheric disturbances; but as we were coming to Norfolk Street, the light suddenly went. There were three flashes of twilight, at intervals of about two seconds, and then complete, inky black darkness.

These "flashes"—as they seemed in comparison with the intense darkness before and after them—mercifully allowed the traffic to pull up without such terrible destruction as might otherwise have occurred; but I heard many crashes and screams and shrieks all around. My bus ran into one in front and was run into by one behind, but without damage to life or limb to myself or my fellow-passengers, though most of the glass broke and fell upon us. The lady sharing my seat was thrown against me, and screamed. Except that she was young and slight, I had no idea what she was like, as she had been buried in a newspaper when I sat down beside her.

"Is it the end of the world?" she asked.

"I don't know," I said. "Either I've gone blind, or something's gone wrong with the world."

"The glass has cut my face!" she gasped.

"Let me feel it," I offered. "I'll be careful not to hurt. I don't find any glass, but there's a nasty cut on your cheek. It's bleeding. Hold my handkerchief to it."

"You are very kind," she acknowledged.

"The light won't turn on," the conductor reported. "Nor anyone else's. It's the end of the world, that's what it is."

"The sun must have blown up," a woman quavered.

"Nonsense!" grunted someone, who sounded like an elderly gentleman. "If the sun blew up, the earth would blow up, and we should all be disintegrated; turned into dust or gas."

"It hasn't reached us yet," said a young man. "When it does we shall just go poof!" He laughed hysterically.

"Perhaps we're dead now," my neighbour suggested, "and don't know it."

She shuddered. I felt her arm knocking against me.

"We aren't," I assured her. "I can feel your shoulder, and my legs when I pinch them. I've just been trying! You feel my hand—flesh and blood, eh? You can hear people talking all round. The world's here, though we can't see it for the moment."

"What shall we do if the light doesn't come back?" she asked. I hadn't any answer, so I said nothing. "I'm trembling so I can't keep still," she went on.

"Hold my arm," I offered. "It *is* a bit creepy."

I tried to laugh, but without much success.

"I *will* hold your arm, if you don't mind," the young lady said. "When you can't see that there's anybody else in the world, you like to feel that there is."

"It's a judgment for our sins!" a woman declared.

"Speak for yourself, madam!" the old gentleman growled.

Several people laughed. One woman said it wasn't a time for joking, and went into hysterics. The driver came round to the conductor "for company." They started singing "Rock of Ages" in a bus near us, and others took it up. I opened the front of my watch and tried to tell the time by feeling the hands. I made it a quarter to six.

"If the light doesn't return," I observed, "they'll have to make watches with stout hands and raised fingers."

"You talk like a fool," the old gentleman roared. "Who's going to make watches in the dark? Who's going to grow food or distribute it? Who's going to do anything but fight for the scraps that are left, till they're eaten? If the light has gone there's nothing for it but to lie down and die."

"Nothing else for those who choose to give in," I said, "but I'm not going to; not for myself or for anybody who'll take my help, either."

"I think you talk like a man," said the girl holding my arm. "I shall try to be brave, too."

"It'll come to the same in the end, missie," said the conductor. "But we may as well die laughing as crying. Who'll come and forage round for a drink?"

He and the driver and some others left the bus. Some people from the roadway who wanted a rest got in to fill the vacant seats.

Presently a man shouted, apparently from the upper window of a shop:

"Government message on the Radio. Royal Observatory reports that there are no signs of any damage to the solar system. Probably the earth is passing through a space in which there is no ether to transmit light rays. All are warned to be very careful about extinguishing matches, etc., as fire still burns, although invisible. Hearers are implored to remain quietly where they are until arrangements have been made for directing them through the dark to their homes. Great care should be exercised in husbanding resources of food, water, fuel, etc., as their production and distribution will present great difficulty. So far as reports have come in, there is no light, natural or artificial, anywhere in Europe. God have mercy upon a darkened world and restore the light."

"Amen," said everyone, like the murmur of a sea.

"All who hear this message are requested to pass it on," the voice concluded.

A number of people started repeating the message from other windows, and from the tops of buses. Afterwards, more distant voices went on reciting it. Then there was silence, except for people asking, "any spare seats?" The girl beside me kept jerking my arm. I patted her hand several times, and whispered that it would all come right.

About half-past six there was a wild shouting. It was a man, who seemed to have gone off his head, yelling that the Day of Judgment had come, and we were the damned, in a hell of darkness. Some fellow-passengers began groaning and wailing, but the old gentleman roared out that it was no use being cowards and fools.

"We make most of our own heavens and hells," he said. "Don't make the darkness any worse than it is."

"Let us pray," a woman in the bus proposed. "Oh, God, give us back the light! Give us back the light!"

"Amen!" we all said. Then there was silence again, except for the continual "any seats in anything!" from the pavements.

At seven there was no further news. Several people left the bus, saying that they should try to make their way home.

"I feel as if I shall faint," the girl on my arm murmured. "I'm not giving way. I went shopping in my lunch hour, you see. So I'm hungry."

"Come on," I proposed. "Let's see what we can find."

"Will you?" she said. "I didn't like to ask. I was afraid to go alone, and I don't even know you by sight."

"Then," said a woman's voice from behind, "don't go with him, duckie! Men ain't to trust in the dark!"

"There's nowhere else to trust them in now," said the old gentleman.

"Are you more afraid to come with me than to go alone?" I asked the girl.

"I am not afraid of you at all," she stated.

So we went. The old gentleman called out:

"Take care of her, my boy, and good luck to you both!"

There was a rush for our vacant seats, and the pushing separated us for a moment. We shouted, "Where are you," and found each other again; asked a number of questions to make sure that we had got the right person. "Are you the gentleman who lent me the handkerchief for my cut face in the bus?" "What did the woman say who called you 'duckie,'" etc.

"I shall hold your arm like a vice in future," she declared. "Isn't it funny to be in a world of voices—and a kind arm!"

"We'd better know each other's names," I suggested, "in case we get separated again. I don't want to get a different voice and arm by mistake. I'm Richard Templeton. Feel my scarf pin. You can identify me by that."

"I'm Marie Eva Rolfe," she told me. "You'll know me by my cut face, won't you? The bottom of my ear just reaches your shoulder. You measure with your hands. Feel my bead necklace. You'll know that."

We moved along the Strand, towards Charing Cross. We kept asking where we were, and stepping into shops to inquire whether they sold things to eat. Presently we found a teashop. After falling over some chairs, we reached the counter. A girl told us to help ourselves to food and gave us tea. She said she'd burnt herself three times, making it in the dark; but if it was the end of the world she was going out doing her job!

After nearly overturning a table and sitting upon some people, we found vacant places and had our tea and discussed finding our way home. I thought I could manage it, as I knew all the streets on my way, and could keep on asking people in them where I was; but it was impossible for her to find her place, as she lived in West Kensington, and didn't know many of the streets leading there.

"You'd better come with me," I proposed, "and I'll get someone to take you in. No doubt some of my neighbours will."

After tea we started, arm-in-arm, but holding out our disengaged hands in front of us to fend people off. We found progress very difficult. We kept slipping off kerbs, and once we got down a side street and had to make our way back. Many people, whom we asked where we were, didn't know, as they had wandered about since the darkness began. Some were calling out wildly for lost companions. One woman in particular was shrieking for "Bob Cartmail." It was half an hour before we got out of reach of her calls. At several places we were blocked by traffic in the side streets. We had to go in one side of a taxi and out of the other to get across one opening. When at last we reached Charing Cross Station, eight struck upon a clock.

"If you hadn't looked after me," Marie said, "I should have gone mad! And how I shall find courage to venture over the big crossings, even with you, I don't know."

However, we found that guidance had been organized there. Strings of policemen and others were holding ropes across, and calling out: "This way for Northumberland Avenue," etc. We followed the Whitehall line and went down Whitehall on the left-hand side.

There we met the first instance of disorder. Apparently some roughs had raided places for drink, and now were plundering and roistering. Several ran into us when I was feeling my watch hands to tell the time, and somebody snatched at the watch and snapped it off the chain. I knocked somebody down, but I doubt if it was the robber. Anyhow, when I got hold of the drunken man I had knocked down, I couldn't find the watch! I lost Marie for half a minute; but found her by her screaming my name. A drunken rough had caught hold of her, but I nearly throttled him and threw him aside. Then she verified me by my scarf pin, etc.—I knew her by her voice—and we walked on. She clung desperately to me.

"Thank Heaven that *you* were sitting next to me!" she said.

I very often do!

Big Ben struck nine just as we reached Parliament Square (now called Mercy Place). I suggested that we should try to get a meal at one of the teashops; but we found them closed. We helped ourselves through a broken window of one. I filled my pockets with buns and pastries, fearing that food would soon be scarce, and Marie took a cake and carried it in her hands, having no pocket and only a tiny handbag.

We got across the square by the aid of a cordon of police calling, "This way to Victoria!" and holding strings from one to the other. Others were calling out, "Beware of pickpockets!" There was a picket at the corner of Great Smith Street which directed us down that. Some people we bumped into tried to rifle my pockets, but I pushed them aside. Someone snatched the cake from Marie, however, and got away into the dark with it.

A little farther on we were almost knocked down by a rush. The crowd were shouting "Fire, fire!" But we did not see it, though we thought we felt heat. Marie said it was like being in a dark forest and hearing wild beasts all round and devils setting it afire.

In Regency Street (according to a person calling from a window) there was a row going on between some men and women as to which belonged to which. We went out into the road to avoid the crowd, and walked up against a cycle-barrow deserted by its rider. It contained groceries and we took some eggs and bacon. We lost our way for a time, but ultimately were told that we were in Vauxhall Bridge Road.

I had great difficulty in finding my block of flats. A motor-car had run upon the pavement and almost blocked the entrance, and I must have passed it several times. I only knew it for certain by my key opening the door. I closed that again. As I did so a voice shouted from above:

"You'll come upstairs at your peril!"

"I'm Templeton," I said. "No. 7."

"How do we know that?" the voice asked. "You might be any-body. We've been warned against letting anyone in, and you don't pass this landing."

I told Marie to get behind me and hold on to my coat-tails while I crawled up, as I should try to grab "the brute" by the legs; but a woman's voice entreated him to come inside their flat and let me pass. He went away warning me that he had a revolver and a chopper for anyone who tried to enter his premises.

"No use asking them to let you stay there," I told Marie. "We'll try on the next floor."

I knocked at the doors of the flats which I believed had ladies living in them. Only two answered, with their doors on the chain. They were hysterical and refused to admit any lady whom they did not know.

"I can't stand it any longer," Marie said at length. "I've tried not to give way, but—but—"

"You must have my flat," I told her. "I'll sleep in the passage if you mistrust me. If not, I'll sleep on the sofa."

"I don't mistrust you," she said. "I think I'm going to faint."

I had to carry her up the next flight of stairs. I dragged her in somehow—I hadn't much strength left myself—and sat her in the armchair. Then I groped about, knocking against things in the familiar rooms, and cut bread-and-butter (and myself as well) and boiled eggs and made tea—burning myself a little, as I could only judge where the burning gas was by the heat.

"Now, Marie," I said. "Feel carefully in front of you for the table. Now feel for the cup and plate and things. And get this into your little head. What ever dangers are before you, there's none from *me*."

"I *have* got that into my head," she declared.

We had supper without misadventure, except that I had filled the salt cellar with castor sugar, and boiled the eggs as hard as stones. Twelve struck on my clock just as we were finishing.

"Perhaps if you phoned to the post-office at the corner of Halston Road they would go round and tell my people I am safe?" she suggested.

She knew the number, and I was able to work it out on my automatic indicator. But the post-office people weren't prepared to go out in the dark. However, they gave me the latest news. Nothing was known as to the cause of the darkness, but it covered the whole earth. Everybody was advised to remain indoors. The Government was endeavouring to arrange to send bread round, while it lasted, but it was feared no more could be made. Strangers should not be admitted unless householders were quite convinced that they were harmless. Various public buildings had been opened as shelters. The news and instructions would be called round the streets.

"Well, Marie," I said, "there's nothing for it but sleep. I'll get a rug and a pillow out of my bed-room. Then you shall have that, and I'll lie down on the couch."

"I'll try to wash up by the feel," she offered, "if you'll lead me where things are."

"We'll do that in the morning," I said. "I'll lead you round the place, so that you'll know where you are before I put you inside your bedroom." When I woke it was six o'clock by my clock, which struck. The darkness was still intense. I prepared breakfast by feel and then called her. We washed up by feel. Marie scalded her hand rather badly. I put butter on the place and bound it up as well as I could in the dark.

Soon after eight someone shouted the news from a window opposite. Those who had wireless sets were asked to do that.

"Government bulletin from memory. Cause of darkness not known. So far as can be judged by rough measurements of gravity no destruction of solar system. Those within range of this message can obtain small quantities of provisions at shops to be notified later. To aid persons travelling, people should call their addresses from upper windows. Lower windows should be guarded, and no one admitted to premises without establishing their identity."

Later in the day we were given the addresses of the milkman opposite, and a neighbouring grocer and butcher and baker. We tied ourselves together with stout cord and went out. We found the butcher's; but we could not reach the shop for the fighting crowd. The butcher kept shouting that he had nothing left. People brushed past knocking us with great joints. Others set upon them and tried to take the meat away. I tried myself to cut a portion off a great piece with my pen-knife, but did not succeed. Marie was struck in the face. So we got out of the crowd and tried the milkman's. He was serving through a partly opened door, blocked with great cases. As I was a regular customer, he gave me a large bottle of milk, some eggs, a loaf of bread, and a few biscuits.

I had taken a stout bag to put the things in and had tied the handle both to Marie and myself, foreseeing that attempts would be made to rob us. They were, but I am a strong man, and managed to force our way through the crowd. I was rather knocked about, however, and as there was a noisy, quarrelling horde at the grocer's, I judged that we were more likely to be robbed of the bag and what we had already obtained, than to get more. So we turned back.

We heard a number of roughs coming along, and went off the pavement to avoid them. Then we heard horses—no doubt abandoned by their drivers—dragging carts about wildly. Marie screamed and staggered against me.

"It was a cart," she cried. "It knocked me in passing. It's hurt my shoulder…"

Then something struck me on the head and stunned me. When next I knew anything I found myself lying upon a bed and heard Marie's voice.

"Richard! Richard! Say your hear! Speak to me, Richard! I'm your little friend Marie!"

"Right-ho!" I muttered. "Where am I?"

"Back at home," she said. "Your flat."

She had carried me—and the bag—to the pavement; found the way by knocking at doors and asking people; got the keys from my pocket and opened the outer door of the flats, carried me upstairs, and got me upon the bed, and I am a big man.

"I didn't think I had the strength left; but I prayed and prayed and it came… I'm only crying because I'm so tired."

In the afternoon there was a bulletin that no more food remained in the shops.

We had only three-quarters of a small loaf, about a pound of bacon, four eggs, three stale pastries, a little butter, and a half-pound slab of chocolate.

The next morning—at least we took it for the morning, but at some time or other we overslept and lost half a day—only a few drippings came from the water-tap. I went round to the other flats to ask for a drop of water, but no one would spare any. A pipe had burst, they said, and run out the tanks. We had only about a pint in the kettle.

When that was gone we decided to make our way to the Embankment to draw up water in a pail, to which I attached a line. We found our way there through the horrible black darkness, after a long while; but the water was brackish. Marie, who was growing weak, cried then—the only time that she gave way. A man called out from the window of a house across the road.

"Leave the woman alone, you brute! You're near enough to judgment!"

Marie cried out a glowing account of my kindness to her. I explained the matter to the man, and he lowered a pail of water from his window. We put our faces to it, one at each side, and drank. We emptied the rest into our pail.

On the return we lost our way completely. When we were almost too tired to stand, we walked against a deserted bus. We sat upon a seat in that and slept for a time. Marie kept her arm in mine, and put her head on my shoulder.

"Don't you dare remember when it's light," she murmured, "if we ever see each other then!"

"If!" I said, and laughed and patted her cheek.

"Don't," she cried. "I mean—that's the cut place, Dick. Pat my head instead… Good-night."

After our sleep—it was five by a church clock, but we did not know if it was morning or afternoon—we tried again to find the flat. We had not had anything to eat since we started out, and we were very hungry. We knocked at several houses and asked for food, but no one had any to spare.

"You may as well starve as us," one said.

"Selfish brute!" I growled.

"He isn't," a woman screamed. "He keeps trying to go without for *us*."

If the Days of Darkness did no credit to universal benevolence they furnished many examples of self-denial for people's families, and near friends.

I was still dizzy from the blow, and Marie had grown weak. The water was heavy; and a number of hungry dogs snapped at us—or perhaps only at the water.

"Dick," Marie said presently. "Do you think we *are* dead; and in hell?"

"'Sh!" I said. "The little arm I've got hold of isn't hell, anyhow. Be brave a little longer. There's someone calling. Perhaps it's good news."

But the report was, "No news at present."

After a couple of hours we found the A flats. The only thing which happened on the way was that two men tried to take our water. They almost overpowered me, but suddenly they yelled and went.

"What was it?" I asked.

"My hat-pin!" said Marie.

When we reached my rooms at last, Marie dropped on to the floor. I could hardly stand, but I managed to get food and crawled to her and fed her, and ate myself. Then I carried her to the bed and covered her, and went to sleep on the sofa.

There was only one bulletin that day.

"It has been found impossible to provide or distribute food to any extent. The only hope is that the darkness may pass. Pray for the mercy of God!"

When we had finished our food, I telephoned to several acquaintances—all whose numbers I could remember—to ask if they could help us, if we reached them. Those who answered had no food or were beyond reach. One tried to console me.

"The Universe is still running," he assured me. "You can tell by the warmth that the sun is still going on. We're just passing through some part of space where there's no ether to transmit light. We shall soon get out of it."

"If there's such a space," I asked, "why hasn't it always made a blind spot in the heavens? It wouldn't have let light pass through it." (This difficulty has never been explained away, though it is suggested that we took the blind space for a cloud.)

"I expect," Marie suggested, "his wife and children are there, and he only said it to cheer them. I'm afraid it's near the end... Dick? I want to say something before I grow too faint and muddled. Your things would have lasted twice as long if you hadn't shared them with a poor girl you don't know; just a voice in the dark to you..."

"A dear voice in the dark," I told her; "and a dear arm in mine... If this passes, Marie, will you marry me?"

She did not answer for some time.

"IF the light comes back," she said at last. "You'll find I am not very good-looking, Dick; only just so-so."

"That's all *I* am," I told her.

"It doesn't matter in a man. If the light returns, I shall be *terrified*; want to run from you for fear you'll be disappointed... I'm not disfigured or *ugly*. I don't mean that, but... Can't you tell I'm only ordinary by feeling my face?... Mind the cut!"

"It feels a dear little face," I told her. "Anyhow, you're you!"

"If the light comes back, and you ask me *then*, I expect I shall say 'Yes.' Let's leave it at that, Dick..."

"Give me one kiss then... One more... One more..."

"That's enough, Dick... If you like me when you see me you shall have quite a lot... Here's just one... Anyhow, no one can ever be to me as much as you have been in these dark days... I don't think there can be worse horrors to come, do you?"

Soon afterwards a man—apparently a chemist who had gone mad—came shouting round the street.

"Bread!" he yelled. "Bread for my children: For a crust I'll give you something to kill you easier than hunger. Bread for poison!"

"I ain't got no bread," someone screamed. "Give me the blooming dope!"

"No bread, no poison," the madman shouted.

"Go out and take it from him," a woman screamed. "It'll be easier."

Then there was a baying like wolves and the man ran; and we heard the patter of dogs—no doubt maddened by hunger and thirst—running down the street; and presently shrieks of the man afar.

Marie held to me and sobbed.

The only other bulletin but one was advice to stay indoors, as dogs were almost all mad from lack of food.

In the morning—if it was morning—we had nothing to eat, and there was only a drop of water left.

We sat upon the sofa holding hands for a long while; and then there came the last bulletin that we heard. Fires had broken out in many places and were spreading. There was no way of extinguishing them, in the absence of light and water, except possibly by blowing up property round them.

After this there were constant false alarms of "fire." Going by the sounds, the street was crowded with people making for Vauxhall Bridge as a refuge from fire. We judged from the uproar which soon arose that this became crowded, and that there was a fight in progress between those trying to remain in possession and those attempting to oust them. (Great loss of life occurred at all the bridges in this manner.)

We slept for intervals, and then woke thirsty and hungry. The thirst was the worst. We should have gone out and tried to get water, but we felt sure that the crowd would not let us get near the river. I tried begging from the neighbours, but no one answered my knocking upon the doors. However we found one door open and the flat empty. In the kitchen there was an ill-smelling liquid in a saucepan. We shared that out between us.

We went back to my rooms and dozed again on the sofa. I was roused by shouts of "Fire." There was a faint smell of smoke, and people were running along the road. I woke Marie and we went out. We found that the smoke seemed to grow more dense Victoria way. So we turned off—I think down Morton Street.

"It's behind us, Marie!" I cried. "There's a sort of faint glare! Look! I can *see* it! *See it!*"

"I can't… Yes, I can! Dick! The light is coming back… Dick? *Don't* expect I'm good-looking, because I'm not… I shall be dirty and draggled and dead-looking, Dick. Don't judge me till I've washed and dressed properly."

"My dear!" I said. "I shall love you anyhow."

Then everything went from me. It was the shock of an explosion blowing up a house we learnt afterwards. Marie was not stunned, she says, only dazed for a time. There was a very faint light, when she "found her senses"; and some policemen came and put me in a cart, and dragged it to a hospital.

"The poor horse was dead, and the dogs had nearly eaten him. I sat beside you, with your head on my lap; and when they turned on the electric lamps I saw the man I expected I was going to marry; and I didn't mind him at all, though he wasn't in the least like I had pictured, and such a dirty, unshaven thing!"

The next I remember was a cheerful young nurse in a hospital; a pretty girl with a saucy little face, and a way of laughing suddenly and tossing her head.

"Well, you know yourself at last, Mr. Sleepy," she said.

"Yes," I agreed. "Where's Marie?"

"The lady who brought you here? Miss Rolfe?"

"Yes," I said. "I'm going to marry her, if she doesn't think I'm too bad when she sees me."

"She has, you know," the nurse told me; "several times." (I had been unconscious for three days.)

"Does she think I'll do?" I inquired anxiously.

"You'd better ask her when she comes. She calls every evening after she leaves business."

"I should think from that she's passed me as a possible," I observed hopefully.

"I fancy," the nurse said, "her trouble is that she's afraid you mayn't admire her."

"I shall," I declared. "I've made up my mind to."

"How good-looking are you expecting her to be?" the nurse asked.

"Well—say about a quarter as good-looking as you. I shall think she is; because I'm in love with her voice. *That's* better than yours even!"

"I'm sure it isn't," the nurse said, tossing her head and laughing—and then I noticed that she was crying too.

"Nurse?" I gasped. "Nurse?... You don't mean—"

"Yes," she said, dropping on her knees beside the bed, "I'm Marie. They let me put these things on so that I could find out if you thought me too dreadful!"

I hugged her up to me.

"Dreadful! My word, no! Tuck your arm in mine and let me feel it again... Let me look at you!... Thank God for the light!"

WITHIN AN ACE
OF THE END OF THE WORLD

Robert Barr

Born in Scotland, Robert Barr (1849–1912) emigrated to Canada with his parents when he was only five, where he later became a teacher. He returned to England in 1881. He had for the previous few years worked as a news editor on the Detroit Free Press *and it was planned that he would establish a weekly English edition of the paper, which proved moderately successful. Barr then turned his skills to creating a new popular magazine,* The Idler, *a title chosen by his co-editor Jerome K. Jerome. The magazine, which first appeared in February 1892, was very successful but later became more of a burden around Barr's neck who took it over as sole proprietor from 1902 to 1911. Barr was a prolific writer, sometimes under the alias Luke Sharp. He is best remembered for his stories featuring the pompous French detective Eugène Valmont, regarded by some as a model for Agatha Christie's Hercule Poirot. The stories were collected as* The Triumphs of Eugène Valmont *(1906). His fiction includes several stories that qualify as science fiction starting with "The Doom of London" (1892) where the capital is suffocated by a severe smog. "The New Explosive" (1893) tells of a weapon too powerful to use. "The Revolt of the —" (1894) is one of his more typical tongue-in-cheek stories of role reversals where women have become dominant in society. The following is far from light-hearted, however, and considers what happens when food production robs the atmosphere of much of its nitrogen.*

THE BEGINNING OF THE END WAS PROBABLY THE ADDRESS delivered by Sir William Crookes to the British Association at Bristol, on September 7th, 1898, although Herbert Bonsel, the young American experimenter, alleged afterward that his investigations were well on the way to their final success at the time Sir William spoke. All records being lost in the series of terrible conflagrations which took place in 1904, it is now impossible to give any accurate statement regarding Sir William Crookes' remarkable paper; but it is known that his assertions attracted much attention at the time, and were the cause of editorial comment in almost every newspaper and scientific journal in the world. The sixteen survivors out of the many millions who were alive at the beginning of 1904 were so much occupied in the preservation of their own lives, a task of almost insurmountable difficulty, that they have handed down to us, their descendants, an account of the six years beginning with 1898 which is, to say the least, extremely unsatisfactory to an exact writer. Man, in that year, seems to have been a bread-eating animal, consuming, per head, something like six bushels of wheat each year. Sir William appears to have pointed out to his associates that the limit of the earth's production of wheat had been reached, and he predicted universal starvation, did not science step in to the aid of a famine-stricken world. Science, however, was prepared. What was needed to increase the wheat production of the world to something like double its then amount was nitrate of soda; but nitrate of soda did not exist in the quantity required—*viz.*, some 12,000,000 tons annually. However, a supposedly unlimited supply of nitrogen existed in the atmosphere surrounding the earth, and from this storehouse science proposed to draw, so that the multitude might be fed. Nitrogen in its free state in the air was useless as applied to wheat-growing, but it could be brought into solid masses for practical purposes by means of electricity generated by the waterfalls which are so abundant in many mountainous lands. The cost of nitrates made from the air by water-power approached £5 a ton, as compared with £26 a ton when steam was used. Visionary people had often been accused of living in castles in the air, but now it was calmly proposed to feed future populations from granaries in the air. Naturally, as has been said, the project created much comment, although it can hardly be asserted that it was taken seriously.

It is impossible at this time, because of the absence of exact data, to pass judgment on the conflicting claims of Sir William Crookes and Mr. Herbert Bonsel; but it is perhaps not too much to say that the actual beginning of disaster was the dinner given by the Marquis of Surrey to a number of wealthy men belonging to the city of London, at which Mr. Bonsel was the guest of the evening.

Early in April, 1899, a young man named Herbert Bonsel sailed for England from New York. He is said to have been a native of Coldwater, Michigan, and to have spent some sort of apprenticeship in the workshops of Edison, at Orange, New Jersey. It seems he did not prosper there to his satisfaction, and, after trying to interest people in New York in the furthering of his experiments, he left the metropolis in disgust and returned to Coldwater, where he worked for some time in a carriage-building establishment. Bonsel's expertness with all kinds of machinery drew forth the commendation of his chief, and resulted in a friendship springing up between the elder and the younger man which ultimately led to the latter's divulging at least part of his secret to the former. The obstacle in the way of success was chiefly scarcity of money, for the experiments were costly in their nature. Bonsel's chief, whose name is not known, seems to have got together a small syndicate, which advanced a certain amount of capital, in order to allow the young man to try his fortune once more in New York, and, failing there, to come on to London. Again his efforts to enlist capital in New York were fruitless, the impending war with France at that period absorbing public attention to the exclusion of everything else. Therefore, in April, he sailed for England.

Bonsel's evil star being in the ascendant, he made the acquaintance of the wealthy Marquis of Surrey, who became much interested in the young man and his experiments. The Marquis bought out the Coldwater syndicate, returning the members tenfold what they had invested, and took Bonsel to his estate in the country, where, with ample means now at his disposal, the youthful scientist pushed his investigations to success with marvellous rapidity. Nothing is known of him until December of that year, when the Marquis of Surrey gave a dinner in his honour at the Hotel Cecil, to which were invited twenty of the richest men in England. This festival became known as "The Millionaires' Dinner"; and although there was some curiosity excited regarding its purport, and several paragraphs appeared in the papers alluding to it, no surmise concerning it came anywhere near the truth. The Marquis of Surrey presided, with Bonsel at his right and the Lord Mayor of London at his left. Even the magnates who sat at that table, accustomed as they were to the noted dinners in the City, agreed unanimously that they had never partaken of a better meal, when, to their amazement, the chair-man asked them, at the close of the feast, how they had relished it.

*

The Marquis of Surrey, before introducing the guest of the evening, said that, as they were all doubtless aware, this was not a social but a commercial dinner. It was the intention, before the company separated, to invite subscriptions to a corporation which would have a larger capitalization than any limited liability concern that had ever before been floated. The young American at his right would explain the discoveries he had made and the inventions he had patented, which this newly formed corporation would exploit. Thus introduced, Herbert Bonsel rose to his feet and said—

"Gentlemen,—I was pleased to hear you admit that you liked the dinner which was spread before us tonight. I confess that I never tasted a better meal, but most of my life I have been poor, and therefore I am not so capable of passing an opinion on a banquet as any other here, having always been accustomed to plain fare. I have, therefore, to announce to you that all the viands you have tasted and all the liquors you have consumed were prepared by me in my laboratory. You have been dining simply on various forms of nitrogen, or on articles of which nitrogen is a constituent. The free nitrogen of the air has been changed to fixed nitrogen by means of electricity, and the other components of the food placed on the board have been extracted from various soils by the same means. The champagne and the burgundy are the product of the laboratory, and not of the wine-press, the soil used in their composition having been exported from the vine-bearing regions of France only just before the war which ended so disastrously for that country. More than a year ago Sir William Crookes announced what the nitrogen free in the air might do for the people of this world. At the time I read his remarks I was engaged in the experiments that have now been completed. I trembled, fearing I was about to be forestalled; but up to this moment, so far as I know, there has been made no effort to put his theories into practical use. Sir William seemed to think it would be sufficient to use the nitrates extracted from the atmosphere for the purpose of fertilizing the ground. But this always appeared to me a most round-about method. Why should we wait on slow-footed Nature? If science is capable of wringing one constituent of our food from the air, why should it shrink from extracting the others from earth or water? In other words, why leave a job half finished? I knew of no reason; and, luckily, I succeeded in convincing our noble host that all food products may be speedily compounded in the laboratory, without waiting the progress of the tardy seasons. It is proposed, therefore, that a company be formed with a capital so large that it can control practically all the water-power available in the world. We will extract from earth, air, and water whatever we need, compound the products in our factories, and thus feed the whole world. The moment our plant is at work, the occupations of agriculturist, horticulturist, and stock-breeder are gone. There is little need to dwell on the profit that must accrue to such a company as the one now projected. All commercial enterprises that have hitherto existed, or even any combination of them, cannot be compared for wealth-producing to the scheme we have now in hand. There is no man so poor but he must be our customer if he is to live, and none so rich that he can do without us."

After numerous questions and answers the dinner party broke up, pledged to secrecy, and next day a special train took the twenty down to the Marquis of Surrey's country place, where they saw in operation the apparatus that transformed simple elements into palatable food. At the mansion of the Marquis was formed The Great Food Corporation (Limited), which was to have such an amazing effect upon the peoples of this earth. Although the company proved one of the most lucrative investments ever undertaken in England, still it did not succeed in maintaining the monopoly it had at first attempted. In many countries the patents did not hold, some governments refusing to sanction a monopoly on which life itself depended, others deciding that, although there were certain ingenious novelties in Bonsel's processes, still the general principles had been well known for years, and so the final patents were refused. Nevertheless, these decisions did not interfere as much as might have been expected with the prosperity of The Great Food Producing Corporation (Limited). It had been first in the field, and its tremendous capitalization enabled it to crush opposition somewhat ruthlessly, aided by the advantage of having secured most of the available water-power of the world. For a time there was reckless speculation in food-manufacturing companies, and much money was lost in consequence. Agriculture was indeed killed, as Bonsel had predicted, but the farmers of Western America, in spite of the decline of soil-tilling, continued to furnish much of the world's food. They erected windmills with which electricity was generated, and, drawing on the soil and the air, they manufactured nourishment almost as cheaply as the great water-power corporation itself. This went on in every part of the world where the Bonsel patents were held invalid. In a year or two everyone became accustomed to the chemically compounded food, and even though a few old fogies kept proclaiming that they would never forsake the ancient wheaten loaf for its modern equivalent, yet nobody paid any attention to these conservatives; and presently even they could not get the wheaten loaf of bygone days, as grain was no longer grown except as a curiosity in some botanist's garden.

*

The first three years of the twentieth century were notable for the great increase of business confidence all over the world. A reign of universal prosperity seemed to have set in. Political questions appeared easier of solution. The anxieties that hitherto had oppressed the public mind, such as the ever-present poverty problem, provision for the old age of the labourers, and so forth, lifted like a rising cloud and disappeared. There were still the usual number of poor people; but, somehow, lack of wealth had lost its terror. It was true that the death-rate increased enormously; but nobody seemed to mind that. The episode at the Guildhall dinner in 1903 should have been sufficient to awaken the people, had an awakening been possible in the circumstances; but that amazing lesson, like others equally ominous, passed unheeded. When the Prime Minister who had succeeded Lord Salisbury was called upon to speak, he said—

"My Lord Mayor, Your Royal Highnesses, Your Excellencies, Your Graces, My Lords, and Gentlemen: It has been the custom of Prime Ministers from time immemorial to give at this annual banquet some indication of the trend of mind of the Government. I propose, with your kind permission, to deviate in slight measure from that ancient custom (cheers). I think that hitherto we have all taken the functions of Government rather more seriously than their merits demand, and a festive occasion like this should not be marred by the introduction of debatable subjects (renewed cheering). If, therefore, the band will be good enough to strike up that excellent tune, 'There will be a Hot Time in the Old Town Tonight,' I shall have the pleasure of exhibiting to you a quick-step I have invented to the rhythm of that lively composition (enthusiastic acclaim)."

The Prime Minister, with the aid of some of the waiters, cleared away the dishes in front of him, stepped from the floor to his chair, and from the chair to the table, where, accompanied by the energetic playing of the band, he indulged in a break-down that would have done credit to any music-hall stage. All the applauding diners rose to their feet in the wildest excitement. His Royal Highness the Crown Prince of Alluria placed his hands on the shoulders of the Lord Mayor, the German Ambassador placed his hands on the shoulders of the Crown Prince, and so on down the table, until the distinguished guests formed a connected ring around the board on which the Prime Minister was dancing. Then all, imitating the quick-step, and keeping time with the music, began circling round the table, one after the other, shouting and hurrahing at the top of their voices. There were loud calls for the American Ambassador, a celebrated man, universally popular; and the Prime Minister, reaching out a hand, helped him up on the table. Amidst vociferous cheering, he said that he took the selection of the tune as a special compliment to his countrymen, the American troops having recently entered Paris to its melodious strains. His Excellency hoped that this hilarious evening would cement still further the union of the English-speaking races, which fact it really did, though not in the manner the honourable gentleman anticipated at the time of speaking. The company, headed by the band and the Prime Minister, then made their way to the street, marched up Cheapside, past St. Paul's, and along Fleet Street and the Strand, until they came to Westminster. Everyone along the route joined the processional dance, and upward of 50,000 persons were assembled in the square next to the Abbey and in the adjoining streets. The Prime Minister, waving his hand towards the Houses of Parliament, cried, "Three cheers for the good old House of Commons!" These being given with a tiger appended, a working-man roared, "Three cheers for 'is Lordship and the old duffers what sits with him in the 'Ouse of Lords." This was also honoured in a way that made the echoes reach the Mansion House.

The *Times* next morning, in a jocular leading article, congratulated the people of England on the fact that at last politics were viewed in the correct light. There had been, as the Prime Minister truly said, too much solidity in the discussion of public affairs; but, linked with song and dance, it was now possible for the ordinary man in the street to take some interest in them, etc., etc. Foreign comment, as cabled from various countries, was entirely sympathetic to the view taken of the occurrence by all the English newspapers, which was that we had entered a new era of jollity and good will.

I have now to speak of my great-grandfather, John Rule, who, at the beginning of the twentieth century, was a science student at Balliol College, Oxford, aged twenty-four. It is from the notes written by him and the newspaper clippings which he preserved that I am enabled to compile this imperfect account of the disaster of 1904 and the events leading to it. I append, without alteration or comment, his letter to the *Times*, which appeared the day after that paper's flippant references to the conduct of the Prime Minister and his colleagues—

THE GUILDHALL INCIDENT

To the Editor of the 'Times':

Sir,—The levity of the Prime Minister's recent conduct; the levity of your own leading article thereon; the levity of foreign reference to the deplorable episode, indicate but too clearly the crisis which mankind is called upon to face, and to face, alas! under conditions which make the averting of the greatest calamity well-nigh impossible. To put it plainly, every man, woman, and child on this earth, with the exception of eight persons in the United States and eight in England, are drunk—not with wine, but with oxygen. The numerous factories all over the world which are working night and day, making fixed nitrates from the air, are rapidly depleting the atmosphere of its nitrogen. When this disastrous manufacture was begun, 100 parts of air, roughly speaking, contained 76·9 parts of nitrogen and 23·1 parts of oxygen. At the beginning of this year, the atmosphere round Oxford was composed of nitrogen 53·218, oxygen 46·782. And here we have the explanation of the largely increased death-rate. Man is simply burning up. Today the normal proportions of the two gases in the air are nearly reversed, standing—nitrogen, 27·319, oxygen 72·681, a state of things simply appalling: due in a great measure to the insane folly of Russia, Germany, and France competing with each other in raising mountain ranges of food products as a reserve in case of war, just as the same fear of a conflict brought their armies to such enormous proportions a few years ago. The nitrogen factories must be destroyed instantly, if the people of this earth are to remain alive. If this is done, the atmosphere will gradually become nitrogenised once more.

I invite the editor of the *Times* to come to Oxford and live for a few days with us in our iron building, erected on Port Meadow, where a machine supplies us with nitrogen and keeps the atmosphere within the hut similar to that which once surrounded the earth. If he will direct the policy of the *Times* from this spot, he may bring an insane people to their senses. Oxford yesterday bestowed a degree of D.C.L. on a man who walked the whole length of the High on his hands; so it will be seen that it is time something was done. I am, sir, yours, etc.,

JOHN RULE, *Balliol College, Oxford*

The *Times* in an editorial note said that the world had always been well provided with alarmists, and that their correspondent, Mr. Rule, was a good example of the class. That newspaper, it added, had been for some time edited in Printing House Square, and it would be continued to be conducted in that quarter of London, despite the attractions of the sheet-iron house near Oxford.

The coterie in the iron house consisted of the Rev. Mr. Hepburn, who was a clergyman and tutor; two divinity students, two science students, and three other undergraduates, all of whom had withdrawn from their colleges, awaiting with anxiety the catastrophe they were powerless to avert. Some years before, when the proposal to admit women to the Oxford colleges was defeated, the Rev. Mr. Hepburn and John Rule visited the United States to study the working of co-education in that country. There Mr. Rule became acquainted with Miss Sadie Armour, of Vassar College, on the Hudson, and the acquaintance speedily ripened into friendship, with a promise of the closer relationship that was yet to come. John and Sadie kept up a regular correspondence after his return to Oxford, and naturally he wrote to her regarding his fears for the future of mankind, should the diminution of the nitrogen in the air continue. He told her of the precautions he and his seven comrades had taken, and implored her to inaugurate a similar colony near Vassar. For a long time the English Nitrogenists, as they were called, hoped to be able to awaken the world to the danger that threatened; and by the time they recognized that their efforts were futile, it was too late to attempt the journey to America which had long been in John Rule's mind. Parties of students were in the habit of coming to the iron house and jeering at the inmates. Apprehending violence one day, the Rev. Mr. Hepburn went outside to expostulate with them.

He began seriously, then paused, a comical smile lighting up his usually sedate face, and finally broke out into roars of laughter, inviting those he had left to come out and enjoy themselves. A moment later he began to turn somersaults round the iron house, all the students out-side hilariously following his example, and screaming that he was a jolly good fellow. John Rule and one of the most stalwart of the divinity students rushed outside, captured the clergyman, and dragged him into the house by main force, the whirling students being too much occupied with their evolutions to notice the abduction. One of the students proposed that the party should return to Carfax by hand-springs, and thus they all set off, progressing like jumping-jacks across the meadow, the last human beings other than themselves that those within the iron house were to see for many a day. Rule and his companions had followed the example set by Continental countries, and had, while there was yet time, accumulated a small mountain of food products inside and outside of their dwelling. The last letter Rule received from America informed him that the girls of Vassar had done likewise.

The first intimation that the Nitrogenists had of impending doom was from the passage of a Great Western train running northward from Oxford. As they watched it, the engine suddenly burst into a brilliant flame, which was followed shortly by an explosion, and a moment later the wrecked train lay along the line blazing fiercely. As evening drew on they saw that Oxford was on fire, even the stonework of the college seeming to burn as if it had been blocks of wax. Communication with the outside world ceased, and an ominous silence held the earth. They did not know then that London, New York, Paris, and many other cities had been consumed by fire; but they surmised as much. Curiously enough, the carbon dioxide evolved by these numerous and widespread conflagrations made the outside air more breathable, notwithstanding the poisonous nature of this mitigant of oxygenic energy. For days they watched for any sign of human life outside their own dwelling, but no one approached. As a matter of fact, all the inhabitants of the world were dead except themselves and the little colony in America, although it was long after that those left alive became aware of the full extent of the calamity that had befallen their fellows. Day by day they tested the outside air, and were overjoyed to note that it was gradually resuming its former quality. This process, however, was so slow that the young men became impatient, and endeavoured to make their house movable, so that they might journey with it, like a snail, to Liverpool, for the one desire of each was to reach America and learn the fate of the Vassar girls. The moving of the house proved impracticable, and thus they were compelled to remain where they were until it became safe to venture into the outside air, which they did some time before it reached its normal condition.

It seems to have been fortunate that they did so, for the difficulties they had to face might have proved insurmountable had they not been exhilarated by the excess of oxygen in the atmosphere. The diary which John Rule wrote showed that within the iron house his state of depression was extreme when he remembered that all communication between the countries was cut off, and that the girl to whom he was betrothed was separated from him by 3,000 miles of ocean, whitened by no sail. After the eight set out, the whole tone of his notes changed, an optimism scarcely justified by the circumstances taking the place of his former dismay. It is not my purpose here to dwell on the appalling nature of the foot journey to Liverpool over a corpse-strewn land. They found, as they feared, that Liverpool also had been destroyed by fire, only a fringe of the river front escaping the general conflagration. So enthusiastic were the young men, according to my great-grandfather's notes, that on the journey to the seaport they had resolved to walk to America by way of Behring Straits, crossing the English Channel in a row-boat, should they find that the shipping at Liverpool was destroyed. This seems to indicate a state of oxygen intoxication hardly less intense than that which had caused the Prime Minister to dance on the table.

They found the immense steamship *Teutonic* moored at the landing-stage, not apparently having had time to go to her dock when the universal catastrophe culminated. It is probable that the city was on fire when the steamer came in, and perhaps an attempt was made to board her, the ignorant people thinking to escape the fate that they felt overtaking them by putting out to sea. The landing-stage was packed with lifeless human beings, whole masses still standing up, so tightly were they wedged. Some stood transfixed, with upright arms above their heads, and death seemed to have come to many in a form like suffocation. The eight at first resolved to take the *Teutonic* across the Atlantic, but her coal bunkers proved nearly empty, and they had no way of filling them. Not one of them knew anything of navigation beyond theoretical knowledge, and Rule alone was acquainted with the rudiments of steam-engineering. They selected a small steam yacht, and loaded her with the coal that was left in the *Teutonic's* bunkers. Thus they started for the West, the Rev. Mr. Hepburn acting as captain and John Rule as engineer. It was fourteen days before they sighted the coast of Maine, having kept much too far north. They went ashore at the ruins of Portland; but embarked again, resolved to trust rather to their yacht than undertake a long land journey through an unknown and desolated country. They skirted the silent shores of America until they came to New York, and steamed down the bay. My great-grandfather describes the scene as sombre in the extreme. The Statue of Liberty seemed to be all of the handiwork of man that remained intact. Brooklyn Bridge was not entirely consumed, and the collapsed remains hung from two pillars of fused stone, the ragged ends of the structure which once formed the roadway dragging in the water. The city itself presented a remarkable appearance. It was one conglomerate mass of grey-toned, semi-opaque glass, giving some indication of the intense heat that had been evolved in its destruction. The outlines of its principal thoroughfares were still faintly indicated, although the melting buildings had flowed into the streets like lava, partly obliterating them. Here and there a dome of glass showed where an abnormally high structure once stood, and thus the contour of the city bore a weird resemblance to its former self—about such as the grim outlines of a corpse over which a sheet has been thrown bear to a living man. All along the shore lay the gaunt skeletons of half-fused steamships. The young men passed this dismal calcined graveyard in deep silence, keeping straight up the broad Hudson. No sign of life greeted them until they neared Poughkeepsie, when they saw, flying above a house situated on the top of a hill, that brilliant fluttering flag, the Stars and Stripes. Somehow its very motion in the wind gave promise that the vital spark had not been altogether extinguished in America. The great sadness which had oppressed the voyagers was lifted, and they burst forth into cheer after cheer. One of the young men rushed into the chart-room, and brought out the Union Jack, which was quickly hauled up to the mast-head, and the reverend captain pulled the cord that, for the first time during the voyage, let loose the roar of the steam whistle, rousing the echoes of the hills on either side of the noble stream. Instantly, on the verandah of the flag-covered house, was seen the glimmer of a white summer dress, then of another and another and another, until eight were counted.

The events that followed belong rather to the region of romance than to a staid, sober narrative of fact like the present; indeed, the theme has been a favourite one with poets and novelists, whose pens would have been more able than mine to do justice to this international idyll. America and England were indeed joined, as the American Ambassador had predicted at the Guildhall, though at the time his words were spoken he had little idea of the nature and complete accord of that union. While it cannot be denied that the unprecedented disaster which obliterated human life in 1904 seemed to be a calamity, yet it is possible to trace the design of a beneficent Providence in this wholesale destruction. The race which now inhabits the earth is one that includes no savages and no war lords. Armies are unknown and unthought of. There is no battleship on the face of the waters. It is doubtful if universal peace could have been brought to the world short of the annihilation of the jealous, cantankerous, quarrelsome peoples who inhabited it previous to 1904. Humanity was destroyed once by flood, and again by fire; but whether the race, as it enlarges, will deteriorate after its second extinguishment, as it appears to have done after its first, must remain for the future to determine.

THE LAST AMERICAN

John Ames Mitchell

John Ames Mitchell (1845–1918) was a man of many talents. He trained as an architect, but after a few years decided that was not for him and so trained as an artist. Looking for outlets for his work and that of others he founded first the American Art Review *in 1879, which proved too expensive, and then co-founded the original* Life *magazine in 1883, remaining its editor until his death. He also turned to writing and several of his works incorporate features of science fiction and the supernatural. His most famous book,* Amos Judd *(1895) deals with a family curse of precognition. Psychic abilities are also experienced by the eponymous child in* Drowsy *(1917), who can read thoughts. Early in his writing career Mitchell produced the following, using humour and parody to satirize the American way of life through the viewpoint of a Persian expedition discovering a ruined and desolate United States years after its collapse. The first edition, published in 1889, included many illustrations by the author, several of which are reproduced here.*

THE LAST AMERICAN

A FRAGMENT FROM THE JOURNAL OF KHAN-LI
Prince of Dimph-Yoo-Chur and Admiral in the Persian Navy

EDITED BY J.A. MITCHELL

———————

*To the American who is more than satisfied with himself
and his country this volume is affectionately dedicated*

———————

A FEW WORDS BY HEDFUL,
SURNAMED "THE AXIS OF WISDOM"

*Curator of the Imperial Museum at Shiraz.
Author of "The Celestial Conquest of Kaly-phorn-ya,"
and of "Northern Mehrika under the Hy-Bernyan Rulers."*

The astounding discoveries of Khan-li of Dimph-yoo-chur have thrown floods of light upon the domestic life of the Mehrikan people. He little realized when he landed upon that sleeping continent what a service he was about to render history, or what enthusiasm his discoveries would arouse among Persian archæologists.

Every student of antiquity is familiar with their history.

But for the benefit of those who have yet to acquire a knowledge of this extraordinary people, I advise, first, a visit to the Museum at Teheran in order to excite their interest in the subject, and second, the reading of such books as Nōfūhl's "What we Found in the West," and Nōz-yt-ahl's "History of the Mehrikans." The last-named is a complete and reliable history of these people from the birth of the Republic under George-wash-yn-tun to the year 1990, when they ceased to exist as a nation. I must say, however, that Nōz-yt-ahl leaves the reader much confused concerning the period between the massacre of the Protestants in 1907, and the overthrow of the Murfey dynasty in 1930.

He holds the opinion with many other historians that the Mehrikans were a mongrel race, with little or no patriotism, and were purely imitative; simply an enlarged copy of other nationalities extant at the time. He pronounces them a shallow, nervous, extravagant people, and accords them but few redeeming virtues. This, of course, is just; but nevertheless they will always be an interesting study by reason of their rapid growth, their vast numbers, their marvellous mechanical ingenuity and their sudden and almost unaccountable disappearance.

The wealth, luxury and gradual decline of the native population; the frightful climatic changes which swept the country like a mower's scythe; the rapid conversion of a vast continent, alive with millions of pleasure-loving people, into a silent wilderness, where the sun and moon look down in turn upon hundreds of weed-grown cities—all this is told by Nōz-yt-ahl with force and accuracy.

"Here's Truth. 'Tis a bitter Pill but good Physic."

———————

ABOARD THE ZLŌTUHB IN THE YEAR 2951

10th May

There is land ahead!

Grip-til-lah was first to see it, and when he shouted the tidings my heart beat fast with joy. The famished crew have forgotten their disconsolate stomachs and are dancing about the deck. 'Tis not I, forsooth, who shall restrain them! A month of emptiness upon a heavy sea is preparation for any folly. Nōfūhl alone is without enthusiasm. The old man's heart seems dead.

We can see the land plainly, a dim strip along the western horizon. A fair wind blows from the northeast, but we get on with cruel hindrance for the *Zlōtuhb* is a heavy ship, her bluff bow and voluminous bottom ill fitting her for speed.

The land, as we near it, seems covered with trees, and the white breakers along the yellow beach are a welcome sight.

11th May

Sighted a fine harbour this afternoon, and are now at anchor in it.

Grip-til-lah thinks we have reached one of the western islands mentioned by Ben-a-Bout. Nōfūhl, however, is sure we are further North.

12th May

What a change has come over Nōfūhl! He is the youngest man aboard. We all share his delight, as our discoveries are truly marvellous. This morning while I was yet in my bunk he ran into the cabin and, forgetting our difference in rank, seized me by the arm and tried to drag me out. His excitement so had the better of him that I captured little meaning from his words. Hastening after him, however, I was amazed to see such ancient limbs transport a man so rapidly. He skipped up the narrow stairs like a heifer and, young though I am, it was faster than I could follow.

But what a sight when I reached the deck! We saw nothing of it yesterday, for the dusk of evening was already closing about us when we anchored.

Right ahead, in the middle of the bay, towered a gigantic statue, many times higher than the masts of our ship. Beyond, from behind this statue, came the broad river upon whose waters we were floating, its surface all a-glitter with the rising sun. To the East, where Nōfūhl was pointing, his fingers trembling with excitement, lay the ruins of an endless city. It stretched far away into the land beyond, further even than our eyes could see. And in the smaller river on the right stood two colossal structures, rising high in the air, and standing like twin brothers, as if to guard the deserted streets beneath. Not a sound reached us—not a floating thing disturbed the surface of the water. Verily, it seemed the sleep of Death.

I was lost in wonder.

As we looked a strange bird, like a heron, arose with a hoarse cry from the foot of the great image and flew toward the city.

"What does it all mean?" I cried. "Where are we?"

"Where indeed!" said Nōfūhl. "If I knew but that, O Prince, I could tell the rest! No traveller has mentioned these ruins. Persian history contains no record of such a people. Allah has decreed that we discover a forgotten world."

Within an hour we landed, and found ourselves in an ancient street, the pavements covered with weeds, grass and flowers, all crowding together in wild neglect. Huge trees of great antiquity thrust their limbs through windows and roofs and produced a mournful effect. They gave a welcome shade, however, as we find the heat ashore of a roasting quality most hard to bear. The curious buildings on either side are wonderfully preserved, even sheets of glass still standing in many of the iron window-frames.

We wandered along through the thick grass, Nōfūhl and I, much excited over our discoveries and delighted with the strange scene. The sunshine is of dazzling brightness, birds are singing everywhere, and the ruins are gay with gorgeous wild flowers. We soon found ourselves in what was once a public square, now for the most part a shady grove.*

* Afterward ascertained to be the square of the City Hall.

The City of Ruins

As we sat on a fallen cornice and gazed on the lofty buildings about us I asked Nōfūhl if he was still in ignorance as to where we were, and he said:

"As yet I know not. The architecture is much like that of ancient Europe, but it tells us nothing."

Then I said to him in jest, "Let this teach us, O Nōfūhl! the folly of excessive wisdom. Who among thy pupils of the Imperial College at Ispahan would believe their venerable instructor in history and languages could visit the largest city in the world and know so little about it!"

"Thy words are wise, my Prince," he answered; "few babes could know less."

As we were leaving this grove my eyes fell upon an upturned slab that seemed to have a meaning. It was lying at our feet, partly hidden by the tall grass, having fallen from the columns that supported it. Upon its surface were strange characters in bold relief, as sharp and clear as when chiselled ten centuries ago. I pointed it out to Nōfūhl, and we bent over it with eager eyes.

It was this:

ASTOR HOUSE

"The inscription is Old English," he said. "'House' signified a dwelling, but the word 'Astor' I know not. It was probably the name of a deity, and here was his temple."

This was encouraging, and we looked about eagerly for other signs.

Our steps soon brought us into another street, and as we walked I expressed my surprise at the wonderful preservation of the stone work, which looked as though cut but yesterday.

"In such an atmosphere decay is slow," said Nōfūhl. "A thousand years at least have passed since these houses were occupied. Take yonder oak, for instance; the tree itself has been growing for at least a hundred years, and we know from the fallen mass beneath it that centuries had gone by before its birth was possible."

He stopped speaking, his eyes fixed upon an inscription over a doorway, partly hidden by one of the branches of the oak.

Turning suddenly upon me with a look of triumph, he exclaimed: "It is ours!"

"What is ours?" I asked.

"The knowledge we sought"; and he pointed to the inscription,

NEW YORK STOCK EXC...

He was tremulous with joy.

"Thou hast heard of Nhū-Yok, O my Prince?"

I answered that I had read of it at school.

"Thou art in it now!" he said. "We are standing on the Western Continent. Little wonder we thought our voyage long!"

"And what was Nhū-Yok?" I asked. "I read of it at college, but remember little. Was it not the capital of the ancient Mehrikans?"

"Not the capital," he answered, "but their largest city. Its population was four millions."

"Four millions!" I exclaimed. "Verily, O Fountain of Wisdom, that is many for one city!"

"Such is history, my Prince! Moreover, as thou knowest, it would take us many days to walk this town."

"True, it is endless."

He continued thus:

"Strange that a single word can tell so much! Those iron structures, the huge statue in the harbour, the temples with pointed towers, all are as writ in history."

Whereupon I repeated that I knew little of the Mehrikans save what I had learned at college, a perfunctory and fleeting knowledge, as they were a people who interested me but little.

"Let us seat ourselves in the shade," said Nōfūhl, "and I will tell thee of them."

We sat.

"For eleven centuries the cities of this sleeping hemisphere have decayed in solitude. Their very existence has been forgotten. The people who built them have long since passed away, and their civilization is but a shadowy tradition. Historians are astounded that a nation of more than seventy millions should vanish from the earth like a mist, and leave so little behind. But to those familiar with their lives and character surprise is impossible. There was nothing to leave. The Mehrikans possessed neither literature, art, or music of their own. Everything was borrowed. The very clothes they wore were copied with ludicrous precision from the models of other nations. They were a sharp, restless, quick-witted, greedy race, given body and soul to the gathering of riches. Their chiefest passion was to buy and sell. Even women, both of high and low degree, spent much of their time at bargains, crowding and jostling each other in vast marts of trade, for their attire was complicated, and demanded most of their time."

"How degrading!" I exclaimed.

"So it must have been," said Nōfūhl; "but they were not without virtues. Their domestic life was happy. A man had but one wife, and treated her as his equal."

In a street of the forgotten city

"That is curious! But as I remember, they were a people of elastic honour."

"They were so considered," said Nōfūhl; "their commercial honour was a jest. They were sharper than the Turks. Prosperity was their god, with cunning and invention for his prophets. Their restless activity no Persian can comprehend. This vast country was alive with noisy industries, the nervous Mehrikans darting with inconceivable rapidity from one city to another by a system of locomotion we can only guess at. There existed roads with iron rods upon them, over which small houses on wheels were drawn with such velocity that a long day's journey was accomplished in an hour. Enormous ships without sails, driven by a mysterious force, bore hundreds of people at a time to the furthermost points of the earth."

"And are these things lost?" I asked.

"We know many of the forces," said Nōfūhl, "but the knowledge of applying them is gone. The very elements seem to have been their slaves. Cities were illuminated at night by artificial moons, whose radiance eclipsed the moon above. Strange devices were in use by which they conversed together when separated by a journey of many days. Some of these appliances exist today in Persian museums. The superstitions of our ancestors allowed their secrets to be lost during those dark centuries from which at last we are waking."

At this point we heard the voice of Bhoz-ja-khaz in the distance; they had found a spring and he was calling to us.

Such heat we had never felt, and it grew hotter each hour. Near the river where we ate it was more comfortable, but even there the perspiration stood upon us in great drops. Our faces shone like fishes. It was our wish to explore further, but the streets were like ovens, and we returned to the *Zlōtuhb*.

★

As I sat upon the deck this afternoon recording the events of the morning in this journal Bhoz-ja-khaz and Ad-el-pate approached, asking permission to take the small boat and visit the great statue. Thereupon Nōfūhl informed us that this statue in ancient times held aloft a torch illuminating the whole harbour, and he requested Ad-el-pate to try and discover how the light was accomplished.

They returned toward evening with this information: that the statue is not of solid bronze, but hollow; that they ascended by means of an iron stairway into the head of the image, and looked down upon us through its eyes; that Ad-el-pate, in the dark, sat to rest himself upon a nest of yellow flies with black stripes; that these flies inserted stings into Ad-el-pate's person, causing him to exclaim loudly and descend the stairs with unexpected agility; that Bhoz-ja-khaz and the others pushed on through the upraised arm, and stood at last upon the bronze torch itself; that the city lay beneath them like a map, covering the country for miles away on both sides of the river. As for illuminating the harbour, Bhoz-ja-khaz says Nōfūhl is mistaken; there are no vestiges of anything that could give a light—no vessel for oil or traces of fire.

Nōfūhl says Jā-khāz is an idiot; that he shall go himself.

13th May

A startling discovery this morning.

By landing higher up the river we explored a part of the city where the būildings are of a different character from those we saw yesterday, Nōfūhl considers them the dwellings of the rich. In shape they are like bricks set on end, all very similar, uninteresting and monotonous.

We noticed one where the doors and shutters were still in place, but rotting from the fantastic hinges that supported them. A few hard blows brought down the outer doors in a dusty heap, and as we stepped upon the marble floor within our eyes met an unexpected sight. Furniture, statues, dingy pictures in crumbling frames, images in bronze and silver, mirrors, curtains, all were there, but in every condition of decay. We knocked open the iron shutters and let the light into rooms sealed up for centuries. In the first one lay a rug from Persia! Faded, moth-eaten, gone in places, it seemed to ask us with dying eyes to be taken hence. My heart grew soft over the ancient rug, and I caught a foolish look in Lev-el-Hedyd's eye.

As we climbed the mouldering stair to the floor above I expressed surprise that cloth and woodwork should hold together for so many centuries, also saying:

"These Mehrikans were not so unworthy as we think them."

"That may be," said Lev-el-Hedyd, "but the Persian rug is far the freshest object we have seen, and that perchance was ancient when they bought it."

On this floor we entered a dim chamber spacious and once richly furnished. When Lev-el-Hedyd pushed open the shutters and drew aside the ragged curtains we started at the sight before us. Upon a wide bed in the centre of the room lay a human form, the long yellow hair still clinging to the head. It was more a mummy than a skeleton. Around, upon the bed, lay mouldering fragments of the once white sheets that covered it. On the fingers of the left hand glistened two rings which drew our attention. One held a diamond of great price, the other was composed of sapphires and diamonds most curiously arranged. We stood a moment in silence, gazing sadly upon the figure.

"Poor woman," I said, "left thus to die alone."

"It is more probable," said Nōfūhl, "she was already dead, and her friends, departing perhaps in haste, were unable to burn the body."

"Did they burn their dead?" I asked. "In my history 'twas writ they buried them in the earth like potatoes, and left them to rot."

And Nōfūhl answered: "At one time it was so, but later on, as they became more civilized, the custom was abandoned."

"Is it possible," I asked, "that this woman has been lying here almost a thousand years and yet so well preserved?"

"I, also, am surprised," said Nōfūhl. "I can only account for it by the extreme dryness of the air in absorbing the juices of the body and retarding decay."

Then lifting tenderly in his hand some of the yellow hair, he said:

"She was probably very young, scarce twenty."

"Were their women fair?" I asked.

"They were beautiful," he answered; "with graceful forms and lovely faces; a pleasure to the eye; also were they gay and sprightly with much animation."

Thereupon cried Lev-el-Hedyd:

"Here are the first words thou hast uttered, O Nōfūhl, that cause me to regret the extinction of this people! There is ever a place in my heart for a blushing maiden!"

"Then let thy grief be of short life," responded Nōfūhl, "for Mehrikan damsels were not of that description. Blushing was an art they practised little. The shyness thou so lovest in a Persian maiden was to them an unknown thing. Our shrinking daughters bear no resemblance to these Western products. They strode the public streets with roving eyes and unblushing faces, holding free converse with men as with women, bold of speech and free of manner, going and coming as it pleased them best. They knew much of the world, managed their own affairs, and devised their own marriages, often changing their minds and marrying another than the betrothed."

"Bismillah! And men could love these things?" exclaimed Lev-el-Hedyd with much feeling.

"So it appears."

"But I should say the Mehrikan bride had much the freshness of a dried fig."

"So she had," said Nōfūhl, "but those who know only the dried fig have no regret for the fresh fruit. But the fault was not with the maidens. Brought up like boys, with the same studies and mental development, the womanly part of their nature gradually vanished as their minds expanded. Vigour of intellect was the object of a woman's education."

Then Lev-el-Hedyd exclaimed with great disgust:

"Praises be to Allah for his aid in exterminating such a people!" and he walked away from the bed, and began looking about the chamber. In a moment he hastened back to us, saying:

"Here are more jewels! also money!"

Nōfūhl eagerly took the pieces.

"Money!" he cried. "Money will tell us more than pages of history!"

There were silver coins of different sizes and two small pieces of copper. Nōfūhl studied them closely.

The face and back of one of the silver coins

"The latest date is 1937," he said; "a little more than a thousand years ago; but the piece may have been in circulation some years before this woman died; also it may have been coined the very year of her death. It bears the head of Dennis, the last of the Hy-Burnyan dictators. The race is supposed to have become extinct before 1990 of their era."

I then said:

"Thou hast never told us, O Nōfūhl! the cause of their disappearance."

"There were many causes," he answered. "The Mehrikans themselves were of English origin, but people from all parts of Europe came here in vast numbers. Although the original comers were vigorous and hardy the effect of climate upon succeeding generations was fatal. They became flat-chested and thin, with scanty hair, fragile teeth, and weak digestions. Nervous diseases unknown to us wrought deadly havoc. Children were reared with difficulty. Between 1925 and 1940, the last census of which any record remains, the population decreased from ninety millions to less than twelve millions. Climatic changes, the like of which no other land ever experienced, began at that period, and finished in less than ten years a work made easy by nervous temperaments and rapid lives. The temperature would skip in a single day from burning heat to winter's cold. No constitution could withstand it, and this vast continent became once more an empty wilderness."

Much more of the same nature he told us, but I am too sleepy to write longer. We explored the rest of the mansion, finding many things of interest. I caused several objects to be carried aboard the *Zlōtuhb*.*

---

* These objects are now in the museum of the Imperial College, at Teheran.

14th May

Hotter than yesterday.

In the afternoon we were rowed up the river and landed for a short walk. It is unsafe to brave the sun.

The more I learn of these Mehrikans the less interesting they become. Nōfühl is of much the same mind, judging from our conversation today, as we walked along together.

It was in this wise:

Khan-li.

How alike the houses! How monotonous!

Nōfühl.

So, also, were the occupants. They thought alike, worked alike, ate, dressed and conversed alike. They read the same books; they fashioned their garments as directed, with no regard for the size or figure of the individual, and copied to a stitch the fashions of Europeans.

Khan-li.

But the close-fitting apparel of the European must have been sadly uncomfortable in the heat of a Mehrikan summer.

Nōfühl.

So probably it was. Stiff boxes of varying patterns adorned the heads of men. Curious jackets with tight sleeves encased the body. The feet throbbed and burned in close-fitting casings of unyielding leather and linen made stiff by artificial means was drawn tightly about the neck.

Khan-li.

Allah! What idiots!

Nōfūhl.

Even so are they considered.

Khan-li.

To what quality of their minds do you attribute such love of need-less suffering?

Nōfūhl.

It was their desire to be like others. A natural feeling in a vulgar people.

15th May

A fair wind from the West today. We weighed anchor and sailed up the Eastern side of the city. I did this as Nōfūhl finds the upper portion of the town much richer in relics than the lower, which seems to have been given up to commercial purposes. We sailed close under one of the great monuments in the river, and are at a loss to divine its meaning. Many iron rods still dangle from the tops of each of the structures. As they are in a line, one with the other, we thought at first they might have been once connected and served as a bridge, but we soon saw they were too far apart.

Came to anchor about three miles from the old mooring. Up the river and down, North, South, East and West, the ruins stretch away indefinitely, seemingly without end.

Am anxious about Lev-el-Hedyd. He went ashore and has not returned. It is now after midnight.

16th May

Praise Allah! my dear comrade is alive! This morning we landed early and began our search for him. As we passed before the brick building which bears the inscription

DELMONICO

high up upon its front, we heard his voice from within in answer to our calls. We entered, and after climbing the ruined stairway found him seated upon the floor above. He had a swollen leg from an ugly sprain, and various bruises were also his. While the others were constructing a litter on which to bear him hence we conversed together. The walls about us bore traces of having once enclosed a hall of some beauty. In idling about I pulled open the decaying door of an old closet and saw upon the rotting shelves many pieces of glass and earthenware of fine workmanship. Taking one in my hand, a small wine-cup of glass, I approached my comrade calling his attention to its slender stem and curious form. As his eyes fell upon it they opened wide in amazement. I also observed a trembling of his hand as he reached forth to touch it. He then recounted to me his marvellous adventure of the night before, but saying before he began:

"Thou knowest, O Prince, I am no believer in visions, and I should never tell the tale but for thy discovery of this cup. I drank from such an one last night, proffered by a ghostly hand."

I would have smiled, but he was much in earnest. As I made a movement to sit beside him, he said:

"Taste first, O my master, of the grapes hanging from yonder wall."

I did so, and to my great surprise found them of an exquisite flavour, finer even than the cultivated fruit of Persia, sweeter and more delicate, of a different nature from the wild grapes we have been eating. My astonishment appeared to delight him, and he said with a laugh:

"The grapes are impossible, but they exist; even more absurd is my story!" and he then narrated his adventure.

It was this:

WHAT LEV-EL-HEDYD SAW.

Yesterday, after nightfall, as he was hastening toward the *Zlōtuhb* he fell violently upon some blocks of stone, wrenching his ankle and much bruising himself. Unable to walk upon his foot he limped into this building to await our coming in the morning. The howling of wolves and other wild beasts as they prowled about the city drove him, for safety; to crawl up the ruins of the stairway to the floor above. As he settled himself in a corner of this hall his nostrils were greeted with the delicious odour from the grapes above his head. He found them surprisingly good, and ate heartily. He soon after fell into a sleep which lasted some hours, for when he awoke the moon was higher in the heavens, the voices of the wolves were hushed and the city was silent.

As he lay in a revery, much absorbed in his own thoughts, he gradually became aware of mysterious changes taking place, as if by stealth, about him. A decorated ceiling appeared to be closing over the hall. Mirrors and tinted walls slowly crept in place of ivy and crumbling bricks. A faint glow grew stronger and more intense until it filled the great room with a dazzling light.

Then came softly into view a table of curious form, set out with flowers and innumerable dishes of glass and porcelain, as for a feast.

Standing about the room he saw solemn men with beardless faces, all in black attire, whose garments bore triangular openings upon the chest to show the shirt beneath. These personages he soon discovered were servants.

As he gazed in bewilderment, there entered other figures, two by two, who took their seats about the table. These later comers, sixty or more, were men and women walking arm in arm, the women in rich attire of unfamiliar fashion and sparkling with precious stones. The men were clad like the servants.

They ate and drank and laughed, and formed a brilliant scene. Lev-el-Hedyd rose to his feet, and moved by a curiosity he made no effort to resist—for he is a reckless fellow and knows no fear—he hobbled out into the room.

They looked upon him in surprise, and seemed much amused at his presence. One of the guests, a tall youth with yellow moustaches, approached him, offering a delicate crystal vessel filled with a sparkling fluid.

Lev-el-Hedyd took it.

The youth raised another from the table, and with a slight gesture as if in salutation, he said in words which my comrade understood, though he swears it was a language unknown to him,

"We may meet again the fourth of next month."

He then drank the wine, and so did Lev-el-Hedyd.

Hereupon the others smiled as if at their comrade's wit, all save the women, whose tender faces spoke more of pity than of mirth. The wine flew to his brain as he drank it, and things about him seemed to reel and spin. Strains of fantastic music burst upon his ears, then, all in rhythm, the women joined their partners and whirled about him with a lightsome step. And, moving with it, his throbbing brain seemed dancing from his head. The room itself, all swaying and quivering with the melody, grew dim and stole from view. The music softly died away.

Again was silence, the moon above looking calmly down upon the ivied walls.

He fell like a drunken man upon the floor, and did not wake till our voices called him.

Such his tale.

He has a clear head and is no liar, but so many grapes upon an empty stomach with the fever from his swollen limb might well explain it.

*

Bear's meat for dinner.

This morning toward noon Kuzundam, the second officer, wandered on ahead of us, and entered a large building in pursuit of a rabbit. He was about descending to the basement below, when he saw, close before him, a bear leisurely mounting the marble stairs.

Kuzundam's narrow escape

Kuzundam is no coward, but he turned and ran as he never ran before. The bear, who seemed of a sportive nature, also ran, and in close pursuit of our friend. Luckily for my friend we happened to be near, otherwise instead of our eating bear's meat, the bear might have lunched quietly off Kuzundam in the shady corridors of the "FIFTHAVENUEHOTEL."

17th May

Today a scorching heat that burns the lungs. We started in the morning prepared to spend the night ashore, and explore the northern end of the city. It was a pleasant walk through the soft grass of the shady streets, but in those places unsheltered from the sun we were as fish upon a frying-pan. Other dwellings we saw, even larger and more imposing than the one we entered yesterday. We were tempted to explore them, but Lev-el-Hedyd wisely dissuaded us, saying the day was waxing hotter each hour and it could be done on our return.

In the northern part of the town are many religious temples, with their tall towers like slender pyramids, tapering to a point. They are curious things, and surprisingly well preserved. The interiors of these temples are uninteresting. Nōfūhl says the religious rites of the Mehrikans were devoid of character. There were many religious beliefs, all complicated and insignificant variations one from another, each sect having its own temples and refusing to believe as the others. This is amusing to a Persian, but mayhap was a serious matter with them. One day in each week they assembled, the priests reading long moral lectures written by themselves, with music by hired singers. They then separated, taking no thought of temple or priest for another seven days. Nōfūhl says they were not a religious people. That the temples were filled mostly with women.

In the afternoon we found it necessary to traverse a vast pleasure-ground, now a wild forest, but with traces still visible of broad promenades and winding driveways.* There remains an avenue of bronze statues, most of them yet upright and in good condition, but very comic. Lev-el-Hedyd and I still think them caricatures, but Nōfūhl is positive they were serious efforts, and says the Mehrikans were easily pleased in matters of art.

We lost our way in this park, having nothing to guide us as in the streets of the city. This was most happy, as otherwise we should have missed a surprising discovery.

It occurred in this wise.

Being somewhat overcome by the heat we halted upon a little hill to rest ourselves. While reclining beneath the trees I noticed unusual carvings upon a huge block against which Lev-el-Hedyd was supporting his back. They were unlike any we had seen, and yet they were not unfamiliar. As I lay there gazing idly at them it flashed upon me they were Egyptian. We at once fell to examining the block, and found to our amazement an obelisk of Egyptian granite, covered with Egyptian hieroglyphics of an antiquity exceeding by thousands of years the most ancient monuments of the country!

Verily, we were puzzled!

"When did the Egyptians invade Mehrika?" quoth Bhoz-jā-khāz, with a solemn look, as if trying to recall a date.

"No Egyptian ever heard of Mehrika," said Nōfūhl. "This obelisk was finished twenty centuries before the first Mehrikan was weaned. In all probability it was brought here as a curiosity, just as we take to Persia the bronze head of George-wash-yn-tun."

---

* Olbaldeh thinks this must be the Centralpahk sometimes alluded to in Mehrikan literature.

We spent much time over the monument, and I think Nōfūhl was disappointed that he could not bring it away with him.

Also while in this park we came to a high tower, standing by itself, and climbed to the top, where we enjoyed a wide-spreading view.

The extent of the city is astounding.

Miles away in the river lay the *Zlōtuhb*, a white speck on the water. All about us in every direction as far as sight can reach were ruins, and ruins, and ruins. Never was a more melancholy sight. The blue sky, the bright sunshine, the sweet-scented air with the gay flowers and singing birds only made it sadder. They seemed a mockery.

We have encamped for the night, and I can write no more. Countless flying insects gather about us with a hateful buzz, and bite us beyond endurance. They are a pest thrice accursed.

I tell Nōfūhl his fine theory concerning the extinction of the Yahnkis is a good tale for those who have never been here.

No man without a leather skin could survive a second night.

18th May

Poor Jā-khāz is worse than sick.

He had an encounter last night with a strange animal, and his defeat was ignoble. The animal, a pretty thing, much like a kitten, was hovering near when Jā-khāz, with rare courage and agility, threw himself upon it.

And then what happened none of us can state with precision. We know we held our noses and fled. And Jā-khāz! No words can fit him. He carries with him an odour to devastate a province. We had to leave him ashore and send him fresh raiment.

This is, verily, a land of surprises.

Our hands and faces still smart from the biting insects, and the perfume of the odorous kitten promises to be ever with us.

Nōfühl is happy. We have discovered hundreds of metal blocks, the poorest of which he asserts would be the gem of a museum. They were found by Fattan-laïz-eh in the basement of a high building, all laid carefully away upon iron shelves. The flood of light they throw upon the manners and customs of this ludicrous people renders them of priceless value to historians.

I harbour a suspicion that it causes Nōfühl some pleasure to sit upon the cool deck of the *Zlōtuhb* and watch Bhoz-jā-khāz walking to and fro upon the ruins of a distant wharf.

19th May

The air is cooler. Grip-til-lah thinks a storm is brewing.

Even Nōfühl is puzzled over the wooden image we brought aboard yesterday. It is well preserved, with the barbaric colouring still fresh upon it. They found it standing upright in a little shop.

The wooden god

How these idols were worshipped, and why they are found in little shops and never in the great temples is a mystery. It has a diadem of feathers on the head, and as we sat smoking upon the deck this evening I remarked to Nōfūhl that it might be the portrait of some Mehrikan noble. Whereupon he said they had no nobles.

"But the Mehrikans of gentle blood," I asked, "had they no titles?"

"Neither titles nor gentle blood," he answered. "And as they were all of much the same origin, and came to this country simply to thrive more fatly than at home, there was nothing except difference in wealth on which to establish a superior order. Being deep respecters of money this was a satisfying distinction. It soon resulted that those families who possessed riches for a generation or two became the substitute for an aristocracy. This upper class was given to sports and pastimes, spending their wealth freely, being prodigiously fond of display. Their intellectual development was feeble, and they wielded but little influence save in social matters. They followed closely the fashions of foreign aristocracies. Great attentions were paid to wandering nobles from other lands. Even distant relatives of titled people were greeted with the warmest enthusiasm."

20th May

An icy wind from the Northeast with a violent rain. Yesterday we gasped with the hot air. Today we are shivering in winter clothing.

21st May

The same as yesterday. Most of us are ill. My teeth chatter and my body is both hot and cold. A storm more wicked never wailed about a ship. Lev-el-Hedyd calls it the shrieking voices of the seventy millions of Mehrikans who must have perished in similar weather.

A street scene in ancient Nhū-Yok [the costumes and manner of riding are taken from metal plates now in the museum at Teheran]

16th June

It is many days since I have touched this journal. A hateful sickness has been upon me, destroying all energy and courage. A sort of fever, and yet my limbs were cold. I could not describe it if I would.

Nōfūhl came into the cabin this evening with some of his metal plates and discoursed upon them. He has no respect for the intellects of the early Mehrikans. I thought for a moment I had caught him in a contradiction, but he was right as usual. It was thus:

Nōfūhl.

They were great readers.

Khan-li.

You have told us they had no literature. Were they great readers of nothing?

Nōfŭhl.

Verily, thou hast said it! Vast sheets of paper were published daily in which all crimes were recorded in detail. The more revolting the deed, the more minute the description. Horrors were their chief delight. Scandals were drunk in with thirstful eyes. These chronicles of crime and filth were issued by hundreds of thousands. There was hardly a family in the land but had one.

Khan-li.

And did this take the place of literature?

Nōfŭhl.

Even so.

20th June

Once more we are on the sea; two days from Nhū-Yok. Our decision was a sudden one. Nōfŭhl, in an evil moment, found among those accursed plates a map of the country, and thereupon was seized with an unreasoning desire to visit a town called "Washington." I wavered and at last consented, foolishly I believe, for the crew are loud for Persia. And this town is inland on a river. He says it was their finest city, the seat of Government, the capital of the country. Grip-til-lah swears he can find it if the map is truthful.

Jā-khāz still eats by himself.

2d July

We are on the river that leads to "Washington." Grip-til-lah says we shall sight it tomorrow. The river is a dirty colour.

Through the streets of "Washington"

3rd July

We see ahead of us the ruins of a great dome, also a very high shaft. Probably they belong to the city we seek.

4th July

A date we shall not forget!

Little did I realize this morning when we left the *Zlōtuhb* in such hilarious mood what dire events awaited us. I landed about noon, accompanied by Nōfūhl, Lev-el-Hedyd, Bhoz-jā-khāz, Ad-el-pate, Kuzundam the first mate, Tik'l-pālyt the cook, Fattan-laïz-eh, and two sailors. Our march had scarce begun when a startling discovery caused great commotion in our minds. We had halted at Nōfūhl's request, to decipher the inscription upon a stone, when Lev-el-Hedyd, who had started on, stopped short with a sudden exclamation. We hastened to him, and there, in the soft earth, was the imprint of human feet!

I cannot describe our surprise. We decided to follow the footprints, and soon found they were leading us toward the great dome more directly than we could have gone ourselves. Our excitement was beyond words. Those of us who had weapons carried them in readiness. The path was little used, but clearly marked. It wound about among fallen fragments and crumbling statues, and took us along a wide avenue between buildings of vast size and solidity, far superior to any we had seen in Nhū-Yok. It seemed a city of monuments.

As we ascended the hill to the great temple and saw it through the trees rising high above us, we were much impressed by its vast size and beauty. Our eyes wandered in admiration over the massive columns, each hewn from a single block, still white and fresh as if newly quarried. The path took us under one of the lower arches of the building, and we emerged upon the other side. This front we found even more beautiful than the one facing the city. At the centre was a flight of steps of magnificent proportions, now falling asunder and overgrown in many places with grass and flowers.

These steps we ascended. As I climbed silently up, the others following, I saw two human feet, the soles toward us, resting upon the balustrade above. With a gesture I directed Nōfūhl's attention

The ruins of the great temple

to them, and the old man's eyes twinkled with delight. Was it a Mehrikan? I confess to a lively excitement at the prospect of meeting one. How many were they? and how would they treat us?

Looking down upon my little band to see that all were there, I boldly marched up the remaining steps and stood before him.

He was reclining upon a curious little four-legged seat, with his feet upon the balustrade, about on a level with his head. Clad in skins and rough cloth he looked much like a hunter, and he gazed quietly upon me, as though a Persian noble were a daily guest. Such a reception was not gratifying, especially as he remained in the same position, not even withdrawing his feet. He nodded his curious head down once and up again, deeming it apparently a sufficient salutation.

The maintenance of my own dignity before my followers forbade my standing thus before a seated barbarian, and I made a gesture for him to rise. This he answered in an unseemly manner by ejecting from his mouth a brownish fluid, projecting it over and beyond the balustrade in front of him. Then looking upon me as if about to laugh, and yet with a grave face, he uttered something in an unmusical voice which I failed to understand.

Upon this Nōfūhl, who had caught the meaning of one or two words, stepped hastily forward and addressed him in his own language. But the barbarian understood with difficulty and they had much trouble in conversing, chiefly from reason of Nōfūhl's pronunciation. He afterward told me that this man's language differed but little from that of the Mehrikans, as they wrote it eleven centuries ago.

When he finally arose in talking with Nōfūhl I could better observe him. He was tall and bony, with an awkward neck, and appeared at first glance to be a man of forty years. We decided later he was under thirty. His yellow skin and want of hair made him seem much older than he was. I was also much puzzled by the expression of his face. It was one of deep sadness, yet his eyes were full of mirth, and a corner of his mouth was ever drawing up as if in mockery. For myself I liked not his manner. He appeared little impressed by so many strangers, and bore himself as though it were of small importance whether we understood him or not. But Nōfūhl since informed me that he asked a multitude of questions concerning us.

What Nōfūhl gathered was this:

This Mehrikan with his wife and one old man were all that remained of his race. Thirty-one had died this summer. In ancient times there were many millions of his countrymen. They were the greatest nation upon the earth. He could not read. He had two names, one was "Jon," the other he had forgotten. They lived in this temple because it was cool. When the temple was built, and for what purpose, he could not tell. He pointed to the West and said the country in that direction was covered with ruined cities.

The man

When Nōfūhl told him we were friends, and presented him at my direction with a hunting-knife of fine workmanship, he pushed out his right arm toward me and held it there. For an instant Nōfūhl looked at the arm wonderingly, as did we all, then with sudden intelligence he seized the outstretched hand in his own, and moved it up and down. This was interesting, for Nōfūhl tells me it was a form of greeting among the ancient Mehrikans.

While all this was going on we had moved into the great circular hall beneath the dome. This hall was of vast proportions, and there were still traces of its former splendour. Against the walls were marble statues entwined in ivy, looking down upon us with melancholy eyes. Here also we met a thin old man, whose hairless head and beardless face almost moved us to mirth.

At Nōfūhl's request our host led the way into some of the smaller rooms to show us their manner of living, and it would be impossible to imagine a more pathetic mixture of glory and decay, of wealth and poverty, of civilization and barbarity. Old furniture, dishes of silver, bronze images, even paintings and ornaments of great value were scattered through the rooms, side by side with the most primitive implements. It was plain the ancient arts were long since forgotten.

When we returned to the circular hall our host disappeared for a few moments into a room which he had not shown us. He came back bringing a stone vase with a narrow neck, and was followed by a maiden who bore drinking-cups of copper and tin. These she deposited upon a fallen fragment of the dome which served as a table.

This girl was interesting. A dainty head, delicate features, yellow hair, blue eyes and a gentle sadness of mien that touched my heart. Had she been ugly what a different ending to this day!

We all saluted her, and the Mehrikan spoke a few words which we interpreted as a presentation. He filled the cups from the stone vase, and then saying something which Nōfūhl failed to catch, he held his cup before his face with a peculiar movement and put it to his lips. As he did this Lev-el-Hedyd clutched my arm and exclaimed:

"The very gesture of the ghost!"

And then as if to himself, "And this is July fourth."

But he drank, as did we all, for our thirst was great and the odour of the golden liquid was most alluring. It tasted hotter than the fires of Jelbuz. It was also of great potency and gave a fine exhilaration to the senses. We became happier at once.

And here it was that Jā-khāz did a fatal thing. Being near the maid and much affected by her beauty, he addressed her as *Hur-al-nissa*,* which, of course, she understood not. This were well had he gone no further, but he next put his arm about her waist with intent to kiss her. Much terrified, she tried to free herself. But Jā-khāz, holding her fair chin with his other hand, had brought his lips almost to hers when the old man raised his heavy staff and brought it down upon our comrade's head with cruel swiftness. This falling stick upon a solid skull resounded about the dome and echoed through the empty corridors.

Bhoz-jā-khāz blinked and staggered back.

Then, with fury in his face, he sprang savagely toward the aged man.

But here the younger Mehrikan interfered. Rapidly approaching them and shutting tight his bony hand, he shot it from him with startling velocity, so directing that it came in contact with the face of Jā-khāz who, to our amazement, sat roughly upon the marble pavement, the blood streaming from his nostrils. He was a pitiful sight.

*   The most angelic of women.

Unaccustomed to such warfare we were seriously alarmed, and thought him killed perhaps. Ad-el-pate, a mighty wrestler, and of powerful build, rushed furiously upon the Mehrikan for whom I trembled. But his arm again went out before him, and Ad-el-pate likewise sat. A mournful spectacle, and every Persian felt his heart beat fast within him.

By this time Jā-khāz was on his feet again, purple with rage. With uplifted scimitar he sprang toward our host. The old man stepped between. Jā-khāz, with wanton cruelty, brought his steel upon the ancient head, and stretched him upon the floor. For an instant the younger one stood horror-stricken, then snatching from the floor the patriarch's staff—a heavy stick with an iron end—he jumped forward, and, quicker than words can tell it, dealt a frightful blow upon the head of Jā-khāz which sent him headlong to the ground with a broken skull.

The slaughter of the Persians

All this had happened in a moment, and wild confusion followed. My followers drew their arms and rushed upon the Mehrikan. The girl ran forward either from terror or to shield her spouse, I know not which, when a flying arrow from a sailor's cross-bow pierced her to the heart.

This gave the Mehrikan the energy of twenty men.

He knocked brave Kuzundam senseless with a blow that would have killed an ox. Such fury I had not conceived. He brought his flying staff like a thunderbolt from Heaven upon the Persian skulls, yet always edging toward the door to prevent his enemies surrounding him. Four of our number, in as many minutes, joined Jā-khāz upon the floor. Kuzundam, Ad-el-pate, Fattan-laïz-eh, and Hä-tāk, a sailor, lay stretched upon the pavement, all dead or grievously wounded.

So suddenly had this taken place, that I hardly realized what had happened. I rushed forward to stay the combat, but he mistook the purpose, struck my scimitar with a force that sent it flying through the air, and had raised his staff to deal a second for myself, when brave Lev-el-Hedyd stepped in to save me, and thrust quickly at him. But alas! the Mehrikan warded off his stroke with one yet quicker, and brought his stick so swiftly against my comrade's head that it laid him with the others.

When Lev-el-Hedyd fell I saw the Mehrikan had many wounds, for my comrades had made a savage onslaught. He tottered as he moved back into the doorway, where he leaned against the wall for an instant, his eyes meeting ours with a look of defiance and contempt that I would willingly forget. Then the staff dropped from his hand; he staggered out to the great portico, and fell his length upon the pavement. Nōfūhl hastened to him, but he was dead.

*

As he fell a wonderful thing took place—an impossible thing, as I look back upon it, but both Nōfūhl and I saw it distinctly.

In front of the great steps and facing this doorway is a large sitting image of George-wash-yn-tun. As the Mehrikan staggered out upon the porch, his hands outstretched before him and with Death at his heart, this statue slowly bowed its head as if in recognition of a gallant fight.

Perhaps it was the sorrowful acceptance of a bitter ending.

The last of the Mehrikans

7th July

Again upon the sea.

This time for Persia, bearing our wounded and the ashes of the dead; those of the natives are reposing beneath the Great Temple.

The skull of the last Mehrikan I shall present to the museum at Teheran.

THE END OF THE WORLD

Simon Newcomb

Simon Newcomb (1835–1909) was born in Canada but later established him-self in the United States as a leading astronomer. He was largely self-taught, as it was not until he was twenty-three that he was able to enrol in a School of Science. He specialized in mathematics and astronomy and in 1861 became professor of mathematics at the United States Naval Observatory in Washington, D.C. He later served as Director of the Nautical Almanac Office and, from 1884, as professor of mathematics and astronomy at John Hopkins University. His major work was on recalculating and refining the tables for the motions of the Moon and the planets. Newcomb had strong views about how certain aspects of science were progressing and, perhaps surprisingly, believed that heavier-than-air flight was impossible. He produced a science-fiction novel, His Wisdom, the Defender *(1900) about a master scientist who, in secret, builds an airfleet, powered by antigravity, and other fighting machines, and uses his power to demand peace. He succeeds becoming, in effect, Master of the World. The following story, however, shows in stark realism what Newcomb anticipated would happen if a rogue body entered the solar system and collided with the Sun.*

"MARS IS SIGNALLING A DARK STAR."

The world to which this news was flashed from the Central Observatory on the Himalayas had long been dull and stagnant. Almost every scientific discovery had been made thousands of years before, and the inventions for their application had been so perfected that it seemed as if no real improvement could be made in them. Methods of conducting human affairs had been brought into such good shape that everything went on as by machinery. Successive Defenders of the Peace of the World had built up a code of international law so complete that every question at issue between nations was settled by its principles. The only history of great interest was that of a savage time, lying far back in the mists of antiquity, when men fought and killed each other in war. The daily newspapers chronicled little but births, marriages, deaths, and the weather reports. They would not publish what was not worth talking about, and a subscriber often found at his door a paper containing little more than the simple announcement, on an otherwise blank page—"Nothing worthy of note has happened since our last issue." Only one language was spoken the world over, and all gentlemen dined in blue coats with gilt buttons, and wore white neckties with red borders. Even China, the most distant nation of all, had fallen into line several thousand years before, and lived like the rest of the world.

To find a time of real excitement it was necessary to go back 3,000 years, when messages had first been successfully interchanged with the inhabitants of Mars. To send a signal which they could see required a square mile of concentrated light as bright as the sun, and experiments extending through thousands of years had been necessary before this result could be brought about by any manageable apparatus. Signals from the plains of Siberia had been made nightly during two or three oppositions of the planet, without any answer being received. Then the world was electrified by hearing that return signals could be seen flashing in such a way that no doubt could exist about them. Their interpretation required more study than was ever expended by our archæologists on a Moabite inscription. When success was at last reached, it became evident by a careful comparison of the records that the people of Mars were more successful watchers of the stars than we were ourselves. It was found that a row of four lights diminishing in intensity from one end to the other, and pointing in one direction, meant that a new star was showing itself in that direction. Some object of this sort had been seen every two or three years from the earliest historical times, but in recent times a star had often been signalled from Mars before even the sensitive photographic plates and keen eyes of our Himalayan astronomers had discerned it.

Ordinary comets were plentiful enough. More than 25,000 had been recorded, and the number was still increasing every year. But dark stars were so rare that not one had appeared for three centuries, and only about twenty had been recorded in astronomical history. They differed from comets in not belonging to the solar system, but coming from far distant regions among the stars, and in being comparatively dark in colour, with very short tails, or perhaps none at all. They were found to be dark bodies whose origin and destination were alike unknown, each pursuing its own way through the immeasurable abysses of space. It had been found that a certain arrangement of five lights in the form of a cross on the planet meant that one of these bodies was flying through or past our system, and the head of the cross showed the direction in which it was to be looked for.

After a dozen generations of men had passed away without seeing a body of this kind, it goes without saying that the news from Mars of a coming dark star excited universal interest. Where is it? What does it mean? What is a dark star? The Himalayan astronomers were nearly buried under telegrams asking these and other questions without numbers. They could only reply that they had not yet succeeded in finding the object, but that the constellation to which the signal pointed was the head of the Dragon.

There was no likelihood that the object was yet visible, even through powerful telescopes, but this did not prevent the family telescope being brought out in every dwelling in the world, in order to scour the heavens for the new star. For some time it evaded the scrutiny even of the Himalayan astronomers. When a week had passed and it had not been sighted, men began to ask whether there was not some mistake in interpreting the signal, and whether it could be possible that the telescopes of another planet were as much better than ours as this failure would seem to indicate. The conviction began to gain ground that the signal had been misinterpreted, and that there was no dark star or anything else unusual coming. But when interest in the subject had about died away, it was suddenly renewed by the announcement that the object had been photographed very near where the signals had indicated it. It was about half-way between the head of the Dragon and the constellation Lyra, moving very slowly toward the East and South.

The problem now was to determine the orbit of the new star, and for this purpose the astronomers began to make the most accurate observations possible. Owing to the slowness of the motion, several days, perhaps two weeks would be required. While waiting for more news curiosity was excited by a new announcement:

"Mars appears to be in a state of extraordinary excitement. The five signal lights which have been seen from time to time ever since the dark star appeared are flashing in a way never before recorded. We cannot imagine what it means."

Our world could only ask: "What can it mean?" and wait patiently.

The astronomers were much puzzled about the orbit, and a month passed before they could reach a decision on the subject. Then Himalaya sent out an announcement more startling than any that had preceded it:

"The dark star has no orbit. It is falling straight toward the sun with a speed that has already reached 30 kilometres a second, and which is continually increasing as it falls. It will reach the sun in about 210 days."

The first man to see the possibilities suggested by this announcement was the Professor of Physics. Although all the scientific discoveries had probably been made, a single great physical laboratory had been established in which experiments were conducted with a faint hope of something new being learned. The laboratory was placed near the southern end of a peninsula, the site of one of the greatest cities of the ancient world, known as Nee-ork, the ruins of which, buried ages before by an earthquake, were known to extend over many square miles. To the north now stood the city of Hattan, the mighty city of the world, whose well-paved streets, massive buildings, public institutions, and lofty towers extended a day's journey to the north and west, whose wealth was fabulous, and whose sights every man in the world wanted to see at least once during his lifetime. Most of the investigations to which the laboratory was devoted had to be carried on where the temperature was the same from one year's end to another. To bring about this result an immense vault hundreds of yards in extent had been excavated at a depth of more than a hundred feet under the ground. Here was stored what one might suppose to be every piece of apparatus that human ingenuity had invented for making physical researches, and every instrument that men could make use of.

Of course the Professor of Physics, like all the rest of the world, heard that a dark star was going to fall into the sun. His proceedings after this announcement would have excited curiosity had it not been that the thoughts of men were too much occupied with the celestial visitor to notice his doings. He proceeded to supplement his immense stock of physical apparatus by a kind of supplies never before known to form the outfit of a laboratory. These consisted of flour, fresh wheat, edibles of every kind, and a supply of the seeds of almost every plant known to Botany. The few people who noticed what he was doing gave the subject no attention, supposing that he was merely extending his experiments into the vegetable kingdom. Having got his supplies all stored away, he called his assistants around him.

"I have something to say to you, and the first condition I impose is that it must be kept an absolute secret. Those who are not willing to pledge themselves to secrecy will please retire."

None retired.

"Will you all hold up your right hands in evidence of your adherence to the pledge which I exact from you?"

All did so.

"Now let me tell you what none but ourselves must hear. You all know that from the beginning of recorded history stars supposed to be new have from time to time blazed out in the heavens. The scientific men know that these stars were not really new. They were simply commonplace stars which, through the action of some cause that no one has yet brought to light, suddenly increased their heat and light thousands of times. Then, in the course of a few months, they faded away into their former insignificance, or rather, perhaps, turned into nebulæ.

"We have also known that dark bodies many times larger than the earth are flying through space like the stars themselves. Now, my theory is that if one of these objects chances to strike a star it bursts through its outer envelope and sets free the enormous fires pent up within, which burst forth in all their fury.

"Next December one of these objects is going to fall into our sun. Now I do not want to frighten you unnecessarily, but I think we may as well look this matter in the face. If my theory is correct, the light and heat of the sun will be suddenly increased thousands of times. Should this result follow, can there be any doubt as to the consequences? The whole surface of the earth will be exposed to a radiation as intense as that in the focus of a burning glass, which, you all know, will not only set fire to wood, but melt iron and crumble stone. The flood of heat will destroy all the works of man and every living being that exists upon the earth. The polar regions alone will be exempt from the radiation, because the sun will not be shining on them at the time of the collision. But they will be visited by such a flood of hot air and steam that their fate can hardly be different from that of the rest of the world.

"Under such circumstances I do not know what to do. For the present I shall merely hope that my theory is all wrong. At the same time I invite you to be in readiness to bring your wives and families here at the critical moment, so that we can all take refuge in our vaults. If nothing occurs, well and good. Nobody need know what we have planned. It is not likely that we shall feel it worth while to live if the rest of the world is destroyed. But we cannot decide that question until we face it. Keep in readiness and say nothing, that is all I have to advise for the present."

During the month that followed the Professor was very much perplexed as to whether he should make his fears known. Against doing this was the consideration that the world could not help itself, and it had better go on to the last moment in ignorance of what was coming. Physicians make it a point of honour not to inform their patient that he has a fatal illness, why should the race be apprised of its inevitable doom? The mental suffering endured in the mean time would be useless, no matter whether they were saved or lost. Why make them suffer to no purpose?

But, in spite of this reticence on his part, the world was much concerned, especially by the signals from Mars. These, instead of ceasing as always before, after one or two nights, now flashed out incessantly night after night. The Martians must be trying to tell us something of unprecedented importance. What could it be? The Professor of Physics was loudly called upon to know if there was not really some danger from the dark comet falling into the sun. The calls became so pressing that he was forced to make some sort of a reply.

"While it is impossible to state with certainty the effect that will be produced by the fall of the dark star into the sun, it is only right to say that it may possibly be followed by an increase in the sun's radiation, which will have reached its height in two or three days, and may continue abnormally great for some weeks. It will therefore be prudent to guard against the possible consequences of an increase in the sun's heat. The roofs of houses, and all combustible objects exposed to the sun's rays, should, as far as possible, be protected by a non-combustible covering. Food and clothing liable to be injured by the heat should be protected by being stored in cellars."

The Professor of Logic in the University of Hattan put all the data bearing on the subject into equations which he proceeded to solve, and then announced his judgment on the view of the Professor of Physics.

"Ten thousand years of recorded experience has led to the conclusion that the sun is one of the most stable bodies in the universe. During all the years through which meteorological records have extended there has not been a change of a single degree in the annual amount of heat radiated to the earth. In favour of the view that a sudden change will be produced by any cause whatever we have only a doubtful physical theory, sustained by no experience whatever. It is, therefore, not logical to be frightened by the prediction of the Professor of Physics, especially when he is himself in doubt about the correctness of his own view. Yet, in view of the magnitude of the interests involved, the prudence of the suggestion made by the Professor cannot be questioned. No harm can be done by taking every possible precaution."

A torrent of dispatches now poured down upon the Professor of Physics from every part of the world wanting to know whether his mathematical theory of the case was really well grounded. After all, was not the Professor of Logic right, and was it not unreasonable to suppose that an order of things which had continued, probably, for millions of years should be so suddenly changed? He could only reply that his theory had never been verified in any known case. He was glad to find his view in doubt. The main fact on which it was based—that the new stars which blazed up every few years were not new, but old stars which had suddenly burst out from some inscrutable cause—he purposely kept in the background.

While this discussion was going on, the terrible object which was darting toward our sun remained for some time invisible in every telescope but the great one of the Himalayas. In a few weeks, however, growing brighter as it came nearer the sun, it could be seen in smaller and smaller telescopes, and at last was clearly made out by every watcher of the heavens. Two months before its occurrence the time of the catastrophe was predicted to a minute by the Himalayan astronomers. It would be in the afternoon of December 12th, after the sun had set in Europe, and while it was still shining on all but the northeastern portion of the American continent and on most of the Pacific Ocean. The sun would have set to regions as far east as Labrador, and would be about an hour high on the middle portions of the Atlantic coast. The star was followed night after night with constantly increasing concern. As each evening approached, men indulged in a vain hope that the black star might prove a phantom—some ghost of the sky which would disappear never again to be seen. But this impression was always dispelled when night came on, and the telescope was pointed. The idea of an illusion vanished entirely when the object became visible to the naked eye, and was seen night after night without any telescope at all.

Every night it was a very little brighter than the night before. Yet there was nothing in the object itself that would excite alarm. Even in the most superstitious age of the world people might never have noticed it, or, if they had, would only have wondered how the star happened to be there when it had not before been seen. Now, however, the very slowness of the increase inflicted a slow torture upon the whole human race, like that experienced by a Chinese prisoner whose shaved head is made to feel the slow dropping of water. What is hardly noticeable at first gets farther and farther beyond the limit of endurance. The slowness with which the light of the star increased only lengthened the torture. Men could scarcely pursue their daily vocations. Notes went to protest on a scale that threatened universal bankruptcy. When December approached it was seen that the fall toward the sun was becoming more rapid, and that the increase in brightness was going on at a greater and still greater rate. Formerly the star had been seen only at night. Now the weird object, constantly growing larger, could be seen in full daylight, like some dragon in the sky.

As December approached the thoughts and sentiments of their remote ancestors, which had been absent for untold ages, were revived in the minds of men. They had long worshipped the invisible, beneficent, and all-pervading Power which informed the universe and breathed into its atoms the breath of life. Now this power became a remorseless Judge, about to punish the men of the present for the sins of ancestors during all time.

December forced its way in, and now the days were counted. Eleven days—ten—tomorrow nine only will elapse before the fate of the world will be decided. It required nerve to face the star; men shut their eyes to it, as if the unseen were nonexistent. Those who dared to point the telescope saw it look as large as the moon to the naked eye. But the mild and serene aspect of our satellite was not there—only a fierce glow, as that of the eye of a beast of prey.

Seven days—six days—five days—fiercer glowed the eye which in waking hours belonged to a being breathing naught but vengeance. Even in sleep men still in imagination saw the eye and felt such terrors as might be inspired by the chase of malignant and pitiless demons of the bottomless pit. They lived over again the lives of their ancestors who had been chased by wild beasts.

Three days—two days—reason began to leave its seat. The insane rushed madly about, but the guardians of the peace heeded them not. In the streets men glared into each other's eyes, but no word was necessary to express the thought.

The last day dawns: tonight—what? Calm and still was the morning; mildly as ever shone the sun, all unconscious of the enemy ready to strike him. His unconcern seemed to calm the minds of men, as if he meant to assure them that nothing was to happen. They plucked up courage to look with eye and telescope. The sun, unmoved as ever, advanced toward the West, the hours were counted—now the minutes.

At every telescope some watcher found the nerve to see what would happen. Every minute the malignant eye grew brighter and glared more fiercely; every minute it could be seen nearer the sun. A shudder spread over the whole city of Hattan as the object seemed to touch the sun's disc. A moment of relief followed when it disappeared without giving any sign. Perhaps, under the fervent heat of the sun, the star had dissolved into the air. But this hope was speedily dashed by its reappearance as a black spot on the sun, slowly passing along its face. Those who considered the case now knew that we were merely looking at the object as seen between us and the sun, and that it had not yet fallen into the latter. For a moment there was a vague hope that the computations of the astronomers had, for the first time in history, led them astray, and that the black object would continue its course over the sun, to leave it again like the planet Mercury or Venus during a transit. But this illusion was dispelled when the dark object disappeared in a moment and its place was taken by an effulgence of such intensity that, notwithstanding the darkness of the glass through which the sun was being viewed, the eyes of the lookers-on were dazzled with the brightness.

No telescope was necessary to see what followed. Looking with the naked eye through a dark-glass a spot many times brighter than the rest of the sun was seen where the black object had just disappeared. Every minute it grew larger and brighter. In half an hour this effulgence, continually increasing and extending, was seen to project away from the sun like a fan or the tail of a comet. An unearthly glow spread over the whole landscape, in the light of which pebbles glistened like diamonds. By the time the sun had set to the Eastern States its size seemed to be doubled and its brightness to have increased fourfold. Before it set on the Pacific coast the light and heat became so intense that every one had to seek the shade.

The setting of the sun afforded a respite for the night. But no sooner had it grown dark than a portentous result was seen in the heavens. It happened that Mars, in opposition, had just risen in the East, while Venus, as the evening star, was seen in the West. These objects both glowed—Venus like an electric light, Mars like a burning coal. Every one knew the cause. Shining by the reflected light of the sun, their brightness increased in the same proportion as the sunlight. It was like seeing a landscape by the light of some invisible conflagration. Its very suggestiveness added a new terror. The beholders could imagine what results were being produced on other continents by the rapidly increasing conflagration, and awaited in calm despair the result when our central luminary should again come around to our longitude.

The earth, continuing its revolution, exposed the oceans and continents in succession to the burning rays. When the sun set at San Francisco the heat was still not unbearable. But from Asia and Europe came the most portentous news through the period of what, for them, was day, while on the American continent it was night. In China and India men could only remain out of doors a few minutes at a time. In the afternoon all had to flee from the heat and take refuge in their houses.

Yet worse was the case in Europe. For a time detailed dispatches came from London. The telegraph offices had all been removed to the cellars of the buildings in which they were located, and men were trying to store everything combustible where the sun's rays could not reach it. Every fire-engine in the city was called out to sprinkle the roofs of the houses. Notwithstanding these precautions, at eleven o'clock a roof in Cheapside took fire, and soon after fires broke out here and there in nearly every quarter. By noon the whole city seemed to be in flames, the firemen fighting heat above them and around them. It would soon become impossible for a human being to live in the streets.

A few minutes later came the news that sudden relief had been experienced. A violent gale came in from the Atlantic, bringing with it a torrent of rain, which, for the time being, extinguished the flames. But a new horror was now added. The wind increased to a hurricane of unexampled force. Houses were everywhere blown down and roofs were flying in mid-air, exposing everything in the interior to the flood of water.

About 3 P. M. it was announced that the sun, having dissolved the clouds with its fervent heat, had again shone forth hotter than ever, and that the telegraph offices would soon have to be abandoned. Not another word was heard from the European side until night. Then it was announced that the heat had again been followed by a torrent of rain, and that, the sun having set, another respite had been obtained. The damage done was incalculable and the loss of life frightful, yet hope would have survived had it not been for what might be expected on the morrow.

The American continent, forewarned, undertook the most vigorous defence possible. Before the sun rose every fire-engine in Hattan was in place ready for action. Everything combustible in the city was covered with woollen cloth and sprinkled with water. The possibility of doing something occupied all minds, and after the sun rose men fought the heat with the courage of despair. Fiercely though the sun poured down its flood of fire, an engine was ready to extinguish the flames wherever they burst forth. As in Europe, they were soon aided by floods of rain. Thus passed the day, while the sun shed a fiercer heat with every passing hour.

The scene while the sun was setting filled all minds with despair. The size of our luminary was multiplied so many times that it was an hour after the lower edge touched the horizon before the upper edge had set. When it finally disappeared the place of twilight was taken by a lurid illumination of the whole heavens, which still left the evening brighter than an ordinary day. Cosmic flames millions of miles in extent, rising from the sun, still appeared above the horizon from time to time. Even at midnight a sort of aurora, tenfold brighter than any that had ever been recorded, seemed to spread over the sky in rising sheets of fiery vapour, which disappeared at the zenith. The trained eye of the Professor of Physics watched the scene from the iron door of his vault. He knew the cause. The exploded sun was sending forth its ions with a velocity almost comparable with that of light to every part of the solar system. In the midst of the illumination the planet Mars could still be seen glowing with supernatural brightness, but no word came from the Himalayan Observatory as to any signals it might be sending to us. Communication from other continents had entirely ceased, and the inhabitants of the whole American continent awaited the coming of what they knew must be the last day.

After midnight, although the ions were flying thicker than ever, a supernatural light seemed to spread over the landscape. The very contrast to what was expected to come in the morning added to the depression and terror. If any vain hope was entertained that the sun might, during its course over the Pacific Ocean and Asia, abate some of its fiery stream, it was dispelled when, shortly after three o'clock, the first sign of the approaching luminary was seen in the East. Still thicker the ions flew, as a bright radiance, far exceeding that of the evening before, heralded the approach of what had always been considered the great luminary, but was now the great engine of destruction. Brighter and brighter grew the eastern horizon, until, long before the actual sun appeared above it, the eye could no longer endure the dazzling blaze. When, an hour later, the sun itself appeared, its rays struck the continent like a fiery flood. As they advanced from the Atlantic to the Pacific everything combustible which they struck burst into flame, stones were crumbled by the heat, towers and steeples fell as if shaken by an earthquake. Men had to take refuge in caves or cellars or beneath any covering which could protect them from the fierce heat. Old and young, rich and poor, male and female, crowded together in the confusion of despair. The great magnates of commerce and industry, whose names were everywhere familiar as household words, on whose wealth and power all the millions that inhabited the continent had looked with envy or admiration, were now huddled with their liveried servants beneath the ruins of falling houses, in the cellars of their own homes, in the vaults of their banks, or under any shelter which could protect them from the burning of a thousand sins.

The Professor of Physics, with his assistants, could only look through a crevice in the covering of his vault and see the fiery radiance which was coming from the East. When the covering grew so hot that he felt refuge must soon be taken in the lowest vaults, the sun was suddenly cut off by a rising cloud of blackness coming in from the Atlantic. The whole ocean was boiling like a pot, and the rising steam was carried over the land by a gale produced by the expansion of the air over the ocean. Moving with inconceivable velocity, the gale passed over the continent, sweeping before it every vestige of human work that stood in its path. Even the stones of the buildings, cracked and pulverized by the heat, were now blown through the air like dust, and, churned with the rain, buried the land under a torrent of mud. The lightning played incessantly everywhere, and, if it did not destroy every being exposed to it, it was only because no living beings survived where it struck. Constantly thickening and darkening clouds poured down their storm of rain upon the ruins. But no relief was thus afforded to the mass of cringing humanity which remained protected in vaults and cellars. The falling flood was boiling hot, scalding to death every one upon whom it fell. It poured through cracks and crevices, flooding cellars, saturating the ruins of buildings, and if a living being remained it scalded him to death.

The Professor and his official family were, for the time being, saved from destruction by the construction of their subterranean chambers. The heat and the wind had effaced every structure at the mouth of the cave, and driven them into the lowest recess of their vaults. Against the iron doors which walled them in the flood pressed like the water against the compartments of a ship riven in two by a collision. The doors burned the hand that touched them, but the boiling water leaked through only in small streams.

The few survivors of the human race here huddled together could only envy their more fortunate fellow-men who, in the sleep of death, had escaped such an imprisonment as they now suffered. Had the question of continuing to survive been put to a vote, all would have answered it in the negative. Hope was gone, and speedy death was the best that could be prayed for. Only the conscience which had been implanted in the race through long ages prohibited their taking their own lives. They had provisions for two years, and might, therefore, survive during that period, if the supply of air and oxygen should hold out. For producing the latter both material and apparatus existed in the vaults. The reflection that such was the case was painful rather than pleasurable. While they did not have the nerve to let themselves be smothered to death, they felt that the devices for prolonging their lives, to which instinct compelled them to resort, could only be the means of continuing their torture. Electric light they had in abundance, but by day or night nothing could be done. They were in the regions of eternal night, except when they chose to turn on the current. From time to time one or another, moved more by the necessity of doing something than by any real object, examined the doors of the cave to see what changes might have taken place in the pressure of the water against them. Long after the latter had ceased to trickle through the cracks the doors continued hot, but as time passed—they could not say whether days, weeks, or months—they found the doors growing cooler.

They at length ventured to open them. A sea of mud, knee-deep, but not quite at a scalding temperature, was found in the passages outside of them. Through this they were at length able to wade, and in time made their way to the open air. Emerging, it was impossible to say whether it was day or night. The illumination was brighter than anything ever known in the brightest day, yet no sun could be seen in the sky. The latter seemed filled with a nebulous mass of light, through and over which the clouds of ions were still streaming like waves of fire. The temperature was barely endurable, but it was no worse than the stifling closeness of their subterranean abode.

The first effect of the outer air was to produce an impression as of waking from a dream. But a glance over the landscape dispelled this impression in a moment. What they saw must be reality, though awful beyond conception. Vainly their eyes looked for the great city. No city, not even a ruin was there. They longed in vain for human help; not an animated being was in sight. Every vestige of man and his works—it might even be said every vestige of the work of Nature was gone. On three sides were what seemed great rivers of slime, while, toward the North, the region which had swarmed with the life and activity of the great world-centre was a flat surface of dried clay, black sand, or steaming mud, in which not even an insect crawled. In the thick and vaporous air not a bird warbled its note. To return to their dungeons was like a prisoner returning to his cell. Farther they must go in a search for some familiar object or some sign of humanity. Is there no telegraph to send a word of news? No railway on which a train may run? No plough with which the furrow may be turned? No field in which wheat can be sown? These questions were asked in silence; had they been asked aloud not even an echo would have answered. When the Professor had stored seeds and provisions in his vaults it was with the thought that, if the worst should happen, he and his companions might repopulate the earth. But now every such prospect dissolved away.

As their strength ebbed, a holy calm spread over the souls of all. The Professor found words:

"Such is the course of evolution. The sun, which for millions of years gave light and heat to our system and supported life on the earth, was about to sink into exhaustion and become a cold and inert mass. Its energy could not be revived, except by such a catastrophe as has occurred. The sun is restored to what it was before there was any earth upon which it could shed its rays, and will in time be ready to run its course anew. In order that a race may be renewed it must die like an individual. Un-told ages must once more elapse while life is reappearing on earth and developing in higher forms. But to the Power which directs and controls the whole process the ages of humanity are but as days, and it will await in sublime patience the evolution of a new earth and a new order of animated nature, perhaps as far superior to that we have witnessed as ours was to that which preceded it."

THE GREAT CRELLIN COMET

George Griffith

In the mid-1890s George Griffith (1857–1906) was the most prolific and best-selling writer of scientific romance in Britain until eclipsed by the popularity of H.G. Wells. Griffith established his reputation in 1893 with his first serialized novel The Angel of the Revolution, *in which a new form of flying machine allows anarchists to take control of Britain. The consequences of their victory are explored in a sequel* Olga Romanoff, or the Syren of the Skies *(1894). These two novels were part of a growing interest in "future war" fiction which was popular in the decades before the First World War. Griffith continued to write future war novels, including* The Outlaws of the Air *(1895),* The Great Pirate Syndicate *(1899) and* The Lake of Gold *(1902), and as a result became rather typecast. It is almost all he is remembered for these days even though he wrote some forty other books ranging from fantasy, crime and historical adventure. He wrote further science fiction including his tour of the solar system,* A Honeymoon in Space *(1901) and a lost-race novel,* A Criminal Croesus *(1904). Of particular interest amongst his shorter fiction is the following story, first published in 1897 and included in his collection* Gambles With Destiny *(1899). Apart from showing his awareness of the works of Verne and Wells, it was the first story to describe a technological solution to fighting the danger of an approaching comet and the first that I know to use the name Terra for Earth.*

Griffith later included much of the story into his final novel The World Peril of 1910 *(1907). Alas, by the time that was published Griffith had died aged only 49, having become an alcoholic.*

I

IN THE FIRST PLACE, PERHAPS IT HAD BETTER BE SAID AT ONCE that the greatest and most imminent peril that the planet Terra has ever been threatened with since it became a world suited to the habitation of men and monkeys, would never have been averted if, in the first place, Mr. Emerson G. Crellin had not made a practically uncountable and ever-increasing pile of dollars by almost every one of the multifarious methods known to the dollar-piling genius of the Great Republic; and if, in the second place, he had not been possessed of two hobbies, upon either of which he was prepared to spend the last dollar in his bottomless pockets.

As it would be difficult to say which of these hobbies was to him the more important, we may take as the first of them that which was calculated to bulk most largely in the eyes of the world. This was astronomy. Among the many millionaire countrymen of his who have so magnificently endowed the temples of this noblest of the sciences, Emerson G. Crellin was determined not to be the least. But what he had done for astronomy was done, not in his native land, but amidst the sylvan beauties of the Surrey hills, and it was here that his second hobby came in. He had a daughter, whom he had somewhat boldly but, as the event proved, justifiably, christened Auriole, and his twin ambition to that of finding the means of making wider and longer excursions into the realms of space than any one else had done was to see the glitter of a coronet—none of your new-creation, bobbed-up-with-the-last-social-earthquake coronets, as he put it, but one that dated back at least to the days when the world had not yet been enriched by the addition of what was some day to be the United States—shining on the brow of his darling Auriole.

It was this that had brought him with his millions and his motherless daughter to the country in which circumstances were most favourable to the making of such an investment, and this was also the reason why the famous Crellin Observatory and the immortal Crellin Reflector with its sixty-four-inch object-glass was located on the Surrey hills instead of on the Alleghanies or the slopes of the Rockies. The observatory was built on the summit of Leith Hill, which had been acquired by the further acquisition and gift in perpetuity to the nation of an addition of about a thousand acres to Hurtwood Common. Leith-hill Place had been included in the purchase and exchange, and here dwelt the millionaire and his daughter with another member of the household who may as well be introduced at once.

This was Arthur Lennox, a man still in the early thirties, who had not only been first of his year in mathematics at London and Cambridge—which is the same thing as saying he was Gold Medallist and Senior Wrangler—but he had so far distinguished himself in original astronomical research that he had gone straight from Cambridge to Greenwich, and he had already made himself one of the most distinguished of the Astronomer Royal's assistants, when Mr. Emerson G. Crellin offered him the seductive prospect of becoming chief of the Crellin Observatory at an almost dazzling salary, and having the finest telescope and one of the best collections of astronomical instruments in the world absolutely at his disposal.

He was a staid, quiet, strong-faced and strong-limbed man, with not much of the student apparent about him save the squareness of his head, the breadth of his brows, and a certain suspicion of dreaminess lurking in the clear grey eyes that looked out from beneath them. But underneath the gravity and chilliness of his scientific exterior there lay the nature of an entirely human man; and this being the case, it was hardly to be expected that he should live for months together under the same roof and in almost constant companionship with one of the most delightful products of the union of the East and the West, the old and the new Anglo-Saxondom, or, in other words, one of the fairest daughters of the Imperial Race of earth, without knowing it as such a man might be expected to know it.

But he also knew the purpose which had brought her to England, and had so given him at once the pleasure and the pain of her acquaintance. His own private opinion of this purpose was by no means an exalted one, but, then, it was a biassed opinion, and he knew it. He knew also that his business at Leith Hill had only just as much to do with this world as was included within the fence which encircled the Observatory buildings. The rest was extra-terrestrial. He recognized, in short, that his proper place was far away in the fields of Space, among planets and suns and stars, star-mists and nebulæ; and that he had a great deal more concern with the eccentricities of the orbits of comets than he had with that of human nature complicated by attractions far more difficult of calculation than that of gravity.

He saw all this clearly, and accepted the situation with perfect loyalty. He did not even admit to himself how powerful this attraction was for him. He only recognized that, to use an astronomical simile, conjunction was an impossibility, and that, so far as human probabilities went, it was not his destiny ever to become the companion of this radiant star, already as far removed from him in one sense as the stars which he could only see with the help of his huge telescope, were in another.

As regards Miss Auriole herself, she also, to all appearances, accepted the situation in the most perfectly sensible fashion. She, too, knew her destiny, and didn't appear to have the slightest objection to it. All that she stipulated for, as she had an absolute and admitted right to do, was that the possessor of the coronet should be, as she put it, a man as well as a lord; and that, as far as possible, she should herself have the unfettered choosing of him. Subject always to this paramount consideration, she and the young astronomer were the very best of friends and even companions, and nothing was more delightful to her quick and comprehensive intelligence than the excursions which they took together from the top of Leith Hill into the star-strewn fields of immensity, wandering among the radiant worlds which make their eternal march along the Milky Way, or visiting planet after planet of the Solar System—a proceeding which, in comparison with their wider travels, seemed almost to resemble the making of a series of calls at the houses of their friends on the country-side.

It was a little after four o'clock one cloudless morning in July that the Professor, as Mr. Crellin took a sort of ceremonious pride in styling his chief astronomer, came out of the Equatorial House and locked the door behind him.

When he had done so, he looked up to the eastward, where the Morning Star hung flashing like a huge white diamond in splendid solitude against the brightening background of the sky. His strong face looked somewhat pale and drawn, his lips were tightly pressed together, and his eyes, which had hardly known three hours' sleep in as many nights, had a look in them that was not to be altogether accounted for by mere weariness.

And yet, tired as he undoubtedly was, he did not take the path which led down to the house after he had let himself out of the inclosure. His work was over for the night, and he might have gone to bed till lunch-time had he chosen. But instead of that, after another long look up at the Morning Star, he turned away with a sigh that might have been one of weariness or something else, and with his hands thrust deep into his trouser pockets, he began to walk with downbent head and slow, irregular strides westward towards Hurtwood Common.

When he sat down to breakfast that morning at half-past eight, Mr. Crellin said to him in the half-paternal, half-deferential tone in which he usually addressed him—

"Say, Professor, I guess I shall have to lock that observatory up and send you over to see how they're getting on with their star-finding and comet-hunting in the States. You're just wearing yourself out body and brain over this new comet of yours. Of course it's very satisfactory that the Crellin Reflector should have got hold of it before any one else has a notion that there is such a thing knocking around; but still, you know, we can't have its discoverer wearing himself to a shadow before the time comes to take the glory of it."

"No, indeed; that's not to be talked about," said Miss Auriole, looking with a just perceptible admiration at the still fairly substantial frame of the shadow; and as she did so, it seemed to her, whether rightly or wrongly, that there was just a suspicion of a stoop in the broad shoulders, and ever so slight a falling forward of the well-poised, erectly carried head. "I do believe, Professor, that this is about the third night that you have had no sleep; and here, instead of getting in forty winks during the day, you've been blinding yourself over those wildernesses of figures and tangling your brain up with equations and cube roots and things. I know something about them, for I shall never forget my struggles with them at Vassar. Would it be impertinent to ask how much longer you are going to make yourself a martyr to science in this way?"

"Perhaps until the end of the—Good Heavens! what nonsense I am talking!" said the Professor, suddenly looking up from his plate with the expression of a man just awakened from a dream. "I really do think I have been going too long without sleep, and I must try to get some today. You see, the man who discovers a new comet is like one of the old discoverers the first time he sighted the shore of a new continent. The temptation to go on is irresistible, and one is apt to forget that, after all, a brain is something else than a machine. Still, I don't think you need have any anxiety about me. You know, I have learnt to take my sleep as a Red Indian takes his meals, and when I have settled the question of this precious comet, I shall probably go to bed and stop there the best part of a week."

"The question?" echoed Mr. Crellin. "What's that? I didn't know there was any question about it. You *have* discovered it, haven't you, Professor?"

"I have made a discovery, Mr. Crellin," he replied, speaking rather more seriously than the circumstances seemed to warrant; "but whether I have found a hitherto unknown comet or not is another matter. What I have done is this: Thanks to that magnificent instrument of yours, I have seen a comet in a part of the heavens where no comet ought to be just now, according to the calculations of all the known orbits and periods; but whether it is a new one or a known one, which, by one cause or another, has been deflected from its orbit and started off on a new course, is the question of which I spoke just now. That I have not yet been able to decide; but, of course, in any case," he went on, with a smile which Miss Auriole thought somewhat lacking in spontaneity, "the discovery will be an important one—very important, I fear—that is to say, of course, I expect—and the honour of the Crellin Reflector cannot fail to be duly vindicated."

"And also that of the discoverer," corrected Miss Auriole; "for, after all, however good the telescope is, it's only a mechanical sort of eye that it needs a brain to use properly, and if the brain doesn't take care of itself, the eye won't be much use; so I want you to promise me just now, Professor, that you are going to lie down the moment breakfast's done, and sleep straight on to lunch-time. You know," she added, colouring ever so slightly, "we're having a garden-party this afternoon, and Lord Westerham and his mother are coming, and I was going to ask you to do the honours of the Observatory, if you hadn't anything else very particular to do."

"I can promise that easily," he replied, looking, as she thought, a trifle earnestly at her out of his tired eyes, "as it is exactly what I was going to do. I shall not have to be at the telescope till nearly eleven tonight, so I shall have plenty of time to get a good nap and do what I can in the way of helping to entertain your friends— and—and his lordship, whom, by the way, I don't think I've told you before, was rather a chum of mine when we were at Trinity together. Westerham's about as good a specimen of the very falsely styled effete aristocracy of this country as a man would wish to call a friend or—a woman—well, something else."

II

The garden-party was both socially and scientifically a great success, and even the young Professor appeared to enjoy it in his usual quiet, grave fashion. The great Reflector was, of course, the supreme object of interest, though nothing was said about the new comet which had been discovered swimming in space far outside the confines of all known systems, for that was still a secret, and was to remain so until all calculations had been completed, and Arthur Lennox was able to tell his brother astronomers, all over the world, how they were to point their telescopes in order to observe the newly arriving stranger from the unknown regions beyond the worlds.

Lennox, as has already been mentioned, had been at Trinity with Lord Westerham, and they had remained good friends since. In fact, it was partly through his lordship's influence as well as his own talents that the young astronomer had got to Greenwich. But even these circumstances hardly seemed to warrant a very direct and intimate question which he put point-blank to him as they were walking together to Ockley Station after the party.

"Westerham," he said, suddenly stopping and looking him straight in the eyes, "I am going to ask you a question which you will probably think a very impertinent one; and, further, whether you answer it or not, I am going to ask you not to ask me why I ask it. There now, there are a good many 'asks' in that, but I wanted to put it plainly, even at the expense of a little tautology."

Lord Westerham was one of the frankest and most open-minded of men, and he stared in a somewhat puzzled fashion at Lennox as he replied—

"My dear fellow, you are at perfect liberty to ask me what question you like; and, if I can, I'll answer it without asking any more questions; but look here, old man," he broke off with a sudden change in his voice, "I hope it's nothing—well, unpleasant—nothing that's going to bring any trouble upon you, for instance—for, 'pon my word, I never saw even you look quite as serious as you do now. But, at any rate, whatever it is, out with it; you can't offend me even if you tried."

"You are about the only man, I think, I should find it possible to ask such a question," Lennox replied, speaking hesitatingly and rather awkwardly, "for it's—it's a precious awkward one for any man to ask another. To put it as shortly as I can, it is just this: Have you made up your mind to marry Miss Crellin; and, if so, is the matter irrevocable?"

Lennox, feeling very like a man in the dock who has just heard the fatal "guilty" spoken by the foreman of the jury, waited with a very plainly depicted expression of mingled apology and apprehension on his slightly flushed face. Lord Westerham's eyes and mouth opened together, but it was a smile that opened his mouth, and there were strong symptoms of a laugh in his honest blue eyes. Then he took a step forward, and his hand fell with a slap on Lennox's shoulder.

"My dear fellow," he said, "why, don't you know—"

"Know what?" said Lennox, with something like a gasp. "You're not—"

"No," said his lordship, shaking his head and trying to look serious—"no, I'm not engaged to her. What I was going to say was, don't you know that I have been engaged to my cousin Lilian Northcote ever since she was old enough—well—to understand the difference between being kissed by a girl and by a boy? No, no; you needn't have any fears of me, old man. Not even Miss Auriole's beauty, with all the glitter of the old gentleman's millions as a halo, would tempt me from that allegiance; and then, you know, happily the Westerham coronet doesn't want regilding. But now that I know what your question is, I am rather sorry that I promised not to ask why you asked it. Still, I dare say I can give a pretty good guess at it, so I suppose I must be content with that."

"A pretty good guess at it!" said Lennox to himself about half an hour later, when he was striding back alone. "A pretty good guess! Good God, if he only could, I wonder what he would think! He with all his splendid prospects and, as he believes, a whole long life of happiness in front of him; and thirteen months today—yes, almost to this very hour—well, for the present, ignorance is bliss.

"And now, I wonder what the old gentleman will say. Anyhow, that's one load off my mind. There won't be anything mean about it. He or she, or both of them, may say 'Yes' or 'No;' but, after all, neither of them will be able to think there is anything dishonour-able in it. A world for a girl! It sounds quite romantic. Fancy me as a hero of a romance, and one, too, if it only comes off, that will put Jules Verne and Flammarion somewhat in the shade! Ah, well! 'sufficient unto the day,' etc. I think I'll tackle the old man first. No, I don't think I will. It is the conventional way, of course; but the circumstances are anything but conventional, and if she won't have anything to do with me, well, there's an end of it—and possibly of the world too. Seems a rather selfish way to put it. In fact, some exalted moralists might call it a bit mean, but—ah! ten o'clock."

He stopped suddenly as the soft chime of an old church clock came drifting along the valley. He listened to the four chimes, and then to the ten slow, clear strokes that tolled but upon the still air of the July evening. At the tenth he started, and a shudder ran through his well-knit, muscular frame. Then, turning his face upwards towards the well-known constellations that were growing brighter in the darkening sky, he began his walk and his reverie again.

"Just fancy! A year and a month from today that very clock may be sounding the death-knell of the human race, striking the hour of Doom, in fact; and forty-six minutes and thirty-eight seconds later—Phew! it isn't a pleasant thing even for the callously scientific mind to contemplate. It seems almost wrong to tell her anything about it, but—rubbish! what an ass I am! It's got to be known, and as soon as the Lick and the Yerkes people get on to it, it won't take them very long to work out the orbit and period; and wouldn't they just score nicely over the discoverer of the Crellin Comet? No, I shall tell her myself; and I may as well tell her tonight as any other time. It's rather lucky I made that promise to show it to her tonight for the first time. I couldn't have a better opportunity."

The result of this resolution was that a little after half-past eleven Miss Auriole was looking wonderingly into the eye-piece of the great Reflector, watching a tiny little patch of mist, somewhat brighter towards one end than the other, like a little wisp of white smoke rising from a very faint spark, that was apparently floating across an unfathomable sea of darkness. She seemed to see this darkness through, and behind a swarm of stars of all sizes and colours. They appeared very much more wonderful and glorious and important than the little spray of white smoke, because she hadn't yet the faintest conception of its true import to her and every other human being on earth; but she was very soon to know now.

While she was watching it in breathless silence, in which the clicking of the mechanism which kept the great telescope moving so as to exactly counteract the motion of the machinery of the universe sounded like the blows of a sledge-hammer on an anvil, Arthur Lennox stood beside her, wondering should he begin to tell her, and what he should say. At last she turned away from the eye-piece, and looked up at him with something like a scared expression in her pretty eyes, and said—

"It's very wonderful, isn't it, that one should be able to see all that just by looking into a little bit of a hole like that? And you tell me all those great big bright stars around your comet are so far away that if you look at them in the ordinary way you don't even see them—and there they look almost as if you could put out your hand and touch them. It's very wonderful, isn't it? And just a little bit awful, too!" she added, with a little shiver.

"Yes," he said, speaking slowly and even more gravely than she thought the subject warranted, "yes, it is both wonderful and, in a way, awful. Do you know that some of those stars you have seen in there are so far away that the light which you see them by may have left them when Solomon was king in Jerusalem? They may be quite dead and dark now, or reduced into fire-mist by collision with some other star. And then, perhaps, there are others behind them again so far away that their light has not even reached us yet, and may never do While there are human eyes on earth to see it."

"Yes, I know," she said, smiling. "You don't forget that I have been to college—and light travels about a hundred and eighty-six thousand miles a second, doesn't it? But come, Professor, aren't you what they call stretching the probabilities a little when you say that the light of some of them will never get here, as far as we're concerned? I always thought that we had a few million years of life to look forward to before this old world of ours gets worn out."

"There are other ends possible for this world besides wearing out, Miss Auriole," he answered, this time almost solemnly. "Other worlds have, as I say, been reduced to fire-mist. Some have been shattered to tiny fragments to make asteroids and meteorites—stars and worlds, in comparison with which this bit of a planet of ours is nothing more than a speck of sand, a mere atom of matter drifting over the wilderness of immensity. In fact, such a trifle is it in the organism of the universe, that if some celestial body collided with it—say a comet with a sufficiently solid nucleus—and the heat developed by the impact turned it into a mass of blazing gas, an astronomer on Neptune, one of our own planets, wouldn't even notice the accident, unless he happened to be watching the earth through a powerful telescope at the time."

"And is such an accident, as you call it, possible, Professor?" she asked, jumping womanlike, by a sort of unconscious intuition, to the very point to which he was so clumsily trying to lead up. "I thought you spoke rather queerly about this comet of yours at breakfast this morning. I hope there isn't any chance of its getting on to the same track as this terrestrial locomotive of ours. That would be just awful, wouldn't it? Why, what's the matter, Professor? You are going to be real ill, I know! You had better get down to the house, and go to bed. It's want of sleep, isn't it? You'll be driving yourself mad that way. Come to the couch and lie down for a moment. You look as if you are going to fall. Shall I call Mr. Sandheim?"

A sudden and terrible change had come over him while she was speaking. It was only for the moment, and yet to him it was an eternity. It might, as she said, have been the want of sleep, for insomnia plays strange tricks sometimes with the strongest of intellects; or, more probably, it might have been that and the horror of his secret working on the great love that he had for this girl who was sitting there alone with him in the silence of that dim room and in the midst of the glories and the mysteries of the universe.

His eyes had grown fixed and staring, and looked sightlessly at her, and his face shone ghastly pale in the dim light of the solitary shaded lamp. Certainly, one of those mysterious crises which are among the unsolved secrets of psychology had come upon him like some swift access of delirium.

He no longer saw her sitting there by the telescope, calm, gracious, and beautiful. He saw her as, by his pitiless calculations, he must do that time thirteen months to come—with her soft grey eyes starting, horror-driven, from their orbits, staring blank and wide and hideous at the overwhelming hell that would be falling down from heaven upon the devoted earth. He saw her fresh young face withered and horror-lined and old, and the bright-brown hair grown grey with the years that would pass in those few final moments. He saw the sweet red lips that had tempted him so often to wild thoughts parched and black, wide open and gasping vainly for the breath of life in the hot, burnt-out atmosphere.

Then he saw—no, it was only a glimpse; and with that the strange trance-vision ended. What must have come after that would in all certainty have driven him mad there and then, before his work had even begun; but at that moment, swiftly severing the darkness that was falling over his soul, there came to him an idea, bright, luminous, and lovely as an inspiration from Heaven itself, and with it came back the calm sanity of the sternly disciplined intellect, prepared to contemplate not only the destruction of the world he lived in, but even the eternal loss of the woman he loved—the only human being who could make that world beautiful or even tolerable to him.

The vision was blotted out from the sight of his soul, the darkness cleared away from his eyes, and he saw her again as she still was. It had all passed in a few moments, and yet in them he had been down into hell, and he had come back to earth and her presence.

Almost by the time she had uttered her last word, he had regained command of his voice, and he began clearly and quietly to answer the question which was still echoing through the chambers of his brain.

"It was only a little passing faintness, thank you, and something else which you will understand when I have done, if you have patience to hear me to the end," he said, looking straight at her for a moment, and then beginning to walk slowly up and down the room past her chair. "I am going to surprise you, perhaps to frighten you, and very probably to offend you deeply," he began again in a quiet, dry sort of tone, which somehow impressed her against all her convictions that he didn't much care whether or not he did any or all of these things; but there was something else in his tone and manner which held her to her seat silent and attentive, although she was conscious of the distinct desire to get up and run away.

"Your guess about the comet, or whatever it may prove to be, is quite correct. I don't think it is a new one. From what I have seen of it so far, I have every reason to believe that it is Gambart's comet, which was discovered in 1826, and became visible to the naked eye in the autumn of 1833. It then crossed the orbit of the earth one month after the earth had passed the point of intersection. After that, some force divided it in two, and in '46 and '52 it reappeared as two twin comets constantly separating. Now it would seem that the two masses have come together again; and, as they are both larger in bulk and greater in density, it would appear that, somewhere in the distant fields of space, they have united with some other and denser body; and the result is, that what is practically a new comet, with a much denser nucleus than any hitherto seen, is approaching our system; and, unless a miracle happens, or there is a practically impossible error in my calculations, it will cross the orbit of the earth thirteen months from today, precisely at the moment that the earth itself arrives at the point of intersection."

So far Auriole had listened to the stiff scientific phraseology with more interest than alarm; but now she took advantage of a little pause, and said—

"And the consequences, Professor? I mean the consequences to us as living beings. You may as well tell me everything now that you've gone so far."

"I am going to," he said, stopping for a moment in his walk. "And I am going to tell you something more than that. Granted that what I have said happens, one of two things must follow. If the nucleus of the comet is solid enough to pass through our atmosphere without being dissipated, it will strike the surface with so much force that both it and the earth will probably be transformed into fiery vapour by the conversion of the motion of the two bodies into heat. If not, its contact with the oxygen of the earth's atmosphere will produce an aerial conflagration which, if it does not roast alive every living thing on earth, will convert the oxygen by combustion into some irrespirable and poisonous gas, and so kill us by a slower, but no less fatal, process."

"Horrible!" she said, shivering this time. "You sound like a judge pronouncing sentence of death on the whole human race. I suppose there is no possibility of reprieve? Well, go on, Professor; is there anything else?"

"Yes," he said, "there is something else. Those are the scientific facts, as far as they go. I am going to tell you the chances now, and something beside. There is just one chance—one possible way of averting universal ruin from the earth, and substituting for it nothing more serious than an unparalleled display of celestial fireworks. All that will be necessary is perfect calculation and unstinted expenditure of money."

"Well," she said, "can't you do the calculations, Professor? and hasn't dad got millions enough? How could he spend them better than saving the whole human race from being burnt alive? There isn't anything else, is there?"

"There *was* something else," he said, stopping in front of her again. She had risen to her feet as she said the last words, and the two stood facing each other in the dim light, while the mechanism of the telescope kept on clicking away in its heedless mechanical fashion, and kept the aperture of the great instrument constantly in such a position that the image of the comet still hovered unseen in the mirror of the Reflector.

"Yes, there was something else, and I may as well tell you, after all; for even if you never see or speak to me again, it won't stop the work being done now. I could have kept this discovery to myself till it would have been too late to do anything, for no other telescope without my help would even find the comet for four months to come, and even now there is hardly a day to be lost, if the work is to be done in time; and then—well, I suppose I must have gone mad for the time being, for I thought—you will hardly believe me, I suppose—that I could make you the price of the world's safety.

"From that, you will see how much I love you, however mad I may have been. Losing you, I would have lost the world with you. If my love lives, I thought, the world shall live; if not, the world shall die. But, just now, when you thought I was taken ill, I had a sort of vision, and I saw you—yes, you, Miss Auriole—as, if my one chance fails, you must infallibly be this night thirteen months hence. I didn't see any of the other millions who would be choking and gasping for breath and writhing in the torture of the universal fire—I only saw you and my own baseness in thinking even for a moment that such a bargain would be possible. That is all."

She had not interrupted him even by a gesture, but as she listened a thousand signs and trifles, which alone had meant nothing to her, now seemed to come together and make one clear and definite revelation. His plainly, almost brutally, spoken words had done the rest. This strong, reserved, silent man had all the time loved her so desperately that he was going mad about her—so mad that, as he had said, he had even dreamed of weighing the possession of her single, insignificant self against the safety of the whole world, with all its innumerable millions of people—mostly as good in their way as she was.

Well, it might be that the love of such a man was a thing worthy to weigh even against a coronet—not in her eyes, for there was no question of that now, but in her father's. But that was a matter for future consideration. She drew herself up a little stiffly, and said, in just such a tone as she might have used if what he had just been saying had had no personal interest for her—had, in fact, been about some other girl—

"I think it's about time to be going down to the house, Professor, isn't it? I am quite sure a night's rest won't do you any harm. No, I'm not offended, and I don't think I'm even frightened yet. It somehow seems too big and too awful a thing to be only frightened at—too much like the Day of Judgment, you know. I am glad you've told me—yes, everything—and I'm glad that what you call your madness is over. You will be able to do your work in saving the world all the better, only don't tell dad anything except—well—just the scientific and necessary part of it. You know, saving a world is a very much bigger business than winning a woman—at least it is in one particular woman's eyes—and I've learnt somewhere in mathematics something about the greater sometimes including the less. And now, don't you think we had better be going down into the house? It's getting quite late."

III

It was about two months later, when Professor Lennox had verified and reverified every figure in his calculations, and made a good many more besides, that he at last sent the news of his discovery to the principal observatories of the world, coupled with the request that his own figures should be checked and any possible errors pointed out.

The results of this ominous communication were instantaneous and terrific. With one accord every powerful telescope in the world was turned upon that portion of the distant fields of space out of which the strange and terrible visitant was rushing at a speed of thousands of miles an hour to that awful trysting-place where it and the planet Terra were to mingle in fiery union. Every astronomer, from California to Greenwich, and from Pike's Peak to Melbourne, set himself to work out the orbit and period of the comet, and a few days later the awful news flashed over the wires of the world, "Lennox figures absolutely correct. Collision with Crellin Comet apparently inevitable. Consequences incalculable."

This was the intelligence which the civilized nations of the earth found in their newspapers on the morning of the first of September. It was followed by digests of the calculations, and these again with speculations of various sorts, some solemn and deliberate, others wild beyond the dreams of phantasy. Those who had for more than a generation made handsome incomes by prophesying the end of the world to occur at about an average of every seven years, gambled with absolute certainty on the shortness of the public memory, revised their figures, and proved to demonstration that this was the very thing they had been foretelling all along.

First there came blank incredulity; then a sort of stupor, which meant that the popular mind was veering round; then panic, wild, universal, and uncontrollable. The earth had only another twelve-month or so to live! The whole human race was doomed to death by fire! What did it matter what anybody did—what *could* anybody do, in fact?

So the planet was in distinct danger of becoming one colossal lunatic asylum, when one morning—it was the fifteenth of September—the *Daily Mail* came out with a double-barrelled interview with Professor Lennox, who was now by far the most famous man in the world, and Mr. Emerson G. Crellin, proprietor of the great Crellin Reflector, and godfather, as it were, of the approaching destroyer.

It was far and away the most interesting communication that had ever appeared in a newspaper, for it informed the world that the discoverer of the worst peril which had ever threatened the human race, and the man whose wealth and devotion to science had made the discovery possible, had all this time been quietly laying their heads together and elaborating a scheme which, as they both confidently asserted, offered the only hope of saving humanity from the impending peril, and would most probably achieve that object.

The idea was simply stupendous, and it lost none of its magnificence by the modesty with which the Professor described it to the interviewer.

"There is nothing new about the idea," he said, "except its application to the present circumstances. Of course you have read Jules Verne's 'Journey to the Moon'? Well, my plan is simply to do the same thing on a much bigger scale, only instead of firing men and dogs and chickens out of my cannon, I am going to fire something like a ton and a half of explosives. The danger is in the contact of the nucleus of the comet with the earth's atmosphere. If that can be prevented, there is no further cause for alarm, so, to put the matter quite shortly, my projectile will have an initial velocity of ten miles a second, and therefore a range that is practically infinite, for that velocity would, if necessary, carry it beyond the sphere of the earth's attraction.

"Hence, if the gun is properly trained and fired at precisely the right moment, and if the fuse does its work, the projectile will pass into the nucleus of the comet, and before the heat has time to melt the shell, the charge will explode and the nucleus—the only dangerous part—will either be blown to fragments or dissipated in gas. Therefore, instead of what I might be allowed to call a premature Day of Judgment, we shall simply have a magnificent display of celestial fireworks, which will probably amount to nothing more than an unparalleled shower of shooting stars, as they are popularly called. The details of the experiment will be practically the same as those which Jules Verne describes—I mean as regards the making and firing of the cannon—only, as we haven't time to get a big-enough hole dug, we have bought a colliery in Durham which has a perpendicular shaft nearly a mile deep, and which is happily exactly in the right latitude and longitude. Everything is arranged, and we shall begin work at once."

Even the *Daily Mail* interviewer was for a few moments paralysed by the quiet and yet stupendous audacity of the scheme; and when he had got his breath back, he turned to Mr. Crellin and said—because just then he could think of nothing else to say—

"And your share in this wonderful work, sir, I presume—"

"Just finding the dollars, sir; that's all," replied the old gentleman soberly. "If we can put the business through, they couldn't be better used; and if we can't, I reckon they won't be much use to me or any one else. Other people can come in, if they like; but, if not, I figure that I can foot the bill myself. It'll be worth the dollars, anyhow, if it's only to show what New-World enterprise combined with Old-World brains can do in the way of bringing off a real big thing. I guess we'll give the planet Terra a new satellite, even if we don't stop the comet; and if we all have to go to glory through a transformation scene of blue blazes, I for one shall go with the comforting knowledge that I've done something to enrich the Solar System. You see, we can't lose much, if the Professor's figures are right, and we do stand in to win something like eternal glory—and that's good enough for me."

The sale of the *Daily Mail* that morning ran far above its own best records, and by noon the news was all over the world, which promptly went mad again, but after a different and more cheerful fashion. Every existing copy of the "Journey to the Moon" was bought up within an hour; Camille Flammarion's wonderful story, "The End of the World," had already been translated into every civilized language, and was selling by millions; while Mr. H.G. Wells's even more extraordinary "War of the Worlds," although it had no actual bearing on the great subject, was bought up in colossal editions with almost equal avidity.

The moment that the Professor's project was made public, money began to flow in from all parts of the world. The iron and steel industries of the north of England were practically bought up for the time being; whole armies of workmen toiled night and day in relays at the preliminary work of making the great cannon. America, not to be behind in the good work of saving the world from its approaching peril, set to work to build an even bigger weapon with which to bombard the still invisible assailant of the earth.

International jealousies and hatreds vanished all the world over; mankind became united in the confronting of the common and the universal menace, and nothing that hands or brains could do to make the great experiment a triumphant success was left undone.

At length, on the first of July, the long and feverishly-awaited word went forth. If the sky on the night of the fourth was clear of clouds, the Crellin Comet, as it was now universally called, would become visible to the naked eye at forty-six minutes and thirty-eight seconds past ten—that is to say, precisely four weeks before the moment at which its nucleus would come into collision with the earth, provided always that the Professor's projectile failed to do its work.

Of course, it had been for some months within range of the tens of thousands of telescopes which had been directed towards it. Photographs of it had been published broadcast over the world, and practically every civilized, and a great many uncivilized, human beings were familiar with its appearance, but this did not diminish the universal interest in the announcement.

While it could only be seen through telescopes or in photographs, there was still a sort of air of unreality about it. It might be coming, but it was still very far away. None but savages now doubted that it was really coming; but civilized humanity as a mass wanted something more than this, and this was supplied on that momentous night when, as the world rolled round, bringing each meridian of longitude within view of that one spot in the skies, millions after millions of eyes were turned upwards and saw the stars shining through a pale, yellow, luminous mist spread out in two vast wings, between which there was a speck of deeper and yellower light.

It was very far away still, but there it was. There could be no doubt now, even in the minds of the most ignorant. Months and months before, the astronomers had prophesied its appearance, and there it was! Henceforth there were but three points of interest for the human race—one, by night, was the comet; the others, by day, were the Hetton Colliery in Durham and the Pittsburg Works.

So the last few remaining days and nights passed. Every night the threatening shape in the heavens grew clearer and bigger and brighter, and every day the newspapers published the most minute details of the progress of the mighty weapons upon which the hopes of humanity, so far as this world was concerned, now rested.

Soon the nucleus of the comet became visible in broad daylight; then the two wings came into view morning and evening, making it look like some colossal bird of prey swooping down from its eyrie, somewhere in the heights of space, upon the trembling and terrified world. The professional prophets naturally said, with the assurance of absolute conviction, that it was nothing less awful than the Destroying Angel *in propriâ personâ*.

At length, when excitement had passed into frenzy, and frenzy into an almost universal delirium, two cablegrams crossed each other under the Atlantic. One was to say that the Pittsburg gun was ready; the other, that the loading of the Lennox gun would commence the following morning. This was just a week before the fatal night; and when the sun set on the evening of the fourth of August, and when many millions had looked upon it, as they thought, for the last time, the Professor set all the wires of the world thrilling with the news that the operation of loading had been carried out with complete success; that the huge projectile with its thirty hundredweight of Lyddite was resting quietly in its place in the potential volcano, which at the touch of a woman's hand was to hurl it through space and into the heart of the swiftly advancing enemy of humanity.

At forty-six minutes past ten exactly the cannon would be fired. Ten seconds later the projectile would strike the nucleus of the comet at a point just one hundred miles above the muzzle of the gun, and the eleventh second would see the fate of the world decided. The mouth of the pit-shaft, which was now the case, as it were, of the colossal weapon which was about to do battle for humanity, lay almost in the middle of a wide oval valley surrounded by ranges of hills. No living thing was permitted to come within five miles of the huge ring of metal out of which that terrific charge was soon to be vomited.

Two electric wires led from the ring over separate rows of poles to the top of a hill five miles away, and ended in two instruments standing side by side on a table. On the same table there were also two chronometers beating time together to the thousandth part of a second.

On all the hills and scattered over the country for miles around was the greatest concourse of human beings that had ever been gathered together on one portion of the earth's surface.

It was numbered by millions, and included nearly every nationality under the sun; and, as the supreme moment drew near, every voice was hushed; and as every eye turned upwards to where the shape of the comet, now vast, menacing, and awful, over-spanned the sky, every heart seemed to beat in unison, as though counting off what might be the last seconds of human life on earth.

Grouped about the table on which stood the two instruments was gathered a concourse of people amongst whom were nearly all the greatest and most celebrated men and women in the world. But rank and honours were already things of the past. In the presence of that appalling menace which flamed across the heavens, all men and women were equal, since within the next few seconds all might be reduced at the same instant to the same dust and ashes.

The ghastly orange-green glare which had now completely obliterated the moonlight shone down alike on the upturned face of monarch and peasant, the good and the bad, the noble and the base, and tinged them all with its own sickly and hideous hue.

There was only one distinction left among all the hosts of men; only one man stood higher than any one else, and this was he upon whom the hopes of the peoples rested.

He stood on one side of the table facing one of the instruments, and opposite to him at the other stood the woman to whom he had first confided the terrible secret of the world's approaching end.

He had honestly kept the unspoken pact that had been made thirteen months before in the observatory on Leith Hill. Neither word nor look of love had, to her knowledge, passed his lips or lighted his eyes, and even now as he stood opposite to her, scanning her upturned face by that awful light, his eyes were as steady and impassive as they had ever been at the eye-pieces of his instruments.

Auriole had a forefinger already resting on a little white button ready to send the kindling spark into the mighty mass of explosives which lay buried nearly a mile down at the bottom of the giant tube.

Lennox, too, had his finger on the button in front of him, but his left hand was in his coat pocket, and his left forefinger was on the trigger of a loaded and cocked revolver.

Auriole knew nothing of this. She only remembered that a few minutes before—it seemed like several weeks ago already—he had promised that, if the worst happened, she at least should be spared the universal agony.

Lord and Lady Westerham were standing close by the table, and his lordship also had a revolver in his pocket.

The chronometers ticked off the seconds, each one seeming more like eternity than the one before it. The comet grew bigger and bigger, and its flaming nucleus blazed out brighter and brighter. A vague, low, wailing sound seemed to be running round the circle of the hills. It was the first utterance of the unendurable agony of the multitudes.

At last Lennox looked up from his chronometer at Auriole, and said in a quiet, dry voice—

"Ten seconds!"

Then he began to count: "Nine—eight—seven—six—five—four—three—two—NOW!"

Their two fingers went clown at the same instant and completed the circuits. The next, the central fires of the earth seemed to burst loose. Such a roar as had never deafened human ears before shook earth and air with a concussion that seemed like the loosening of the foundations of the world, and a mighty column of pale flame sprang up to the zenith over which the nucleus of the comet was now exactly impending.

Then came ten more seconds of mute and agonized suspense; and then, such a sight as no other human eyes will ever see, saving only those which, in the fulness of time, may look upon the awful pageantry of the Last Day.

High up in the air there was a shrill, screaming sound following the roar of the great gun. Something like a white flash of light streamed upwards straight at the heart of the descending destroyer.

Then the whole heavens were illumined by a blinding glare of unearthly light. The nucleus of the comet seemed to fling out long rays of many-coloured light, and then, like some vast globe of electric fluid, it burst into myriads of atoms.

The watching millions on earth instinctively clasped their hands to their ears, expecting such a sound as would deafen them for ever; but none came, for the explosion had taken place beyond the limits of the earth's atmosphere. The whole sky was now filled from zenith to horizon with a pale, golden, luminous mist, and through this the moon and stars began to shine dimly.

Then a blast of burning air swept shrieking and howling across the earth, for now the planet Terra was rushing at her headlong speed of nearly seventy thousand miles an hour through the ocean of fire-mist into which the shattered comet had been dissolved. Then this passed; the cool wind of night followed it, and the moon and stars shone down once more undimmed through the pure and cloudless ether.

So far there had been silence; but now there rose from earth to heaven such a burst of triumphant thanksgiving as had never welled up from human hearts through human lips before.

A north-country miner with a mighty baritone voice had somewhere started the Old Hundredth Psalm, and away it went, rolling through the now still night over hill and vale, echoing from village to village, and from town to town, until the whole United Kingdom was with one voice giving thanks for the Great Deliverance.

But the man who, under Providence, had wrought it, heard nothing of this. He only felt a soft, trembling clasp closing round his right hand, and he only heard Auriole's voice whispering a single word—and that word was his own name.

The next moment a stronger grip pulled his left hand out of his coat pocket—bringing the revolver with it—and the somewhat hard, practical voice of Emerson G. Crellin, for the first and only time shaken by emotion in public, said—

"We may thank God and you, Professor, that there is still a world here with living men and women on it—and there's one woman who's going to live henceforth for you and no one else. She told me all about it last night. You've won her fair and square, and you're going to have her. I did have other views for her; but I've changed my mind—and, anyhow, you're the biggest man on earth just now."

Before daybreak the next morning there was put into the Professor's hand a cablegram from Pittsburg, worded as follows:—

LENNOX, ENGLAND.

Well aimed! As you left no pieces for us to shoot at, we have sent our projectile to take its chance in space. No use for it here. Hope it will hit and stop next comet of same sort coming this way. America thanks you. Any terms you like for lectures.

Arthur Lennox so far accepted the invitation as to spend his honeymoon in a triumphal progress through the States and Canada; but not even the Crellin Reflector has been able to discover anything of the whereabouts of the famous Pittsburg Projectile. Probably it is still speeding on its lonely way through the silent fields of space—for it left the earth endowed with the enormous initial velocity of fifteen miles a second—and it is within the limits of possibility that, at some happy moment in the future, and somewhere far away beyond the ken of human vision, its gigantic charge of explosives may do for some other threatened world what the Lennox Projectile did for this one when it shattered the nucleus of the now happily vanished Crellin Comet.

TWO BY TWO

John Brunner

For over forty years John Brunner (1934–1995) was one of the leading British writers of science fiction, and one of the most prolific. From the early exuberance of his space operas and adventures through time published in the 1950s he developed, in the 1960s, a more cynical view of how mankind seems incapable of looking after itself and may prove to be a "nonviable species". Out of this came some of his best work, notably the award-winning Stand on Zanzibar *(1968), a bleak view of an overpopulated Earth and the machinations of government in population control and genetic engineering. Other major works include* The Jagged Orbit *(1969) with its even bleaker vision of the year 2014 where drugs and weapons are taking over;* The Sheep Look Up *(1972) where the deterioration of the environment leads to famine, civil unrest and war; and* The Shockwave Rider *(1975), a proto-cyberpunk novel portraying a world where hackers can control and manipulate computer networks. Brunner was always experimenting, and from time to time, to recharge his batteries, he reverted to writing the flamboyant adventures on which he had first made his reputation, such as* Threshold of Eternity *(serial, 1958),* To Conquer Chaos *(serial, 1963) and* The Wrong End of Time *(1971). Brunner was such a capable and diverse writer that there is something for everyone amongst his works. The following story from early in his career, reflects that early flamboyance showing how hope may emerge from chaos. Brunner may also be given some credit for getting the first two letters of the name of the first man on the moon correct!*

The same day were all the fountains of the great deep broken up, and the windows of heaven were opened. And the rain was upon the earth forty days and forty nights.

———

T HE CIRCUIT WAS FUZZY; THERE WERE ALL KINDS OF NOISES coming out of the speaker that should not have been there. Arkwright experienced a momentary surge of panic, and threw a quick glance over his shoulder at the viewport which happened to be turned towards the sun. There was a broad shallow bite out of the left-hand edge.

Then Costello's high, rather over-carefully accented tones sorted themselves out of the hubbub. "Hello, Moon One! Arkwright, can you hear me?"

Arkwright breathed a gusty sigh. "Yes—just!"

"What's the trouble?" the reply came back; the time-lag was almost at maximum now, for the ship was dropping towards the landing. "Would you check your transmitter?"

"The fault's not in the equipment," said Arkwright sourly. "Have you taken a look at the sun lately?"

"I haven't left the blockhouse since you blasted off." A splutter of interference muffled the last syllable. "Why, what's happened to it?"

"There's the biggest sunspot I've ever seen coming around the disc," Arkwright reported. "Can you check with the observatory?"

"Well, yes, but I don't see there's much they could do about it."

"They may be able to tell us how long this blasted interference is liable to go on for."

"Possibly. Okay, I'll do that." Costello was silent for a moment, as if he had covered the mike to speak to someone else. "How far are you from the surface now?"

"About six hundred and twenty seconds," Arkwright answered, glancing at the chronometer. "Braking procedure should start at a hundred fifty."

"Fine. You're on schedule." Even Costello's formal, clipped speech didn't hide the intense excitement he felt. "We'll be watching and listening. Good luck!"

"Thanks," said Arkwright, and pushed himself away from the handholds he had been gripping. The straps of the acceleration couch floated in mid-air; he caught the nearest and drew himself down on to the air-filled pad. Giving a final look round to make sure he hadn't left anything out which the deceleration would knock to the floor and break, he wrapped the straps around him and fastened the clips.

Well, for better or worse, this was it.

Behind him, in the heart of the atomic reactor, relays were answering the second-by-second click of the master chronometer; dampers were winding out on their screw rods, the radiation level was building up and dashing a deluge of gamma against the shielding of the pilot compartment.

Precisely and exactly at the hundred and fifty second mark, the pumps leapt into life and thundered a cataract of propellant into the centre of the cylindrical "firebox". The temperature there approximated four thousand degrees Centigrade.

At once the propellant, heated in a fraction of a second from the coldness of the ship's sunless side, expanded with explosive force, and a white-hot tongue of dissociated molecules sprang out towards the barren surface of the moon.

A slap of deceleration, like being brought up short on a breaking rope: Arkwright sank with a gusty sigh into the cushions. His eyes were fixed on the plumb-bob which indicated the ship's attitude as it poised perilously on its tenuous pillar of gas, his hands ready to slam home the emergency accelerator if by mischance the gyros precessed and the ship toppled.

The plumb-bob remained steady; yard by yard, and at last foot by foot, the ship settled to the smooth floor of the *Mare*; the main hydraulic landing leg met solidity; the weight of the ship compressed a telescopic section at the top of the leg and closed a relay; four other extensible legs shot out and found a purchase, and the engine's roar died away into a sigh and then into silence.

A man was on the moon.

Stiffly—after nearly four days without gravity at all, even the lunar pull tried his muscles—Arkwright got up and walked uncertainly towards the viewport. The one he chose showed the stark black-and-whiteness of a ringwall, scattered mountains, hillocks and jagged rocks—and Earth, like a blue-green fruit against the unbearable blackness of the sky.

"I made it!" he shouted across the cabin, as if the microphone were a listening man. "D'you hear me? *I made it!*"

A torrent of solar static laughed back at him from the speaker; when it cleared, Costello and many other people—it seemed that everyone on the project must be singing and shouting behind him in the blockhouse—were already calling their congratulations into the circuit.

Finally, when things had quietened down a little, Costello said, "Okay! We'll go ahead and make the announcements now. Arkwright, how's it feel to be the most famous man in the world?"

"Ask me when I get back," said Arkwright dryly. "I'm not over the shock of finding myself here in one piece yet."

A burst of static interrupted him, and the speaker spat and crackled loudly. Glancing up towards the sun, he saw that the stain on its edge was visibly creeping across the disc. It was as sharp as if a transit were beginning—but he knew there were no transits due.

There were almost too many things to be done for him to think about his achievement during the first twenty-four hours of his stay. Donning his spacesuit, he went out—first to try the sensation of moving under light gravity, then to attend to serious business. The greater part of his cargo consisted of scientific devices connected to a recorder and a telemetry unit; he had to set them up far enough from the ship to be unharmed by the blast-off later.

He aligned their antennae towards Earth and set them to working; Costello informed him that their signals were muddy, which was hardly surprising—his own voice could at times scarcely be made out through the intervening noise. With growing anxiety Arkwright looked towards the stained face of the sun.

"What's going on with old Sol?" he demanded.

"We don't know," confessed Costello. "Practically every observatory on Earth has been besieged by thousands of visitors wanting to see your ship for themselves—it's visible in a decent-sized instrument. I got on to Dutrey of the Astrophysical Foundation, though, to see if he could tell"—sputtering and crackling—"going to go on. It's a damned nuisance it picked this time of all times to happen."

"How is it"—crash!—"how is it with you down there?"

"Bad! Ordinary radio is bearable, but television stations are having to suspend operations. All you get on the screen is interference—and I mean *all*."

This time the noise was like a tidal wave. It seemed to flood out of the speaker and hit Arkwright with almost physical force. He waited for it to die down.

"There's no future in this," he said wryly. "I'll see if I can pick"— crackle—"pick a time when the spot's not delivering so strongly. Have"—splutter—"have someone listen out for me."

"Of course. Don't worry about that."

Interference was mounting to a steady pulse and surge in the background; Arkwright signed off and looked at the sun. It was like a suet pudding, he thought irrelevantly—stuffed with enormous, black currants.

He couldn't explore very far from the ship in the time available; however, he had a Geiger counter to carry with him on the off-chance, and a fairly complete and exceedingly compact laboratory at one end of the cabin, so that he could run quick analyses on sample rocks which looked interesting. Any data gained at first hand on the composition of the moon was important, of course, but rocks containing water of crystallization, for example, might make the difference between a self-supporting lunar colony soon, or never.

The storm of solar radiation boiled slowly towards a climax. He had landed about a week before sunset, and he kept wishing ridiculously that the lunar night would fall early, so that the setting of the sun would relieve the unceasing interference.

It was torture to listen to the faint, indistinct voices which reached him from Earth; many times he gave up in disgust, unable to unravel the tangled skeins of sound. He had looked to a constant contact with the people at base to alleviate tedium which might arise during his stay; there would be very little to do once he had explored his immediate neighbourhood. The instruments looked after themselves.

Still, he had samples of rock to break down in his test-tubes, and when he found the water he was looking for, he set up a small solar still to prove it could be extracted.

He went back continually to the radio, hoping to find at least a temporary lull in the racket. When he got his chance, he voiced his frustration to Costello, who tried to cheer him.

"After all, it won't last forever," came the words indistinctly from the crackling speaker. "We've reached the moon once, and it'll still be there for the next trip. It doesn't matter tremendously if all the data we get are what you can actually bring back with you. Inci"—crackle.

"Repeat please! Repeat!" Arkwright shouted, but the speaker spat at him like an angry cat, and after waiting five minutes he gave up.

He knew that the world must have been thrown into turmoil by the news of his landing; Costello had read him extracts from news reports and articles about him. It was all very fine and large to be hailed as a second Columbus, but Arkwright was finding that the spluttering of the radio got on his nerves. The rest of it could wait till his return.

He fetched out the biological kit which formed part of his equipment, and went to see if a certain strange stain he had noticed on the rocks could possibly be a living organism.

The urgent signal came about six hours before sunset; he was away from the ship, still working on the stain, and had just come to the conclusion that it was only a corrosive compound. He shut up the biokit and returned to the cabin.

The words could barely be distinguished through the hum and thunder on the circuit. But he made out enough to tell that it was Costello calling him and that the man seemed in a hurry.

"What is it?" he demanded loudly and clearly.

"We can't get any readings from your spectrographs," Costello shouted back.

"I'm not surprised!" said Arkwright. It was a scanning transmission of the television type.

"Can you read a spectrogram?"

"I don't know if I could without a line-chart, I'm afraid. Why do you want to know?"

"Would you go out anyway and see what you can do?"

"What's the hurry? When the sun sets in a few hours, interference should drop off enough for you to get the data."

"That's exactly what we can't wait for. We need a free-space reading of the solar spectrum."

Arkwright was silent for a moment. "You must have heard from Dutrey, I take it. What's his opinion?"

"He wants that spectrogram to help him make up his mind. Make a note of what he wants you to look for, will you?"

Arkwright got a pencil and scratchpad, and took down the several dozen code numbers Costello read out; on many of them he had to ask for repetitions. At the end he whistled. "Tell Dutrey not to be silly," he requested. "There just *aren't* that many hydrogen lines in sunlight!"

"In a free-space spectrogram there may be," returned Costello after a pause. "Apparently it'll mean something if there are."

"Okay," shrugged Arkwright. "You're in charge. I'll have to be quick about this—the sun'll be down soon."

He clamped his space-helmet back into position and went outside again.

The spectrographs were four in number; one was focussed on the sun, the others on interesting stars whose spectra should furnish valuable data on stellar processes. Of course, thought Arkwright dryly, I would have put the solar one furthest from the ship, wouldn't I?

He dropped into shadow of the instrument and thrust up the shaded visor before his face-plate to look at the blindingly bright pattern on the visual object-glass. He gave a grunt of surprise as he began to see it clearly.

Dutrey was right; there *were* that many lines.

He set his notepad on his knee and checked the code numbers against the visible spectrum; as he found them he ticked them off, and then he added a few more which Costello hadn't given him. Something about these last tickled his memory, and he sat back, rapping his pencil against his helmet.

If he remembered rightly, they couldn't possibly have been there at all.

When he returned to the ship, he was frowning.

"Well?" said Costello with barely concealed eagerness. "What did you find?"

"Everything you asked for, and more besides," Arkwright told him, and thought he heard a gusty sigh through the static. "I don't quite know what's happened, but something must have punched the sun right in the solar plexus." He wondered if Costello found the joke amusing. "Some of these lines belong down in the million-degree region. What in hell are they doing on the surface?"

"I don't know," said Costello. "But I hope Dutrey does."

Anything else he might have added was lost in a welter of noise.

Arkwright returned worriedly to the spectrograph and took another careful look at it before the sun finally settled behind the mountains of the crater ringwall. It looked by now as if the legendary beast reputed to devour it at eclipses had been taking wholesale bites out of the limb.

As soon as it had disappeared completely, he re-aligned the solar spectrograph on to the next star on his list. It was a long job, involving the retiming of the precessing clockwork and the fitting of a larger lens with a longer focus. It was getting bitterly cold even inside his insulated suit by the time he finished, but he stuck with it, and it was two hours past sunset before he got back to the ship.

The solar interference should be masked by the moon to some extent by now, he figured. He raised Costello and was rewarded to find the noise slightly less nerve-racking.

"Well, what's Dutrey got to say?" he demanded.

"Have a heart, man! How long do you think he's had to digest the information? Wald of Mount Palomar has been on to us too; I gave him the same data. Seems that the mess it's made of international communications has finally taken people's minds off you. There's the usual hooha demanding why the government doesn't *do* something—"

"I guess there would be," said Arkwright. "Well, let me know what they say, won't you? I'm bothered by that spectrum."

He signed off to break out a meal for himself; he ate with his scratchpad open before him, staring at the symbols and trying to read some sort of meaning into them.

When he finished, he decided to go out and take a look at Earth.

The shining shape of the planet was dazzling because of the brightness lent by air and water; now that the sun had gone it stood out in true relation to the brilliance of the moon as seen from Earth. Arkwright had been intellectually aware of the difference, but seeing it was something altogether different again.

He gazed up at it for a long time.

And then, as suddenly as if a switch had been pulled, a light turned on, the illuminated part of the disc became blindly, incredibly bright.

The glare made him cry out and throw up his hand in front of his eyes; a purple afterimage burned like fire on his retinae. It was only when he had blinked uncomprehendingly at it through the dark visor that he realized what might—what *must* have happened.

He turned and ran up the ladder to the airlock, cursing the slowness with which the mechanism cycled. As soon as the door opened, he tore across the cabin, shouting at the implacable black maw of the microphone.

"Costello! Anyone! Can you hear me? What happened?"

The voice which came back through a clamour of noise greater than any before was that of a stranger; it was hysterical, raging futilely into the void.

"The sun's blown up!"

The pitiless glare of the swollen sun played across the face of Earth like a flamethrower. Numbly, stirring neither to eat, drink nor sleep, Arkwright sat and watched it.

For a little while—during the first few hours, while there were still places on the surface of the planet unscarred by the finger of flame—he managed to patch together a few facts from men who, in the midst of destruction, had remained calm enough to tell what was happening—not caring who was listening, not even certain that there was anyone to hear them.

They told of fantastic hurricanes devastating continents as the atmosphere at the noon meridian was flash-heated to boil it into wind; of the surface of the sea steaming and breaking into slow, sullen bubbles as if the bed of the ocean were one gigantic saucepan; of tidal waves roaring up the beach to roll twenty, fifty, a hundred miles inland. They told of acres of summer-dried plain and forest blazing in a moment into flame; of cities crumbling, of people seared to death more certainly than by atomic blast.

After the first complete revolution the icecaps had gone; the sea-level had risen enormously. The cold eternal waters of the Great Deeps must have been approaching boiling point by then; there would be no snowcaps left on mountains, no water running in the shallower rivers...

Later, the air was too full of steamy clouds for him to see more than a featureless disc, as blank and barren as the face of Venus.

Looking towards the horizon in the first hour, he had seen the last of the lunar peaks to catch the sunlight glow into sombre red; a few of them had crumbled. Seismic shocks still indicated that on the side no man had yet seen Earth's satellite too was being seared by the flaming heat.

He had expected momently that the tide of outflung gas from the sun would lick out and absorb the Earth-Moon system—but if that was going to happen, it would have happened in the first few hours. As nova explosions went, this was a small one; the expanded frontier of the sun would have engulfed Mercury, perhaps even Venus, but no further.

And yet its work was as final as it needed to be. The thermo-couple he had with him was a poor instrument for use over a quarter million miles; still, he made the attempt, and the dial told him silently that the equatorial temperature of Earth had risen by six hundred degrees.

At last he fell asleep at his post; head slumped back, limbs limp, he dived gladly into the unawareness of sheer exhaustion.

After that, time passed for him in a sort of daze. He would look up at the gleaming, featureless ball of clouds and not really remember what it signified; listen to the roar of static without any stir of hope that there might be a voice calling somewhere.

He wondered why he himself was taking the trouble to stay alive, and remembered that when the sun rose again on the moon, he would be denied the chance.

The long lunar night passed away. When the chronometer told him it was almost over, he donned his spacesuit again, his hands moving over the fastenings as if they belonged to someone else, and left the spaceship to watch for the final dawn. It seemed logical to him to do it that way, instead of cowering in the useless protection of the ship, or hiding in a cave among the rocks.

Standing on the plain of the *Mare*, he turned his eyes achingly towards Earth again. It was so brilliant in its new disguise of clouds that it seemed like a new giant star in the heavens, and not a world.

He thought of things he had done, places he had been, people he had called his friends—whom he would never see again. He wished he were a poet, perhaps, to write an epitaph, create a masterpiece for some unknown alien being to find and decipher in a million years, and learn how a race had died...

Well, or badly? He wondered.

And that was the end of Hitler and Napoleon, of Attila and Genghis Khan—so much the better. But it was also the end of Jesus, Buddha and Confucius; of Galileo, Newton and Einstein; of Beethoven, Kreisler and Armstrong; of Pheidias, Michelangelo and Picasso; of Homer and Shakespeare—

How could you simply pick up a pen and write THE END across a story that had lasted about two million years?

He had stood for so long in a trance, remembering, that it was some time before a single fact penetrated his regret-drugged mind, and he looked about him with a start.

The landscape lay in sunlight; long dawn shadows slanted towards the horizon. But he was still alive.

Unbelieving, he turned and looked full at the low, rising sun. It was misshapen; it was diffuse, clothed in its own erupted gases, and it seemed larger than before. But it was no longer bright enough to kill him.

After so long a resignation to the inevitability of death, it took him a while to grow accustomed to the idea of staying alive. When he did so, he spent a while in frenzied, joyful shouting, until exhaustion sobered him and the thought what use he might make of his reprieve.

It could only be a reprieve. His release from the bond of Earth was temporary; he could not live out his life up here without food, water, oxygen…

Perhaps there were people who had lived through the hell of the nova in underground refuges: in deep mines, in H-bomb shelters. *Perhaps*.

There was only one way to find out. He would have to go back.

The face of Earth was changed beyond recognition. The heaving, oily seas; the blasted and scarred grasslands; the ruined cities poking up from newly inundated bays—it was a vision of Inferno, masked by thick, coiling clouds of steam and great black drifts of slowly dispersing smoke.

Flying the spaceship on its glider wings, he looked anxiously down whenever the fierce buffetings of the tortured air allowed, seeking a sign of life.

But what kind of life could have survived the storm of heat and radiation which had poured down from the sun?

He chose a landing ground on what had been a swamp; the ground had been parched to smooth dry mud, interrupted only by the remnants of a few scattered trees scorched into charcoal. Fantastic electrical storms raged on the horizon; he did not dare fly on further and face them.

It was good, as landings go; he rolled a thousand yards expecting every moment that his wheels would find a fissure and drop him crashing to the ground, but he halted safely.

As soon as he could leave the control panel, he got out his chemical kit and went to make some tests. They dealt the final blow to his hope that men might have survived.

There was no oxygen in the air; foetid water vapour and carbon dioxide in incredible abundance from the gigantic burning that had taken place made up the balance with the nitrogen and hydrogen. Without oxygen, there could be no animal life; without animal life, vegetation was doomed.

He put on his spacesuit and plodded to the edge of the sea which glistened leadenly a mile away. It had been fifty miles distant before the icecaps melted—if he had recognized his present location correctly; the coastlines were so changed it was difficult to tell.

The sea rolled steaming against the beach; it was full of carrion. Fragments of fish were cast up by one wave and taken back by the next. He tried its temperature; it was within ten degrees of boiling, even now.

Without any real hope, he exposed some culture plates, thinking at least that airborne spores might be revealed by them. Sitting and waiting for them to show results, he looked out towards the steam-masked skyline.

"And the waters prevailed upon the Earth," he murmured. It must have been like this in the Beginning—the air full of carbon dioxide from the dying volcanoes and steam from the cooling oceans. And both continents and oceans alike barren of life.

"This has all happened before," he told the world. "And every living substance which was upon the face of the ground was destroyed—"

Where did that come from, anyway? He thought a moment, and remembered. Of course: from the description of Noah's flood.

Had that flood really happened? He wondered. He knew that the story was widespread—almost too widespread to be a legend. The Jews had called him Noah; the Greeks, Deucalion; the Babylonians, whose version was the most ancient of all, had known him as Ut-Napishtim. Yes, that had been a great flood—but this was a more final one. Noah had carried with him his family and representatives of every species of bird and beast and insect. He was ready to start over.

Whereas he himself—and he looked at the culture plates to find them barren—was alone.

Later, before his laboratory bench, he faced the facts. The sea was sterile; the air was unbreathable; the land was bare. He was not only the last human being; he was the last living creature on Earth.

He picked up one of the culture slides again listlessly, and gave an incredulous cry. A tiny colony of bacteria stained its surface.

Which medium had he exposed that one to? Feverishly he consulted his notes, and drew back in disappointment. It had been blank when he brought it into the ship.

It had been blank when he brought it into the ship.

But he was not the only living creature on Earth.

And out there things were as they had been in the Beginning, when life appeared on Earth: the sea sterile, the air unbreathable, the land bare—but *waiting*.

Smiling, certain now of what he must do, Arkwright got to his feet and opened the airlock.

———

And Noah went forth, and his sons, and his wife, and his sons' wives with him;

Every beast, every creeping thing, and every fowl, and whatsoever creepeth upon the Earth, after their kinds, went forth out of the Ark.

FINIS

Frank Lillie Pollock

Frank Lillie Pollock (1876–1956?) was a prolific writer of adventure stories both for the boys' magazines and pulps at the start of the twentieth century. Of Irish descent, although born in the United States and so had American citizenship, his family had settled in Canada and Pollock later returned to Canada where he married and, amongst other things, raised bees. One of his earliest stories, "The Man Who Ran Europe" (1898) may well be the first story of a hacker, as it concerns a man who taps into a telegraph line between two countries and rewrites messages, almost causing a war. His fertile imagination occasionally led him to write stories classifiable as science fiction, such as "The Invisible City" (1901), an ingenious story of a city in the desert hidden from the outside world by hypnosis. "World-Wreckers" (1908) shows how the discovery of a process to make gold leads to civil unrest and financial collapse. The following, first published in 1906, has been reprinted several times but I make no apology for including it here because it is such a powerful image of Earth's cosmic fate.

"I 'M GETTING TIRED," COMPLAINED DAVIS, LOUNGING IN THE window of the Physics Building, "and sleepy. It's after eleven o'clock. This makes the fourth night I've sat up to see your new star, and it'll be the last. Why, the thing was billed to appear three weeks ago."

"Are *you* tired, Miss Wardour?" asked Eastwood, and the girl glanced up with a quick flush and a negative murmur.

Eastwood made the reflection anew that she certainly was painfully shy. She was almost as plain as she was shy, though her hair had an unusual beauty of its own, fine as silk and coloured like palest flame.

Probably she had brains; Eastwood had seen her reading some extremely "deep" books, but she seemed to have no amusements, few interests. She worked daily at the Art Students' League, and boarded where he did, and he had thus come to ask her with the Davis's to watch for the new star from the laboratory windows on the Heights.

"Do you really think that it's worth while to wait any longer, professor?" enquired Mrs. Davis, concealing a yawn.

Eastwood was somewhat annoyed by the continued failure of the star to show itself and he hated to be called "professor", being only an assistant professor of physics.

"I don't know," he answered somewhat curtly. "This is the twelfth night that I have waited for it. Of course, it would have been a mathematical miracle if astronomers should have solved such a problem exactly, though they've been figuring on it for a quarter of a century."

The new Physics Building of Columbia University was about twelve storeys high. The physics laboratory occupied the ninth and tenth floors, with the astronomical rooms above it, an arrangement which would have been impossible before the invention of the oil vibration cushion, which practically isolated the instrument rooms from the earth.

Eastwood had arranged a small telescope at the window, and below them spread the illuminated map of Greater New York, sending up a faintly musical roar. All the streets were crowded, as they had been every night since the fifth of the month, when the great new star, or sun, was expected to come into view.

Some error had been made in the calculations, though, as Eastwood said, astronomers had been figuring on them for twenty-five years.

It was, in fact, nearly forty years since Professor Adolphe Bernier first announced his theory of a limited universe at the International Congress of Sciences in Paris, where it was counted as little more than a masterpiece of imagination.

Professor Bernier did not believe that the universe was infinite. Somewhere, he argued, the universe must have a centre, which is the pivot for its revolution.

The moon revolves around the earth, the planetary system revolves about the sun, the solar system revolves about one of the fixed stars, and this whole system in its turn undoubtedly revolves around some more distant point. But this sort of progression must definitely stop somewhere.

Somewhere there must be a central sun, a vast incandescent body which does not move at all. And as a sun is always larger and hotter than its satellites, therefore the body at the centre of the universe must be of an immensity and temperature beyond anything known or imagined.

It was objected that this hypothetical body should then be large enough to be visible from the earth, and Professor Bernier replied that some day it undoubtedly would be visible. Its light had simply not yet had time to reach the earth.

The passage of light from the nearest of the fixed stars is a matter of three years, and there must be many stars so distant that their rays have not yet reached us. The great central sun must be so inconceivably remote that perhaps hundreds, perhaps thousands of years would elapse before its light should burst upon the solar system.

All this was contemptuously classed as "newspaper science" till the extraordinary mathematical revival a little after the middle of the twentieth century afforded the means of verifying it.

Following the new theorems discovered by Professor Burnside, of Princeton, and elaborated by Dr. Taneka, of Tokyo, astronomers succeeded in calculating the arc of the sun's movements through space, and its ratio to the orbit of its satellites. With this as a basis, it was possible to follow the widening circles, the consecutive systems of the heavenly bodies and their rotations.

The theory of Professor Bernier was justified. It was demonstrated that there really was a gigantic mass of incandescent matter, which, whether the central point of the universe or not, appeared to be without motion.

The weight and distance of this new sun were approximately calculated, and, the speed of light being known, it was an easy matter to reckon when its rays would reach the earth.

It was then estimated that the approaching rays would arrive at the earth in twenty-six years, and that was twenty-six years ago.

Three weeks had passed since the date when the new heavenly body was expected to become visible, and it had not yet appeared.

Popular interest had risen to a high pitch, stimulated by innumerable newspaper and magazine articles, and the streets were nightly thronged with excited crowds armed with opera-glasses and star maps, while at every corner a telescope man had planted his tripod instrument at a nickel a look.

Similar scenes were taking place in every civilized city on the globe.

It was generally supposed that the new luminary would appear in size about midway between Venus and the moon. Better informed persons expected something like the sun, and a syndicate of capitalists quietly leased large areas on the coast of Greenland in anticipation of a great rise in temperature and a northward movement in population.

Even the business situation was appreciably affected by the public uncertainty and excitement. There was a decline in stocks, and a minor religious sect boldly prophesied the end of the world.

"I've had enough of this," said Davis, looking at his watch again. "Are you ready to go, Grace? By the way, isn't it getting warmer?"

It had been a sharp February day, but the temperature was certainly rising. Water was dripping from the roofs, and from the icicles that fringed the window ledges, as if a warm wave had suddenly arrived.

"What's that light?" suddenly asked Alice Wardour, who was lingering by the open window.

"It must be moonrise," said Eastwood, though the illumination of the horizon was almost like daybreak.

Davis abandoned his intention of leaving, and they watched the east grow pale and flushed till at last a brilliant white disc heaved itself above the horizon.

It resembled the full moon, but as if trebled in lustre, and the streets grew almost as light as by day.

"Good heavens, that must be the new star, after all!" said Davis in an awed voice.

"No, it's only the moon. This is the hour and minute for her rising," answered Eastwood, who had grasped the cause of the phenomenon. "But the new sun must have appeared on the other side of the earth. Its light is what makes the moon so brilliant. It will rise here just as the sun does, no telling how soon. It must be brighter than was expected—and maybe hotter," he added with a vague uneasiness.

"Isn't it getting very warm in here?" said Mrs. Davis, loosening her jacket. "Couldn't you turn off some of the steam heat?"

Eastwood turned it all off, for, in spite of the open window, the room was really growing uncomfortably close. But the warmth appeared to come from without; it was like a warm spring evening, and the icicles were breaking loose from the cornices.

For half an hour they leaned from the windows with but desultory conversation, and below them the streets were black with people and whitened with upturned faces. The brilliant moon rose higher, and the mildness of the night sensibly increased.

It was after midnight when Eastwood first noticed the reddish flush tinging the clouds low in the east, and he pointed it out to his companions.

"That must be it at last," he exclaimed, with a thrill of vibrating excitement at what he was going to see, a cosmic event unprecedented in intensity.

The brightness waxed rapidly.

"By Jove, see it redden!" Davis ejaculated. "It's getting lighter than day—and hot! Whew!"

The whole eastern sky glowed with a deepening pink that extended half round the horizon. Sparrows chirped from the roofs, and it looked as if the disc of the unknown star might at any moment be expected to lift above the Atlantic, but it delayed long.

The heavens continued to burn with myriad hues, gathering at last to a fiery furnace glow on the skyline.

Mrs. Davis suddenly screamed. An American flag blowing freely from its staff on the roof of the tall building had all at once burst into flame.

Low in the east lay a long streak of intense fire which broadened as they squinted with watering eyes. It was as if the edge of the world had been heated to whiteness.

The brilliant moon faded to a feathery white film in the glare. There was a confused outcry from the observatory overhead, and a crash of something being broken, and as the strange new sunlight fell through the window the onlookers leaped back as if a blast furnace had been opened before them.

The glass cracked and fell inward. Something like the sun, but magnified fifty times in size and hotness, was rising out of the sea. An iron instrument-table by the window began to smoke with an acrid smell of varnish.

"What the devil is this, Eastwood?" shouted Davis accusingly.

From the streets rose a sudden, enormous wail of fright and pain, the outcry of a million throats at once, and the roar of a stampede followed. The pavements were choked with struggling, panic-stricken people in the fierce glare, and above the din arose the clanging rush of fire engines and trucks.

Smoke began to rise from several points below Central Park, and two or three church chimes pealed crazily.

The observers from overhead came running down the stairs with a thunderous trampling, for the elevator man had deserted his post.

"Here, we've got to get out of this," shouted Davis, seizing his wife by the arm and hustling her toward the door. "This place'll be on fire directly."

"Hold on. You can't go down into that crush on the street," Eastwood cried, trying to prevent him.

But Davis broke away and raced down the stairs, half carrying his terrified wife. Eastwood got his back against the door in time to prevent Alice from following them.

"There's nothing in this building that will burn, Miss Wardour," he said as calmly as he could. "We had better stay here for the present. It would be sure death to get involved in that stampede below. Just listen to it."

The crowds on the street seemed to sway to and fro in contending waves, and the cries, curses, and screams came up in a savage chorus.

The heat was already almost blistering to the skin, though they carefully avoided the direct rays, and instruments of glass in the laboratory cracked loudly one by one.

A vast cloud of dark smoke began to rise from the harbour, where the shipping must have caught fire, and something exploded with a terrific report. A few minutes later half a dozen fires broke out in the lower part of the city, rolling up volumes of smoke that faded to a thin mist in the dazzling light.

The great new sun was now fully above the horizon, and the whole east seemed ablaze. The stampede in the streets had quieted all at once, for the survivors had taken refuge in the nearest houses, and the pavements were black with motionless forms of men and women.

"I'll do whatever you say," said Alice, who was deadly pale, but remarkably collected. Even at that moment Eastwood was struck by the splendour of her ethereally brilliant hair that burned like pale flame above her pallid face. "But we can't stay here, can we?"

"No," replied Eastwood, trying to collect his faculties in the face of this catastrophic revolution of nature. "We'd better go to the basement, I think."

In the basement were deep vaults used for the storage of delicate instruments, and these would afford shelter for a time at least. It occurred to him as he spoke that perhaps temporary safety was the best that any living thing on earth could hope for.

But he led the way down the well staircase. They had gone down six or seven flights when a gloom seemed to grow upon the air, with a welcome relief.

It seemed almost cool, and the sky had clouded heavily, with the appearance of polished and heated silver.

A deep but distant roaring arose and grew from the south-east, and they stopped on the second landing to look from the window.

A vast black mass seemed to fill the space between sea and sky, and it was sweeping towards the city, probably from the harbour, Eastwood thought, at a speed that made it visibly grow as they watched it.

"A cyclone—and a waterspout!" muttered Eastwood, appalled.

He might have foreseen it from the sudden, excessive evaporation and the heating of the air. The gigantic black pillar drove towards them swaying and reeling, and a gale came with it, and a wall of impenetrable mist behind.

As Eastwood watched its progress he saw its cloudy bulk illumined momentarily by a dozen lightning-like flashes, and a moment later, above its roar, came the tremendous detonations of heavy cannon.

The forts and the warships were firing shells to break the water-spout, but the shots seemed to produce no effect. It was the city's last and useless attempt at resistance. A moment later forts and ships alike must have been engulfed.

"Hurry! This building will collapse!" Eastwood shouted.

They rushed down another flight, and heard the crash with which the monster broke over the city. A deluge of water, like the emptying of a reservoir, thundered upon the street, and the water was steaming hot as it fell.

There was a rending crash of falling walls, and in another instant the Physics Building seemed to be twisted around by a powerful hand. The walls blew out, and the whole structure sank in a chaotic mass.

But the tough steel frame was practically unwreckable, and, in fact, the upper portion was simply bent down upon the lower storeys, peeling off most of the shell of masonry and stucco.

Eastwood was stunned as he was hurled to the floor, but when he came to himself he was still upon the landing, which was tilted at an alarming angle. A tangled mass of steel rods and beams hung a yard over his head, and a huge steel girder had plunged down perpendicularly from above, smashing everything in its way.

Wreckage choked the well of the staircase, a mass of plaster, bricks, and shattered furniture surrounded him, and he could look out in almost every direction through the rent iron skeleton.

A yard away Alice was sitting up, mechanically wiping the mud and water from her face, and apparently uninjured. Tepid water was pouring through the interstices of the wreck in torrents, though it did not appear to be raining.

A steady, powerful gale had followed the whirlwind, and it brought a little coolness with it. Eastwood enquired perfunctorily of Alice if she were hurt, without being able to feel any degree of interest in the matter. His faculty of sympathy seemed paralysed.

"I don't know. I thought—I thought that we were all dead!" the girl murmured in a sort of daze. "What was it? Is it all over?"

"I think it's only beginning," Eastwood answered dully.

The gale had brought up more clouds and the skies were thickly overcast, but shining white-hot. Presently the rain came down in almost scalding floods and as it fell upon the hissing streets it steamed again into the air.

In three minutes all the world was choked with hot vapour, and from the roar and splash the streets seemed to be running rivers.

The downpour seemed too violent to endure, and after an hour it did cease, while the city reeked with mist. Through the whirling fog Eastwood caught glimpses of ruined buildings, vast heaps of debris, all the wreckage of the greatest city of the twentieth century.

Then the torrents fell again, like a cataract, as if the waters of the earth were shuttlecocking between sea and heaven. With a jarring tremor of the ground a landslide went down into the Hudson.

The atmosphere was like a vapour bath, choking and sickening. The physical agony of respiration aroused Alice from a sort of stupor, and she cried out pitifully that she would die.

The strong wind drove the hot spray and steam through the shattered building till it seemed impossible that human lungs could extract life from the semi-liquid that had replaced the air, but the two lived.

After hours of this parboiling the rain slackened, and, as the clouds parted, Eastwood caught a glimpse of a familiar form halfway up the heavens. It was the sun, the old sun, looking small and watery.

But the intense heat and brightness told that the enormous body still blazed behind the clouds. The rain seemed to have ceased definitely, and the hard, shining whiteness of the sky grew rapidly hotter.

The heat of the air increased to an oven-like degree; the mists were dissipated, the clouds licked up, and the earth seemed to dry itself almost immediately. The heat from the two suns beat down simultaneously till it became a monstrous terror, unendurable.

An odour of smoke began to permeate the air; there was a dazzling shimmer over the streets, and great clouds of mist arose from the bay, but these appeared to evaporate before they could darken the sky.

The piled wreck of the building sheltered the two refugees from the direct rays of the new sun, now almost overhead, but not from the penetrating heat of the air. But the body will endure almost anything, short of tearing asunder, for a time at least; it is the finer mechanism of the nerves that suffers most.

Alice lay face down among the bricks, gasping and moaning. The blood hammered in Eastwood's brain, and the strangest mirages flickered before his eyes.

Alternately he lapsed into heavy stupors, and awoke to the agony of the day. In his lucid moments he reflected that this could not last long, and tried to remember what degree of heat would cause death.

Within an hour after the drenching rains he was feverishly thirsty, and the skin felt as if peeling from his whole body.

This fever and horror lasted until he forgot that he had ever known another state; but at last the west reddened, and the flaming sun went down. It left the familiar planet high in the heavens, and there was no darkness until the usual hour, though there was a slight lowering of the temperature.

But when night did come it brought life-giving coolness, and though the heat was still intense it seemed temperate by comparison. More than all, the kindly darkness seemed to set a limit to the cataclysmic disorders of the day.

"Ouf! This is heavenly!" said Eastwood, drawing long breaths and feeling mind and body revived in the gloom.

"It won't last long," replied Alice, and her voice sounded extraordinarily calm through the darkness. "The heat will come again when the new sun rises in a few hours."

"We might find some better place in the meanwhile—a deep cellar; or we might get into the subway," Eastwood suggested.

"It would be no use. Don't you understand? I have been thinking it all out. After this, the new sun will always shine, and we could not endure it even another day. The wave of heat is passing round the world as it revolves, and in a few hours the whole earth will be a burnt-up ball. Very likely we are the only people left alive in New York, or perhaps in America."

She seemed to have taken the intellectual initiative, and spoke with an assumption of authority that amazed him.

"But there must be others," said Eastwood, after thinking for a moment. "Other people have found sheltered places, or miners, or men underground."

"They would have been drowned by the rain. At any rate, there will be none left alive by tomorrow night.

"Think of it," she went dreamily, "for a thousand years this wave of fire has been rushing towards us, while life has been going on so happily in the world, so unconscious that the world was doomed all the time. And now this is the end of life."

"I don't know," Eastwood said slowly. "It may be the end of human life, but there must be some forms that will survive—some micro-organisms perhaps capable of resisting high temperatures, if nothing higher. The seed of life will be left at any rate, and that is everything. Evolution will begin over again, producing new types to suit the changed conditions. I only wish I could see what creatures will be here in a few thousand years.

"But I can't realize it at all—this thing!" he cried passionately, after a pause. "Is it real? Or have we all gone mad? It seems too much like a bad dream."

The rain crashed down again as he spoke, and the earth steamed, though not with the dense reek of the day. For hours the waters roared and splashed against the earth in hot billows till the streets were foaming yellow rivers, dammed by the wreck of fallen buildings.

There was a continual rumble as earth and rock slid into the East River, and at last the Brooklyn Bridge collapsed with a thunderous crash and splash that made all Manhattan vibrate. A gigantic billow like a tidal wave swept up the river from its fall.

The downpour slackened and ceased soon after the moon began to shed an obscured but brilliant light through the clouds.

Presently the east commenced to grow luminous, and this time there could be no doubt as to what was coming.

Alice crept closer to the man as the grey light rose upon the watery air.

"Kiss me!" she whispered suddenly, throwing her arms around his neck. He could feel her trembling. "Say you love me; hold me in your arms. There is only an hour."

"Don't be afraid. Try to face it bravely," stammered Eastwood.

"I don't fear it—not death. But I have never lived. I have always been timid and wretched and afraid—afraid to speak—and I've almost wished for suffering and misery or anything rather than to be stupid and dumb and dead, the way I've always been.

"I've never dared to tell anyone what I was, what I wanted. I've been afraid all my life, but I'm not afraid now. I have never lived; I have never been happy; and now we must die together!"

It seemed to Eastwood the cry of the perishing world. He held her in his arms and kissed her wet, tremulous face that was strained to his.

The twilight was gone before they knew it. The sky was blue already, with crimson flakes mounting to the zenith, and the heat was growing once more intense.

"This is the end, Alice," said Eastwood, and his voice trembled.

She looked at him, her eyes shining with an unearthly softness and brilliancy, and turned her face to the east.

There, in crimson and orange, flamed the last dawn that human eyes would ever see.

THE MADNESS OF PROFESSOR PYE

Warwick Deeping

Warwick Deeping (1877–1950) was one of the best-selling novelists of the 1920s, best known for his novel Sorrell and Son *(1925), which caught the mood of the nation in the years after the First World War. A decorated war hero struggles to survive in the changing post-war society. Deeping first established himself as a writer of historical romances, including the Arthurian fantasy* Uther and Igraine *(1903). This interest remained because at the start of the Second World War he wrote* The Man Who Went Back *(1940) where, following a car accident, the protagonist finds himself back in Roman Britain and his fate there subsequently helps him cope with the War. The following story, first published in 1934, reflects Deeping's frustrations with the modern-day world. Some readers may notice that it is set in the same part of Surrey as Griffith's "The Great Crellin Comet".*

I

PROFESSOR PYE'S HOUSE WAS VISIBLE FROM ONE POINT ON the Dorking-Guildford road as a cube of concrete rising above the dark foliage of a group of old yews. Standing upon the chalk ridge and reached only by a steep and flinty lane whose privacy was emphasized by a notice board, it suggested the isolation of an iceberg. Professor Pye's message to humanity carried no sense of uplift. His notice board did not challenge the casual crowd to climb the heights and speak of Plotinus and Einstein.

It was a rude and abrupt notice board. It said—or rather, it snarled—

> *Private.*
> *Keep out!*
> *Yes, you!*

A serious hiker in shorts, shirt and spectacles, happening upon that notice board, remarked upon it to his mate.

"That's the sort of thing that puts my back up. Let's trespass, Maisie."

Maisie was less politically minded than her mate. It was a hot day, and the lane was steep and stony.

"I don't see any sense, Fred, in climbing a hill just to have a row."

"It's one's duty to have a row with a fellow who—"

The lady fanned herself with a piece of bracken.

"Too many flies, and I want my tea."

They passed on, but happening upon a roadman trimming a hedge the young man in spectacles paused to ask questions.

"Excuse me, who lives up there? The fellow who put up that notice board."

The roadman ran a thumb along the edge of his swaphook.

"That there white house?"

"I suppose so. Sort of chap who owns the earth."

The roadman grinned.

"Chap named Pye—Professor Pye. Very particular about his privacy."

"I should say so."

"Down there in the village they call him Old Crusty."

The hiker's spectacles glimmered approvingly.

"Bit of a misanthrope, what!"

The roadman was not familiar with the word, but he divined its meaning.

"All crust and no apple."

The hikers applauded this piece of rustic humour and passed on in search of tea.

Now, Professor Pye was a very distinguished physicist, but to the public he was not even a name. As a scientist he had not received from his confrères the recognition that is acceptable to a philosopher, and when the simple things of life go wrong there can be no more unphilosophic person than your philosopher. Things had gone wrong for Professor Pye. Someone had once described him as "A man whom nobody liked, a piece of cold flat-fish," which was both true and an exaggeration. There had been moments in his life when Alfred Pye had been furiously eager to be liked. As a man he had fallen in love with women and friendship and success and the swagger of it, and all of them had flouted him. He possessed a great brain and an unfortunate exterior, a certain resemblance to an undersized grey he-goat.

Women actually shrank from him as from something that was both cold and unpleasantly libidinous. As a young man he had been shocked and wounded and enraged by this shrinking. He could remember sitting on a seat in a moonlit garden, burning to utter the words that other men could utter, and suddenly the girl had risen to her feet. Actually, she had shuddered.

"I think it's too cold out here."

And poor Pye's passion had flopped like a fallen angel into bitter and icy waters.

He was strangely repellent to anything with warm blood, women, children, dogs, his fellow-men, and at one period of his life he had—with bitter irony—made pets of a snake and a tortoise. These cold-blooded creatures had accepted him, and had fed out of his hands. He might have said that they recognized the brother reptile.

II

But one thing he did possess, and that was money. The Pyes *père* and *grandpère* had been Birmingham men, successful manufacturers of hardware, and Alfred had been an only son. Being interested in pure science, he had sold the business on his father's death, and retired into his laboratory with two hundred thousand pounds in gilt-edged securities. He was somewhat sensitive about his money. He knew that though the world had no affection for Alfred Pye it would smile upon Alfred's pile of cash.

The making of a misanthrope may be a complex business, and if at the age of sixty Professor Pye hated humanity he had his reasons for this hatred. A man who has lived alone with himself for fifteen years can turn sour in the process, and Pye's uncontestable brilliancy made scorn easy. As a younger man he had carried out experimental work as a subordinate, only to have his very suggestive discoveries exploited by his senior. Professor Gasson, in claiming the younger man's researches for the honour of a particular University, had seen to it that much of the honour had materialized as a personal halo. Professor Gasson had an international reputation. He was a facile writer, one of those men who can popularize the abstruse and the mysterious. He was now Sir Philip Gasson.

Pye had never forgotten or forgiven the ingenious fraud. It had taught him secretiveness, made him even more lone and separative. He had withdrawn from the world of men, academic and otherwise. He had purchased thirty acres of land on the North Downs and built himself a kind of little concrete fortress, a strong place that was as complete and self-supporting as money and brains could make it. It contained a laboratory; it possessed its own water supply, a powerful electric installation, an oil storage tank, a miniature observatory. Even Professor Pye's dietary was eccentric. He drank nothing but water or strong coffee, and lived on grape-fruit, oranges, apples, nuts, bread and cheese. Life in all its details was simplified and subordinated to his work. The laboratory was his holy of holies, and in it he functioned like a priest.

He possessed one temple-servant, a curious creature named Hands, an ex-service man who had lost his hearing and half a face in the war. Life's disfigurements and frustrations had made Hands as much a recluse as his master. He was a queer, sedulous slave who lived with a small mongrel dog in the kitchen, and who made beds, and stoked the furnace, and ran the oil engine and dynamo, and controlled the stores, and pottered about in a very small garden of his own. There was nothing of the spy about Hands. A large, gentle, tame creature who smoked a pipe, and liked to feel his hands licked by his dog's tongue, he could resign himself to his environment. He attached himself like a neuter cat. So attached had he become to the solitary place on the downs that semi-suburban Surrey had become as wild to him as a jungle.

Between these two men there existed the kind of affection that had united Robinson Crusoe and good Man Friday. Isolation held them together. Hands had a disfigured face, the professor a warped soul. Hands hated nothing; to the professor hatred of the world of men had become a sinister inspiration. Pye was so malignantly sober in his scorn for all the follies and hypocrisies and conventions of the social scheme that he was too sober to be sane as carnal man understands sanity. Year by year Pye was becoming nothing but a brain, a concentration of pure and merciless intelligence, an intelligence that was hostile to his fellows.

If he had any affection for any creature it was for Hands. Hands could lip-read, and being deaf he never heard the rasp of Alfred Pye's voice, nor did he feel the abruptness with which his master spoke to him.

"Hands—turn off that radiator."

"Hands—more bread."

"Hands—the oil's too low in the storage tank. When are those damned fools coming to refill it?"

Hands would nod his head reassuringly.

"Yes, sir."

He had a flat and toneless voice, and eyes that were not unlike the eyes of his dog.

"Yes, sir—I'll see to it, sir."

According to Trade Union standards he was one of the most overworked men upon earth, a meek automaton with a curious capacity for devotion. He was sure that Professor Pye was a very wonderful person, a kind of super-man. That, too, was Professor Pye's conviction. The outer world was full of damned fools, monkeys, mountebanks, people who would be better dead. The professor's egotism had grown like some monstrous fungus, or like a fantastic brain uncontrolled by any of the human reactions. In his younger days—like all normal men—he had wanted to be liked, and the world had not liked him. A bitter and solitary egotism cherished hate.

Sometimes on a summer day he would go up to the little white tower of his house and stand there looking down into that deep, green, beautiful valley. He could command a short strip of the road, and observe the procession of cars passing along the tarmac surface. To the satanic Pye upon his height they looked like tin toys, absurd little mechanisms that crawled and tooted.

"Beetles, ants."

So—that was civilization, a procession of little standardized robots running around in their little machines, people who had no more originality than flies. An insect world, grubs that daily consumed the pulp of a popular press. Professor Pye's scorn was cosmic. If he felt himself to be a creature living in a world of other dimensions to those clerks and shopmongers he had some justification for his arrogance. He had a wonderful intelligence. He was living on the brink of catastrophic revelations. He had worked for years in that fascinating atmosphere where things physical melt into the seemingly miraculous. Like Professor Rutherford and his disciples he had been analysing the atom. His dream had been to dissociate the atom, and somewhere he had read that centuries would elapse before man could split and control atomic energy.

Professor Pye had smiled over that particular paragraph in a learned article.

"Damned fools!"

He knew what he knew. The lightning was in his hands. He had but to discover how to control and to project it.

And then? No Jove upon Olympus would be so potent as this little grey man of sixty standing alone upon his concrete tower.

The world had misliked him, ignored him, cheated him.

"Damned fools!"

He would give the world thunder and lightning.

III

It happened on an afternoon in June. Hands had carried an ancient basket chair into his piece of garden, and was proposing to enjoy a pipe and a little relaxation. His dog lay at his feet and blinked up at him through the sunlight. It was a warm and gentle summer day, but for Hands it had been a day of toil and trial.

A lorry full of stores had arrived from Garrod's. The professor purchased everything in bulk in London, and Hands had had to deal with those stores and pack them away in the store-room.

The oil-tanker had laboured up the lane to recharge the storage tank. Also, it happened to be charging day, and the oil engine had behaved temperamentally. So, in fact, had the professor. When Hands had knocked at the door of the laboratory and attempted to inform his master that the stores had arrived and been checked and put away, the professor, forgetting Hand's deafness, had screamed at him:

"Get out. Don't interrupt me."

Not hearing the order, Hands had continued to knock at the locked door.

"I've had trouble with the engine, sir."

And suddenly the door had flown open, and Professor Pye, red lidded, wild as to the head, and in nothing but shirt and grey flannel trousers, had raged at him.

"Get out, you fool. Don't come worrying here. I'm busy."

The meek Hands, watching his master's mouth, had repeated his news about the engine.

"Accumulator's low, sir."

"What!"

"I dare say I'll get it going soon."

The professor had gibbered at him.

"You'd better. Most damnably important. Telephone to Guildford for a mechanic."

"Oh—I'll get it right, sir."

"You had better."

And Professor Pye had slammed the door and locked it.

Hands, sucking his pipe, felt pleasantly sleepy. After all, some gentlemen were funny, just as colonels and sergeant-majors had been funny in the army, but this life suited Hands. Professor Pye might be a little grey bit of wire and wisdom, with a tufted chin and red-lidded eyes, an irritable gentleman, but after all he was a great man. He paid Hands generously. There were days when the professor was as smooth as silk. The dog was asleep with his head resting against his master's right foot, and Hands himself was on the brink of dozing.

Then, something startled both man and dog. Hands straightened in his chair; the dog, up and quivering, emitted three sharp barks, and stood whimpering. There had been no sound, but both dog and man had felt a curious vibration like an earth tremor. Hands could have sworn that his chair had moved under him.

He stood up, holding in his right hand a pipe that had gone out. He looked at the quivering dog.

"What was it, Jumbo?"

Jumbo, tail down, whimpered and looked up obliquely at his master.

"I don't know," he was saying; "but whatever it was—I didn't like it."

Neither did Hands. He put his pipe away in his pocket. He stared at the white wall behind him. He was a man whose mind worked slowly.

"Anything wrong in there?"

He remembered reading somewhere that strange things sometimes happened to learned gentlemen who experimented in laboratories. Had anything happened to Professor Pye? The suggestion was a sufficient stimulus, and Hands became the man of action. He rushed into the house and found himself staring at a glazed door at the end of the corridor. The glass in the door had been smashed, blown out upon the floor.

Hands pushed it back, and crunching broken glass, made for the laboratory. He sniffed the air. No, there was no strange smell. The door of the laboratory was painted white, and down the two upper panels ran dark scars. They were cracks where the panels had been split.

Hands rushed at the door, seized the handle, and shook it.

"What's happened, sir? Are you all right?"

Silence, an inevitable silence so far as Hands was concerned. The door was locked. He put his face close to one of the cracks and tried to see into the laboratory. He could distinguish a table, and he realized that the table, a stout, deal bench, was lying on its side. There was a foot visible beside it, or rather—a black boot, toe upturned and everted.

Hands put a shoulder to the door and heaved. It defied him.

He drew back a yard and charged it. He was a heavy man, and the lock plate gave, and Hands and the door went in together. Recovering himself, he stood and stared. The laboratory looked as though a bull had been active in a glass and china shop. The windows were smashed; everything seemed on the floor.

Professor Pye was on the floor, surrounded by what appeared to be the glass and metal fragments of some complicated apparatus.

Hands bent over his master. Professor Pye's face was the colour of old vellum; his eyes were closed, and from his nostrils blood oozed. Hands had seen dead men in the war; Professor Pye looked like death, and Hands was frightened.

He knelt down, and put his head close to the professor's chest. No, his master was breathing. And Hands lumbered up and off into the dining-room. The professor did indulge occasionally in old French brandy. Hands extracted the bottle from the sideboard and hurried back.

But he paused in the laboratory doorway, and stood staring. The professor was sitting up, looking bemused, ghastly and bewildered. The fingers of his right hand were stroking his forehead. He gazed at Hands, and his eyes were vacant.

"My God—you gave me a shock, sir!"

The professor's lips moved, mumbling something. He looked round the shattered room.

"What happened, sir? Something exploded? Have some brandy, sir."

The professor looked at the brandy bottle, nodded, and allowed Hands to trickle some of the spirit between his lips. He gurgled, he spluttered, and suddenly, clutching Hands's arm and shoulder, he struggled up. He still looked ghastly, but his very ghastliness was exultant.

"Eureka!"

Hands blinked at him.

"Where shall I find it, sir? In your shaving cupboard?"

And suddenly Professor Pye laughed, a strange, creaking and discordant laugh.

"No, I've got it, Hands, I've got it. Eureka, Eureka!"

IV

When the Masters of Science speak of protons, electrons and neutrons, and describe strange bombardments, and streams of particles shooting at high speed through a substance that has every appearance of being solid, the plain man must listen and accept the strange things that these adepts tell him. At home in the suburbs the plain man may fiddle with his wireless, and repeat some of the jargon of the technical press, but in the matter of knowledge he is but a child. His may be the right to say, "Well—I'm damned! What will these scientific fellows do next?" The marvels of research may leave him gaping, and feeling perhaps vaguely uncomfortable, and certainly had any John Citizen been allowed to peep into the mental workshop of Professor Pye he would have felt supremely uneasy.

For, Professor Pye had taken a leap beyond his contemporaries. He had discovered and isolated a little creature that he called the "On." It would not be possible for an untechnical scribbler to describe the manifestations and mysteries of this child of the atom. Professor Pye had brought a little stranger into the world of man's awareness, and with a complex of glass tubes, electrical force and certain chemicals had caused the On to manifest. That the On or congeries of Ons had nearly killed him was neither here nor there. Professor Pye, working upon certain hypotheses, had taken risks. His idea was not only to isolate the On, but to control and use it.

A minute manifestation of On-force had blown a screen of argonil to atoms, but the protecting tube of palmyrium had stood the shock. Apparently palmyrium was impervious to the On. That—of course—had to be proved and tested with an increasing stress of On-force, but if a palmyrium box or tube could be produced that could contain and confine the streams of Ons when Professor Pye's process produced them, then—! Professor Pye, standing on his concrete tower and looking out across this peaceful English valley, smiled a truculent little smile, and rubbed his beard. He, Alfred Pye, granted that his hypotheses were correct, would have under his hand a strange new force that could be controlled and projected into space. What its ultimate effects would be upon things organic and inorganic he could not yet say, but judging by his experience of a minute release of the On-force, a larger dose would be lethal to creatures of protoplasm. It would annihilate—silently and secretly. It might be potent over a thousand miles. The German gun that bombarded Paris would be a mere crude and barbaric toy compared with it.

For some time after the wrecking of the laboratory Jack Hands was worried and nervous. Apparently, Professor Pye had been immensely excited over the result of some particular experiment, and it was probable that the experiment would be repeated. Hands, simple soul, was more worried about his dog than about himself. He spoke to the professor.

"Are there going to be any more—explosions, sir?"

For Professor Pye was working far into the nights. Hands, worried and restless, had seen the laboratory windows lit up at two in the morning, and fear is more fearful at night.

"You see—I could put Jumbo to sleep in the tool-house."

Alfred Pye had no sense of humour, or any feeling for pathos. Moreover, he was becoming more and more the little megalomaniac swollen with a sense of imminent and catastrophic power. In fact, Professor Pye was not quite sane in that he represented pure and pitiless intelligence divorced from all emotion and the social urges. He spoke curtly to Hands.

"Don't be a fool, man. Bring me my lunch in here."

Professor Pye was in apron and shirt-sleeves, and standing by his electric furnace. Hands could see that some queer apparatus was in process of construction, for Pye had so great a contempt for his man's intelligence that he let him stand and stare. The professor was not only an inspired physicist but an expert mechanic. He had small, strong, delicate fingers, hands of infinite dexterity and precision. He was capable of manufacturing a watch or turning out the most sensitive of instruments. Being a separatist and secretive he had trained himself to do these things.

Hands went for the professor's lunch, an apple, six dry biscuits and two wedges of Swiss Gruyère cheese. He was placing the tray on a laboratory table when the professor—who had quick ears—heard the sound of a car in the little courtyard behind the house.

"Who's that?"

Hands—of course—had heard nothing. Pye, who was beginning to nourish acute suspicion now that his researches were nearing fruition, went to one of the laboratory windows. It was a high window, and Pye had to stand on a stool to look out.

"A woman in a car. Go and see what she wants."

The professor pulled down the blinds on the side next the courtyard, and Hands hurried out to interview the visitor. She was elderly, plump and pleasant. She looked compassionately at Hands's disfigured face, and produced a little book.

"I am sure you will excuse me calling at this hour, but could I see Professor Pye?"

Hands, with his eyes watching her lips, explained some-what apologetically that the professor was not easy of approach. The lady smiled upon Hands.

"But won't you go and ask him to see—me?"

"What name, ma'am?"

"Mrs. Millard."

Hands returned to the laboratory where Pye, sitting on a stool, was eating cheese and biscuit.

"A lady named Millard, sir. Her compliments and would you—?"

"What does she want?"

"I don't know, sir. She's got a little book."

"A damned journalist! Go and tell her to go to—"

Hands did not deliver the message as he had received it from Professor Pye. He explained that the professor was busy in his laboratory and could not be disturbed.

Mrs. Millard smiled her social-service smile.

"I—quite—understand. I called to see if Professor Pye would subscribe to the S.P.C.C. I'm collecting subscriptions for our committee."

Hands was puzzled but wishing to be helpful.

"The S.P.C.C., ma'am?"

"Yes, the Society for Prevention of Cruelty to Children."

Hands took the book, and ventured once more into the laboratory.

"The lady wants a subscription, sir."

"A subscription?"

"Yes, sir, to the Society for the Prevention of Cruelty to Children."

The professor was eating his apple. His face registered a curious, twisted little smirk. He cackled, and the sound was sinister.

"Quite superfluous. Sadism is an interesting human trait. Well, I'll give her something. Pass me my coat."

Hands fetched it from the hook on the laboratory door.

"She's quite a nice lady, sir."

"That's not unusual, Hands, when they are after favours."

Professor Pye picked a pound note from his wallet and passed it to Hands.

"Give her that. No, I don't want to put my name in her wretched little book. Get rid of her."

Hands went out to announce the good news to the nice lady, and Professor Pye resumed the eating of his apple. His nostrils expressed scorn.

"Prevention of Cruelty to Children! Better that most of the little wretches shouldn't be born. Cruelty! Is an earthquake cruel? Can my intelligence be cruel—to ants?"

V

During the whole of that summer Professor Pye was at work upon what may be described as his Atomic Gun. Externally it consisted of a tube of palmyrium mounted on a tripod stand, and in appearance not unlike a machine-gun. Its mouth could be closed by a diaphragm of palmyrium, and to the centre of the tube electric leads were attached. The apparatus's interior could have been described only by Professor Pye himself, and the description was set down in cypher in a note book which he kept locked in a safe.

Also, during the whole of August he kept the laboratory locked, and Hands, brooding over his exclusion, was both a little grieved and tempted. Moreover, Professor Pye's temper had become like the English weather, absolutely unpredictable in its moods and phases. He was extraordinarily taciturn. He emerged from the lab. to munch his biscuits and apples in the dining-room, and the lab. key was in his pocket.

Hands, who after all was human, did make one attempt to play Peeping Tom one day while the Professor was at lunch. Undoubtedly, the old boy was up to something, and Hands had not escaped the world's passion for sensationalism. Since the laboratory door was locked, and the key in the professor's pocket, he would have to attempt the windows, but when Hands sneaked round with an empty grocery box for a stool he found that the windows were shut and the blinds drawn. Obviously, Professor Pye had something to hide, and he was not taking any chances.

And Hands wondered. He was not without education in the matter of lurid literature. Like many simple souls and children he had a fantastic fancy. Now—just what would a very ingenious gentleman create in a lonely and a sexless spot like this? Sex and its bitter and baffled urges vexed Hands not a little. Supposing an old man like the professor had dreamed amorous dreams and was proposing to create a sort of mechanical Venus?

"Damn it," said Hands—"why not?"

The fantastic notion piqued him. He even chortled over it. Certainly, this would be a species of creation that a man like Professor Pye would keep draped and screened. And then Hands had a feeling that somehow his carnal fancy had overstepped the bounds of decency.

Eminent scientists should be allowed to transcend the erotic. Professor Pye might be planning to fly to the moon.

Hands felt bothered by a certain personal turgidity, and when the flesh vexed him he dug hard in his garden or took Jumbo for a walk. On occasions he would ramble along the downs for miles, finding solace and solitude, while Jumbo discovered rabbits, imaginary and otherwise. To Hands his dog was a dumb but eloquent preceptor. The little beast had attached himself to a lone man to the exclusion of all canine calls.

"Marvellous!" Hands would exclaim, "Jumbo, you can teach me something."

It was a Thursday in September when Hands asked Professor Pye to grant him leave of absence for the afternoon, and though he did not know it, the request toned with the professor's plans. He was in a state of concealed excitement. He had been wanting to get rid of Hands for the afternoon.

"I'd like to take the dog for a walk, sir."

Pye was affable.

"Certainly, Hands, certainly. You can have the whole afternoon. By the way, you haven't had a holiday since you've been here."

"No, sir."

"You must take a holiday, Hands. Haven't you any relations?"

"I've a brother in Brighton, sir."

"Well, arrange to take a holiday. I may be going to stay at my London club for a week."

"Holidays aren't much in my line, sir. You see—"

The professor was emphatic.

"Everybody needs a holiday sometimes. Change of environment. You must go for a holiday, Hands."

Hands took Jumbo out on the downs towards Dorking. Now, just what was the old fellow at? Was he really going to London, or did he desire Jack Hands's absence for a period? Hands had taken a

Thermos with him, and a parcel of bread and butter and cake. The professor allowed him grocer's cake, the yellow stuff with cherries in it, but on that day Jumbo consumed most of the cake. Hands was feeling strangely depressed. Almost, he seemed to be suffering from some unpleasant premonition.

Not so Professor Pye. He carried that four-foot tube of alloy with its tripod to the top of the observation tower, and linked it to a power plug by long flexes that ran from one of the lab. windows and were raised by a cord to the top of the little concrete tower. It was a serene and perfect September day, windless and golden, but Professor Pye had no eyes for the beauty of the landscape. His hands trembled as he attached the wires to the apparatus. He was face to face with his crisis, and he was facing more than a critical experiment. He was confronting death, personal annihilation. He could regulate his current, and release what he might estimate to be a small charge of On-force, but he could not swear that the new force would not shatter the apparatus and kill its creator.

But he needed a target, something protoplasmic and obvious upon which he could train the atomic gun. He stood looking down over the low parapet, and the target offered itself, some cows in a field in the hollow of the valley. These cows belonged to Mr. Honniset of Fox Farm, and they were pastured in two different fields separated by a strip of arable. One of the fields was less than three hundred yards away, the other more than a quarter of a mile. Professor Pye trained the gun on the farther field, and stood back behind it with his foot on the contact-maker.

For one moment he hesitated. There was a faint click as a flexible wire operated the diaphragm, a second click as his foot pressed the make and break. The palmyrium tube remained motionless; there was no sound, no suggestion of vibration. Professor Pye stood with his eyes fixed on the apparatus. He had been prepared for a possible catastrophe, blackness, oblivion.

Apparently, nothing that could be registered by the senses had happened. Professor Pye kept his foot on the contact maker for three seconds, released it, and closed the diaphragm. A curious little grin seemed to trickle into his beard. What had happened? Had anything happened? He was conscious of furious excitement and a feeling of personal reprieve. He had let the thing loose, and he was alive.

He walked to the parapet and looked down into the valley. The cows in the farther field had been grazing in a group, and every beast in that field was down. Dead? The animals were lying on their sides, legs and heads extended. The cows in the near field were still grazing. Professor Pye's face expressed a kind of demonic exultation. His hair stood up like the crest of a cockatoo. But were those cows dead, or merely shocked and temporarily helpless? He dashed downstairs for a pair of field-glasses, returned, and crouching behind the parapet, focused his glasses on the field.

He realized that he was looking at carcasses. The flaccid, inert posture of the bodies was unmistakable. He watched them intently for five minutes, and not one of the animals gave any sign of life.

Professor Pye stood up. His face was the face of a man who was not quite sane. It might have been the face of a Biblical Satan, or of a mischievous, malignant and amoral boy who had perpetrated some cunning outrage and who gloated over its success. What were a few cows compared with the discovery that he could kill, silently, swiftly, secretly? He possessed power, power such as no other man had ever commanded. He had evolved that power. It was his.

VI

But it was not merely a question of dead cows.

The beasts in the near field had not been touched, and Professor Pye, reflecting upon that fact, realized that for some unknown reason there was a non-lethal zone surrounding his gun. Queer, that! The area of the dispersion of the On-force would have to be studied and tabulated.

What was its range?

His gaze travelled beyond the farther field, and then it was that Professor Pye realized that something unusual was happening down there in the valley. The projected line of force had traversed the strip of high road that was visible from the tower, and in the roadway, or rather in the hedges, the professor could distinguish what appeared to be the wreckage of motor-cars. One of them was alight and burning brightly.

He raised his glasses and crouched.

Other cars were piling up in the road to left and right of the wreckage. Little figures were active. A man could be seen squirting the burning car with a fire extinguisher. Another man joined him.

And then Professor Pye understood, and drew swift and stark conclusions. The On-force had caught those two cars, killed the drivers, and the machines had run off the road and crashed! For a moment his face showed bleak and sharp, lips retracted, nostrils pinched. He crouched there. He had killed more than a few cows. And what—exactly—had he killed? How far had the force travelled? Had it sped for miles and left a death track behind it?

If ever a man was taken to a high place by the Satan that is self and tempted, Professor Pye was that man. He crouched between compassion and the consciousness of unrestrained and intoxicating power. He was tempted perhaps as few men of science have been tempted. He could bless or he could curse. But whereas most men of science are also social men, Professor Pye was not a social creature. He was one of the world's paranoiacs, a man who had cherished a sense of his own infinite significance, and the conviction that the world had persecuted him and denied him greatness. His was a case in which a malignantly sane intelligence was socially insane. He was a little, venomous Jehovah looking down upon the world of men and finding it vile and hateful.

He stood up. He extended his arms like some prophet cursing his generation. Almost his face was maniacal. He slavered into his beard.

"You legion of swine. Mine—is the power. It shall not spare you."

VII

He was like a man possessed.

The immensity of the thing intoxicated him. He seemed to shake with a cold rage; the urge to prove his power became a merciless and ordered frenzy. For a little while he stood observing through his glasses that minor catastrophe in the valley. He focused those agitated and active ants on that tarmac road. And then he observed in particular two figures—one that of a police constable, the other that of a chauffeur in a linen coat. They were standing together looking up at his white house. And one of them raised an arm and pointed. He was pointing out the white tower and the little figure poised there.

They were pointing at him! How dared they point at him? Did these slaves suspect?

Professor Pye stepped back behind the palmyrium tube. He rearranged the tripod and trained the gun on the road below. He released the diaphragm and switched on the current, and with an air of sardonic glee awaited the result.

There was sudden stillness down yonder. The man in the dust-coat was lying on his back in the middle of the road. The police constable had crumpled into an inert blue heap.

They had dared to point at him, had they, he—the great Professor Pye, god of the On-force, the greatest man alive!

His self-exaltation was in full flood. Inevitably he was challenged to prove the extent of his new power. Men were no more than ninepins to be bowled over. Was it not possible for him to efface humanity or as much of it as he pleased, or perhaps to permit a remnant to crawl to him and hail him as god and master? The passion to prove his power became a frenzy. He must choose some particular ant-heap and reduce it to nothingness so far as man was concerned. He stood brooding in the September sunlight, while at Newlands Corner and on Leith Hill hikers and motorists and children played and made love and picnicked in ignorance of the menace.

What ant-heap should he choose?

London?

No, London would be too immense, too large and luscious a fruit to begin with. He would prefer gradualness, a subtle crescendo.

Brighton—Hands's Brighton—flashed into his mind.

Why not Brighton?

And then he remembered Hands.

Confound the fellow! He would have to get rid of Hands, and to that deaf and disfigured creature Professor Pye allowed his one moment of compassion. Hands had been a good creature. Should he keep the fellow here? But, no, that was impossible. He could permit no man to witness his humbling of humanity. Hands must go. He would give the fellow money and tell him to go—but where? Professor Pye's pity shrugged its shoulders. After all—this was fate.

And then he heard the voice of Hands, calling to his dog.

"Jumbo—Jumbo—come on, old lad."

The dog had loitered, and Professor Pye, crossing to the back of the tower and looking over the parapet, saw Hands standing in the courtyard. The decision was made and taken. He would have to play the autocrat with Hands.

He locked the door of the tower staircase and descended. Hands was just entering the house with the dog at his heels.

"Hands, you must go for your holiday."

Hands stared.

"When, sir?"

"Now."

"Now, sir?"

"Yes, at once."

"But, sir—"

"I'm going to London tonight in the car. I insist on your taking a holiday, Hands. I shall pay for your holiday."

The professor went into the laboratory and opened his safe. When he returned to the hall he had six five-pound notes in his hand. He thrust them at Hands.

"Here's the money. Pack a suit-case. Catch a bus to Guildford. No, better still—I'll drive you to Guildford."

Hands looked bothered. He took the money, and stood hesitant.

"I'll go to Brighton, sir."

The professor's face expressed exasperation. Damn the fellow! He couldn't go to Brighton. By midnight there might be no Brighton in any human sense.

"Don't be a fool, Hands. Go and see something. Go to Scotland. Get some mountain air. Good for the dog, too."

"But where'll I stay, sir?"

"Stay? Why—at hotels—of course. Enjoy yourself, eat, drink and be merry."

It occurred to Hands that the professor would have to be humoured. He could allow the professor to drive him into Guildford and leave him at the station. He could take a train to London, and another train to Brighton. Scotland? No, he was not going to Scotland, and the professor need not know about it. Besides, he would be pretty welcome at Brighton, with thirty pounds in his pocket. He and Brother Jim could have a bit of a beano on thirty quid. He could buy the kids presents.

The professor himself opened the door of the garage and backed the two-seater into the yard. Hands hurried in to pack. Years of intimate experience had taught him that when some bee buzzed in Professor Pye's bonnet, it was necessary to let that bee buzz itself to death. Besides, thought Hands, as he tossed his belongings into an old fibre case, the Brighton idea with thirty quid to blow was a bit of all right. He could take Jumbo down to the beach and introduce the dog to the sea. Jumbo had never seen the sea.

He hurried out to the waiting car. The professor, hatless, was sitting in the driving seat. It struck Hands that Professor Pye's hair looked more turbulent and fierce than usual.

"Do you want your hat, sir?"

Professor Pye looked contemptuous. Need the world's new god and master be reminded of the conventional hat?

"Get in, Hands. Better nurse your dog."

Hands slung his suit-case into the dickey, and got in, holding Jumbo in his arms.

The private lane struck the main road about a quarter of a mile from where the On-force had acted, but even here cars were strung out and people were standing talking. Professor Pye threaded his way through the crowd. He took the Merrow road, and on the long hill to Newlands Corner they met a couple of ambulances.

Hands was interested.

"Must have been an accident, sir."

"Probably, Hands, probably."

"A pretty bad smash, I should say, sir. Road blocked, and two ambulances."

"The roads are full of fools, Hands."

"Must have been a motor-coach, sir."

"Perhaps two motor-coaches, Hands."

The professor drove into Guildford, and in his state of mental exaltation he drove rather carelessly. He ignored or did not observe the signal of a policeman on point duty, and the constable whistled to him and came and said rude and sarcastic things to the professor. He was a tall and superior young man with thin lips and a Roman nose.

"Careless driving—dangerous driving. Ignoring signals——"

The professor went red.

"I didn't see you."

"You were not looking, sir."

"I've something more important to do," said Pye, "than look for fools in uniform."

That put the official back up. The professor had to produce his licence. The policeman took notes and told Mr. Alfred Pye that the case would be reported.

The professor smiled a little sneering smile.

"Think so, do you? Poor idiot!"

The policeman waved him on.

"You might watch your manners, sir."

Manners—indeed! The professor drove on to the station and deposited Hands, dog, and suit-case. He was abrupt with Hands.

"Enjoy yourself. Go and see Loch Lomond."

Hands saluted the professor as he drove off. Gosh, but the old lad had put it across the bobby! Would he—Hands—be hauled up as a witness? Probably, but not till after he had completed a classic week at Brighton. He watched the two-seater disappear, and with Jumbo on the lead, he walked into the booking-office, and took a third-class ticket and a dog ticket for London.

The professor left Guildford by the Shalford road. He had no desire to repass that insolent young officer, but so poor a thing was his philosophy that it pleased him to think that all such insolent and obstructive fools would soon be effaced, with all courts and cross-roads. Alfred Pye's return was without adventure. Certainly, he did pass a number of cars whose occupants had the serious and subdued faces of people who had seen some strange and rather terrible thing. In fact, by the Albury fork a scout signalled to the professor and shouted a warning to him.

"Better go slow, sir—there's been a bad accident along there."

Professor Pye, head in air, smiled at him.

"Thank you. I will be exceedingly careful."

VIII

Professor Pye left his car parked at the bottom of the lane and walked along the high road to observe in a proper scientific spirit the results of his experiment. There was still a considerable crowd here, and both the crowd and the traffic were being controlled by the police. Professor Pye wormed his way as far as the nearest policeman, but when he attempted to pass the officer he was ordered back. There were some twenty tenantless cars along that section of road. Police, ambulance men and volunteers had had to extract the dead motorists and lay them on the grass beside the road. Some of the bodies were still there.

It was a shocked, sober, quiet crowd. The whole business was a mystery, and Professor Pye was able to savour the elements of the sensation he had produced. He was not shocked by the tragedy. He was immensely curious as to the lethal effects of the On-force on the human body.

He listened to two men talking, educated men.

"It couldn't have been carbon monoxide. How could it have been?"

"Well—what else? People just dead in their cars. The doctors tried artificial respiration."

"No use. Something extraordinarily sinister and strange. Apparently, there was no explosion of any kind, nothing to be seen or heard. Just as though poison gas had been released."

"Could there have been anything in one of those first cars?"

"What's the idea?"

"I'm not a chemist, but supposing one of those cars had contained a carboy of some chemical that vaporized easily, and the gas was lethal?"

"It's possible—I suppose."

"People just collapsed where they sat or stood. Something very potent and deadly."

"Anyhow it's pretty ghastly."

Someone was shouting in the field above the road, a farm hand who had come to collect those cows for milking, and had found them dead. The hedge happened to be a high one, and no one in the road had seen those dead beasts. The farm hand ran down to the hedge and shouted to one of the policeman.

"Hi—come and look, all our cows dead!"

People scrambled up the bank and tried to peer through the hedge. The driver of a van found a gate and climbed over it. The crowd followed him, and suddenly some premonition warned Professor Pye of possible complications. He hurried back to his car, drove it up and into the garage, and locking all doors, ascended to the top of the tower.

He crouched and looked over the parapet. The lower field was stippled with human figures. He saw faces turned towards the house on the hill. Someone was pointing, and sweeping an arm as though to indicate the direction and drift of a gas cloud. People were arguing.

"If you take that house on the hill, and these dead cows and the road—they line up, so to speak. What is that place up there?"

Someone pointed to the live cows in the upper field.

"What about those beasts? If your gas idea—"

"I'm thinking of that affair in Belgium when people were gassed by the emanations from a factory."

"But that was foggy weather. Besides, who would emit a lethal gas on the top of the downs?"

"Yes, but supposing someone was experimenting? A heavy gas would roll downhill on a still day like this."

"But, my dear sir—those other cows there are none the worse."

"That's so. Anyway it's a pretty ghastly puzzle."

"The autopsies on those poor devils ought to show something."

"I suppose so."

Professor Pye was thinking rapidly and logically, and for the first time his demonic egotism was tinged with fear. He had let death loose. He had stirred up the social hive, and these angry insects would be buzzing hither and thither seeking—what? No, the simile of the hive and the insect swarm did not apply. He and mankind were at war, and man was a creature of intelligence who could think, reflect and explore. His wits were at war with the wits of mankind.

At any moment he might have that crowd pouring up the hill to investigate. His experiment went to prove that for some unexplained reason his On-force did not exert its effect until it had travelled four hundred yards. If those people advanced into the non-lethal zone he and his discovery would be at their mercy.

His ruthlessness was reinforced by fear. After all—this was war, Alfred Pye *contra* Mundum. Was he—the new Jove—to flinch with the lightning in his hand? He stood up. He trained the atomic gun on the people in the field. He opened the diaphragm and switched on the current. With a kind of cold and frozen glee he saw that death was there—painless, sudden death.

For some minutes a kind of frenzy possessed him. The gun was mounted on a ball and socket joint and roller bearings and could be slewed in any direction. He swung it south, west, north, east, keeping the hypothetical range low. He would create about him a circle of silence and security. He would efface any near possible interference. He must have time to think, time to act.

Was he aware of the silence that fell upon all that part of Surrey, such a silence as had not been known since the glaciers of the ice age piled up their deposits of gravel and sand? Motor-cars, suddenly released from control, ran on till they ended in hedges or ditches. Guildford High Street with its chaos of cars and of shoppers was a place where people seemed to have fallen asleep in cars and on pavements. At the foot of the steep hill runaway motors had piled themselves. Shop assistants lay dead behind their counters. There was not a sound to be heard, save perhaps the ticking of hundreds of clocks. Even the dogs and the cats and the birds were dead. At Newlands Corner the turf was covered with the figures of men, women and children who seemed to sleep. Spectral trains ran for a while past signal boxes and through stations where life had ceased. In a thicket a quarter-mile from the white house two lovers lay dead in each other's arms.

Professor Pye walked down to the field where the dead lay. There was no anguish here, no distortion, merely the semblance of sleep. It would appear that the On-force acted upon the central nervous system, producing shock and syncope. The human heart ceased beating.

Professor Pye looked at the first dead in the war between a mad scientist and humanity. Almost, he felt kindly towards these victims. Had not they helped to prove his power?

Moreover, might he not be regarded as a beneficent being? He could give peace and sudden painless oblivion to a world of disease, and futile little strivings, discontents, poverty, bitternesses. The class war, votes, the dole, demos stupid and arrogant, politicians orating, the sensational puerilities of the press! He could put an end to all this. He could cleanse the earth, efface all the fools and mental deficients, and leaving perhaps a hardy remnant in some corner of Canada or Japan, renew the human experiment on scientific lines. He, Professor Pye, would be its god, and dictator.

Returning, he crossed the upper field where those live cows were still grazing. One of the beasts raised a head and stared at him with large, liquid eyes.

Professor Pye raised a hand as though blessing the beast.

"Behold your god, my dear. You shall be retained in his service."

His madness had reached its zenith. It transcended even a great man's folly. It was egotism that forgot both the bull and the cowherd. Who would milk those beasts? Or—did Professor Pye propose to live in a desert on wild apples and honey? But even the bees were dead. The only survivals were the trees and the grasses and all green things, and certain low forms of life whose central nervous system was not sufficiently sensitive to be shocked by the On-force.

IX

But the alarm was being sounded. Professor Pye had silenced everything within a radius of fifteen miles, but into that reservation other humans were beginning to penetrate. Waterloo Station was all crowds and chaos. Telephone operators, tired of calling, "Hallo, Guildford," and finding themselves repulsed by a most strange silence in all that part of Surrey, left their instruments and became part of a London that stood in the streets and listened to monstrous rumours. The bus depots were disorganized. Such and such a bus had never returned. Scared motorists who had passed through that zone of death, pulled up when they rediscovered people who were living, and with white faces spread the incredible news.

"Half Surrey's dead."

"Miles of derelict cars and buses."

"At Addlestone a train had stopped at the level crossing. Full of dead people. Signalman dead in his box. We couldn't get through that way."

The thing seemed too ghastly and immense to be true.

But already police cars and pressmen and adventurous motorists, and agonized city men were penetrating into that circle of death. The Prime Minister had called an emergency meeting of the Cabinet at No. 10, Downing Street. Scotland Yard was at work. The Press rushed out alarmist editions. Almost, they were fought for by the crowds in the streets. Press agencies were telephoning from all over the world.

"What Has Happened in Surrey?"

"Is it an Attack from Mars?"

Police cars, returning from the dead area, had to force their way through scared and eager crowds. Rumour became actuality, and as the news spread a shocked and bewildered silence seemed to spread over London. People were inarticulate. The thing was too vast, too terrible, too astounding. It was said that the P.M. himself had hurried down into Surrey. Aldershot had been wiped out as well as Guildford and Godalming. Woking, Byfleet and the districts along the river were full of dead people. The Guards were being paraded. The whole of the available police were being mobilized.

People rushed to their wireless sets. What had the B.B.C. to say?

The little voice of the announcer was official.

"The Prime Minister appeals to everyone to remain calm. He asks you to mistrust all wild rumours, and to avoid panic. All the possible causes of this unprecedented and terrible tragedy are being explored."

Night.

Professor Pye had been sitting at his wireless set. It had an extensive range and he could listen in to London, Paris, Berlin, Milan. He picked up fragments of Continental agitation. Paris was commenting upon the incredible cataclysm in England. Had there been an escape of some strange subterranean gas through a crack in the earth's crust? No seismic shock had been recorded. Milan was speculating as to cosmic dust. Or had the lethal atmosphere of some passing comet brushed across a portion of Great Britain? Eminent scientists were being asked to give their views upon a catastrophe that was of startling significance to the whole world.

Professor Pye went up to his tower. He looked out over Surrey. He heard the lowing of those abandoned and unmilked cows in the field below. He heard the sound of a car in the valley, and saw its headlights clearing the darkness. That ingenious and irrepressible insect man was buzzing back into the death zone. The car stopped in the valley. And then Professor Pye heard the drone of an aeroplane overhead.

His madness became cunning. He had left the lights in the laboratory, and he hurried downstairs and switched them off. If he showed a light—especially a stationary light—his enemies might infer that someone was alive. Life itself would inspire curiosity—suspicion. He had other brains pitted against his.

He returned to the tower. He had hurried up the staircase. He was agitated. That aeroplane was droning overhead, and its sound was angry and menacing. He would have to deal with aeroplanes. Just before dusk he had taken his bearings and left the atomic gun trained upon Brighton. Yes, he would try more current. It was a risk, but he would have to take that risk. He stood in the darkness behind the tube and released a larger volume of On-force.

The gun had stood the strain.

But just how far would its lethal effect carry? Supposing that the range was limited by the size of the apparatus? What then? Yes, he would have to experiment and discover how far this power extended. By listening in he would be able to define the dead zone from the living. If Paris remained vocal he would have discovered the limitations of his gun. What then? To maintain about him a zone of death, to repulse all penetration, until he had built a more powerful apparatus.

Ruthlessness, a kind of divine ruthlessness, was inevitable.

Meanwhile, these explorers, these angry human insects in cars and aeroplanes were beginning to buzz about him. They would have to be dealt with—and that instantly. He must make his desert so deadly that no human creature would dare to venture into it. It was necessary for him to have leisure, breathing space, security. He had food and water, electricity, oil.

Inexorably, but with a slight and significant tremor of the hands he slewed the gun this way and that. There had been voices, in the valley, but suddenly they were stilled, though the cars' head-lights continued to blaze. Crouching, he pointed the gun skywards towards the sound of the cruising plane. The drone did not cease, but it seemed to slip and to descend. There was a sound of a crash in the valley, and presently a knot of flame sprang up.

X

Terror upon terror, sensation after sensation.

The Prime Minister had not returned from Surrey. None of those who had hurried down to investigate had returned.

Heston Aerodrome, which had sent out two scouting planes, reported both machines as missing.

Moreover, doctors in the area surrounding that centre of dark-ness and of silence were being summoned to hundreds of people who had fainted and remained unconscious for short periods of time. The On-force, lethal over a definite field, weakened upon dispersal until it produced nothing more than syncopic attacks, giddiness, nausea.

A telephone operator, speaking to the Brighton exchange, was left stranded in sudden silence.

"Hallo—Brighton, hallo."

Brighton did not reply.

Other people who were speaking to friends in Brighton experienced the shock of that same silence. Voices died away, and did not return.

Trains that had left Brighton after dark, or were in the Brighton area, failed to arrive.

Horsham, Cuckfield, Hassocks were equally silent. So were Peacehaven and Shoreham, Steyning and Lewes. Worthing and Eastbourne reported hundreds of cases of people fainting in the streets, on the sea front, in cinemas, hotels, houses.

The area over which the On-force was active had the shape of an elongated egg. It spread gradually from its point of origin, reached a certain extreme width, and then contracted. Earth contours, hills and valleys, appeared to have no obstructing effect upon the force. It penetrated wherever there was air. People were killed in tunnels, subways and cellars.

During that first night very few people slept. A venturesome aviator, flying in the early morning over Surrey and Sussex, returned safely to Croydon Aerodrome. He and his observer had the stark faces of men who had looked upon some horror.

"Brighton's a vast morgue. Yes, we flew low along Brighton front. Thousands of people lying dead there."

The Cabinet, sitting at No. 10, Downing Street, received the news of this latest cataclysm. Already they had called in scientific experts, among them Professors James and Beddington. Maps were spread. With such facts as they could command, these ministers and experts attempted to define the area of death and to arrive at some explanation of the mystery.

There was the problem of a public panic and the Press.

"Better stop all the morning papers."

"Wouldn't that be more likely to produce a panic? Press has been asked to refrain from publishing too much detail."

Professor Beddington, bending over a map, was shading certain portions of it with a blue pencil. He had a police report beside him.

The Chancellor of the Exchequer bent over Beddington's shoulder.

"Any theory, Beddington?"

Beddington was a dispassionate, large-headed man who had the appearance of a farmer.

"There seems to be a definite focus. Our information goes to show that the focus is on the North Downs between Guildford and Dorking."

The Leader of the House, standing by a window and smoking a pipe, asked the question that was at the back of every mind:

"It might happen—to London?"

Professor Beddington looked up.

"Yes. Obviously—so."

Somewhere in the room a voice sounded a note of fear.

"What—is—the damned thing? My God—we must find out!"

"Any views on the Martian theory, Beddington?"

The man at the table tapped his teeth with the end of the blue pencil.

"Not very likely. If Mars was bombarding us with some kind of cosmic ray—there would be more dispersion. I mean, I think the area covered would be larger. We have had no reports from the Continent, have we, of similar happenings?"

"No."

The Leader of the House, his pipe in his right hand, came and stood at the table.

"Then the thing's—human?"

"Inhumanly human. Satanic."

"Well?"

Professor Beddington leaned back in his chair.

"Supposing some individual who was anti-social and not quite sane had discovered how to control and use such a thing as—shall we say—atomic energy."

There was a moment's silence.

"Is that possible? Of course, Beddington, you are one of the few men—"

"It is what we have been working for—but beneficently so."

"Then, the inference is that if some malignant genius had evolved something of the kind he could wipe out humanity?"

"Exactly."

"Good God! how would one deal with him?"

Professor Beddington smiled.

"Ah—how?"

Professor James had been scribbling on a writing-pad. He raised his head suddenly and spoke.

"I have been jotting down names, Beddington, alphabetically. I have just come to Pye. Did you ever meet Pye?"

"Once."

"Rather a poisonous little person, but infernally clever. I happen to know that Pye lives in Surrey. He had a grievance against—everybody and everything. He was supposed to be researching on his own. Now, supposing, for argument's sake, a man like Pye—?"

Professor Beddington nodded his large head.

"That's my feeling too, James. I think we have to deal with some infernally clever super-megalomaniac. One ought to try and put one's hand on every physicist in the country."

Said the Man with the Pipe, "Why not begin with this fellow—Pye? He can be located; he can be—"

Once again Professor Beddington smiled his quiet smile.

"Yes—but supposing Pye to be the man—Pye will be—unapproachable. We cannot raise Pye to the Teeth—by—just deciding to do so. Pye can elevate us all to Paradise—before—"

"Good God!" said the frightened voice—"we are like a lot of doomed rats in a ship."

The Man with the Pipe relit it.

He said, "I never felt less like a rat."

XI

Professor Pye had not slept. He had been listening to the aerial voices of the earth.

Soon after dawn he carried a chair to the top of the tower and sat down beside his infernal gun.

He was like a little grey spider in the midst of a web of silence.

Brighton—human Brighton—had ceased to be. He had picked up that news from French sources. He was able to infer that his On-force had not reached the coast of France.

He sat with a map on his knees. He looked haggard, and his eyelids were red. If London shivered on the edge of panic, Professor Pye was not very far from strange terror. His discovery was catastrophic, but in the clarity of that September dawn he confronted his limitations. Obviously, the range of his atomic gun was lethal up to perhaps a hundred miles, but beyond that point society was safe. The problem posed him. Either the gun as it was designed would have to be made mobile, or a larger and more powerful apparatus be constructed. If he mounted the gun on a car and lorry, he would need more current than a portable battery could supply. He might connect, of course, with local generating stations. But when he had dealt with England, Wales and Scotland, he would arrive at the sea. A fast motor-boat and a dash across the Channel! but he could infer that the air would be thick with patrolling aeroplanes waiting for "It" to emerge from England. He would have to clear the sky as he went.

He began to shrink inwardly from the vastness of his war upon society. It began to scare him. He went below and heated up some coffee, and into it he poured some of his old brandy. A little knot of warmth hardened in his stomach. He lit a cigar, and with a faint suggestion of swagger he walked up and down the laboratory. How silent the world was! Sounds that he would not have reacted to on a normal day now impressed themselves on him by their absence. No trains, no traffic on the road, no birds, no Hands, no dog. Even those few live cows had stampeded in a panic, crashed through hedges, and had ceased to be. He heard nothing but the ticking of the laboratory clock, and the sound of his own footfalls. When he stood still to listen he could hear his own breathing.

But what was that?

He was growing jumpy. He stiffened and bristled like a scared cat.

Yes, there was some sound, a vibration in the air. Aeroplanes—not one, but several! The distant roar of the engines and the hum of the propellers roused qualms in his stomach. Big drums beating, war-drums. He rushed up the stairs to the tower; he crouched. He saw five planes in formation flying from the north-east. Soon they would be over the tower.

He crawled to the gun, slewed it round and up, and covered those planes. He released the On-force. For a second or two the planes held on before their formation broke; they appeared to drift this way and that like errant leaves. They dived, spun—disappeared beyond the hill. He counted five faint crashes.

Professor Pye left the gun pointed skywards and rose to his feet. He had wiped out that R.A.F. squadron, but the appearance of that squadron over the North Downs gave him furiously to think. Did the world suspect? Had other brains than his spent sleepless hours over the elucidation of the problem, and were approaching the most probable solution? They were postulating the manifestations of some new form of energy controlled and applied by a human being who was hostile to his fellows. They were searching for the focus of the On-force and the man who controlled it. They were sending out planes to scout over Surrey.

A sudden frenzy took possession of Alfred Pye. They suspected him! They were trying to locate the new demigod. These fools thought that they could destroy him and his discovery, a discovery that if wisely used could efface an idiot democracy and cleanse the earth of demagogues and claptrap. He had in his hands the power to create a new earth, to decide what should live and what should die. He was the new dictator, a super-eugenist who could purge the earth of the little people who preached the palsy of Socialism. Equality! Brains like so many peas in a pod! Preposterous nonsense! He would demonstrate to the mob that it had a master.

His ruthless sanity may have been inspired, for those who have vision look for an autocracy of science, a just and beneficent tyranny exercised by the enlightened few over the inferior many. Science will mount its Olympus and rule, holding perhaps the menace of lightning in its hands. But Professor Pye had no Olympian smile. He was both ruthlessly sane and malignantly mad. He was a megalomaniac in a hurry to impress a destructive ego upon a society that opposed him.

London?

Yes, London was the enemy. London must be destroyed, for its destruction would send such a shudder over the earth that civilization would fall on its knees and surrender.

He would hear aerial voices appealing for mercy.

"O Thou Unknown God and Master, have pity on us. Spare us and we will serve you."

His face was the face of a man in a frenzy. He trained the atomic gun on London, and then suddenly he paused. He had a sardonic inspiration. He possessed a small portable wireless set which he used when the more powerful apparatus was not needed. He went below and carried the little cabinet up into the tower. He placed it beside the gun.

Was London speaking?

He switched on. London was speaking. He heard the little, refined and carefully standardized voice of the B.B.C. announcer. It was telling England that Mr. Percy Haldane—the Leader of the House—was about to broadcast on the crisis. Mr. Haldane wished to appeal to the country for calmness and courage. There must be no panic. The Government and its body of experts were convinced that they were on the brink of locating the origin of the catastrophe and also its originator.

Professor Pye moistened his thin lips. So, they thought, did they—that he would wait to be located? Fantastic fools! But he would hold his hand for a moment and listen in to that prince of platitudinarians, Mr. Percy Haldane. It was Mr. Percy Haldane's Government that had presented Sir Philip Gasson with his knighthood. A tribute to science! Gasson a scientist? He was just an academic sneak-thief.

The announcer's voice ceased. There was a short pause, and then the deliberate and slightly sententious and rolling voice of Mr. Haldane was heard.

"I am speaking to England. I am speaking to those who, in a crisis, have never failed to meet it, however acute and ominous that crisis has been. Within the last forty-eight hours this country has experienced a series of mysterious catastrophes, but may I once say that the mystery is on the point of being—resolved. We—the Cabinet and our body of experts—are confident—that there is—in this country a monstrous offender against—civilization and humanity. We believe and are sure—that we can deal—with this evil spirit in our midst. I have just left a conference in which several eminent scientists, Professors Beddington and James, and Sir Philip Gasson—"

Professor Pye's head gave a jerk. A little malevolent smile shimmered over his face. So, Gasson was there, Gasson the slimy and debonair, Gasson of the black velvet coat and the cerise-coloured tie, Gasson who, when lecturing, posed as though all the women must think him Zeus. Professor Pye licked his lips. Mr. Haldane's voice was still booming.

Click! Professor Pye switched on the current. The wireless cabinet produced four more words from Mr. Percy Haldane.

"We English are people—"

Silence! Not a murmur. The little wooden cabinet was mute, and Professor Pye's face malignantly triumphant. Exit—London, exit Mr. Percy Haldane, and Philip Gasson, and Whitehall and Somerset House, and Lambeth Palace, Whitechapel, all that suppurating sore which fools called a great city. Eros, on his pedestal in Piccadilly Circus, would be posing above an exhibit of corpses. For a few seconds there must have been infinite mechanical chaos, buses and cars running amok, charging each other and crashing through shop-fronts. The trains in the tubes had continued to circulate like toy trains until a confusion of collisions had jammed the tunnels.

Professor Pye's cold frenzy continued. He swept the whole horizon with his gun. He would efface everything within the limit of its range, and then wait for the earth to surrender.

He would listen in to Europe's terror and anguish.

Soon, they would be appealing to the Unknown God for mercy.

America, Asia, Africa, Australia, all would be on their knees to him in their transmission stations.

The world would surrender to him by wireless.

XII

Over the whole South-East of England, a large portion of East Anglia, the Midlands and the West there was silence. The death zone covered Bournemouth, Bristol, Gloucester, Birmingham, Leicester, Peterborough, Ipswich, Dover. Exeter, Cardiff, Derby, Nottingham and Norwich were alive. Calais and a small segment of the French coast had been affected. Just beyond the zone, life had been shocked but not effaced. There had been the same symptoms of nausea, giddiness, and in some cases temporary unconsciousness.

For some days panic prevailed. A few adventurous or anguished souls attempted to penetrate the lethal zone, only to be effaced by Professor Pye's drenching of that area with On-force. Once every hour the atomic gun covered every point of the compass. Half Somerset, Devon and Cornwall were isolated between the Channel and the Irish Sea. From villages and towns near the borderline the population fled, pouring into Wales, Cheshire, Lancashire and Yorkshire. Cardiff, Liverpool, Manchester and Sheffield were flooded with refugees. During those first few days organized government, the very social scheme itself seemed in danger of dissolution.

It was in Manchester that resistance hardened. The Lord Mayor of Manchester and the city council formed themselves into a species of provisional government. The crisis was unprecedented, and improvisations were urgent and inevitable. The mayors of all the Yorkshire and Lancashire towns were gathered in. York proposed that the centre of authority should be located at Edinburgh.

Meanwhile, the whole world was in agitation.

Moscow both trembled and gloated. Bourgeois England had received a death-blow.

New York was all head-lines. Crowds filled the streets.

France, wounded at Calais, so near the terror, was arming with all its expert intelligence to combat the horror.

A deputation flew from Manchester to Paris to discuss with the French Government the confrontation of this crisis. Europe's international quarrels were forgotten for the moment. Berlin, Prague, Rome, Madrid, each sent a body of representatives and experts to Paris. Signor Mussolini flew in person to the French capital, bringing with him a little Italian physicist from Turin, Professor Pirelli. The discussions were informal and held at the Elysée. It was Mussolini's little professor who was in a position to bring forward data that might explain the cataclysm. He too was working on the atom. He had released from it certain energy that when controlled was lethal to mice and rats. His work was as yet an affair of the laboratory, but he postulated that the earth was being assailed by some inspired lunatic who had discovered how to release and control atomic energy.

The English members could produce certain facts. London, before its destruction, had telegraphed confidential information to the municipal authorities in the provinces, The source of the mysterious force was centred in Surrey, and probably on the North Downs within a few miles of Guildford. It was known that a certain eccentric scientist had a house there, and that he lived the life of a misanthrope and a recluse. Professor Pye was under suspicion.

Europe's Council of War debated the problem. It was evident that the field of force was limited. The death area had not extended. It was like a spider's web, and in the centre of it crouched the spider.

Signor Mussolini was for instant action.

"Aeroplanes—bombs."

Reminded that the air was controlled over that area, he was not to be dissuaded.

"We must attack. Let our aeroplanes go out by the hundred, swarm after swarm, to observe, and to make sure. We must take risks, every risk."

Those round the table looked to Professor Pirelli. Had he anything to suggest? He smiled whimsically. No, he had nothing more subtle to propose. Crude explosives, or perhaps gas bombs, were the only retort science could provide at the moment. Even if one aeroplane survived, and discovered one live human being in that death area, it might be assumed that that one live man was the monster who was attacking humanity.

One German delegate suggested the construction of long-range guns that could be mounted on the French coast to bombard Surrey.

The French President, with certain unhappy memories in his mind, asked the German to say how long it would take to manufacture those guns, and the German was silent.

No, action must be instant and co-ordinated. The terror might spread. They must make what use they could of the instruments that were to hand. Every country must supply its quota of planes. It would be better to call for volunteers as aviators and observers.

Signor Mussolini flew back to Rome, the Germans to Berlin. Orders were issued to the French Air Force. To begin with the air squadrons would patrol the outskirts of the death zone, observe and report, before attempting to locate and destroy the enemy.

XIII

Professor Pye waited for the earth to broadcast its appeal for mercy. The aerial voice might be English, French or German, but Alfred Pye spoke both French and German, and perhaps he expected the voice to be French.

Meanwhile, he had not had his clothes off for three days, nor had he slept, save in brief snatches. He was looking distinctly worn and dishevelled. He had omitted to shave that part of his face that was accustomed to be razored, and his eyes were the eyes of a man short of sleep.

He had carried a mattress and bed-clothes to the top of the tower. He took his perfunctory meals there beside his gun, with the portable wireless switched on, and a pair of binoculars slung round his neck. A dispassionate observer would have described him as a scraggy little man who was both scared and irritable, a grey rat on the alert. Professor Pye was feeling the strain of playing the part of Jupiter.

He was becoming more and more aware of the dreadful silence. He looked out upon a green world that was empty of all sound and movement, save the movement of the clouds and the trees. He was surrounded by a ghastly, stagnant greenness, and at night he was alone with the stars. Almost, he began to hunger for the sound of a human voice. The craving was illogical and absurd, but so strong was it that he carried a gramophone up to the tower and played Bach and Beethoven.

Moreover, the air was unaccountably silent. Even his large installation could pick up no voices. What was the earth doing? Had his On-force gradually penetrated over the whole globe, and had man ceased to be? But if so he himself should be dead, for the force would have circled the earth and returned to destroy him.

Most strange—this silence.

Or was it deliberate? Was civilization conspiring to isolate him? Were all the earth's transmitting stations wilfully mute? Paris and Berlin and New York might be conferring by cable.

Now and again he would patrol the top of the tower and turn his glasses on the green emptiness of Surrey, and scan the whole horizon. There were moments when he imagined movement upon some hill-side, or fancied that he could spot an aeroplane in the distance. He would rush to his gun and apply On-force to the imagined menace.

He was beginning to look very wild about the eyes.

September continued warm and sunny. A gentle breeze blew from the east, and at noon the mercury stood at seventy.

It happened that Professor Pye had gone below to make himself some tea. He was using tinned milk. He carried the tea tray to the top of the tower, and as he reached it he became aware of a faint odour, sickly and strange. It was as though the whole atmosphere was tainted. He put the tray down on a table, and stood with his nose to the wind.

An odour of death, of decay? Yes, that was it, millions of dead bodies swelling in the September heat. He was scenting London, Greater London, all those towns and villages, the dead cows in the field below, the dead men and women in the valley. And Professor Pye's face looked suddenly bloodless and ashy. Almost, it was the face of a corpse. He left his tea untouched. He had not seen the horror he had perpetrated, but he could savour it.

Nausea attacked him. He went below and poured out two ounces of brandy.

XIV

Would nothing happen?

This silence was becoming unbearable.

He was possessed by a febrile and busy restlessness. He went out and walked along the downs—but that sickly smell of decay was everywhere. Even in green and solitary places he blundered upon death—bodies lying around a cloth with cups and plates and cushions, a dead lad and a girl, an old man with a book, a child and not far away a man and woman. He saw a dead dog lying in some rough grass. Was he himself alive or dead? More than once his fingers went to his throat. War, yes, war, but the silence and stench of a field after a battle! He slunk back to the white house. He found himself hungry for the face of Hands, yes, even for a disfigured face.

And what had become of Hands?

He fell into a kind of frenzy. He drank more brandy. Where were his enemies? Why did they not attack?

But the war of the world against Professor Pye was developing. To begin with the reconnaissance in force was crudely conceived. A hundred aeroplanes flying in a vast half-circle crossed the Channel and passed over Sussex. The hour was about noon on a clear day and the planes had the sun above and behind them. Professor Pye heard the faint roar of the massed machines as they crossed the

South Downs, for his ears had been straining to catch some sound that might break the stagnant silence. He turned his field-glasses on that stretch of sky. He saw the little black silhouettes strung out across the horizon. The planes were flying fast and low.

Here—at last—was something tangible to deal with. The earth was alive, and it had not surrendered. Those planes were coming to attack him. Anger and hatred revived. Insolent fools! Did they imagine that an aerial cavalry charge could contend with his On-force.

He sat by his gun. He waited until that half-moon of flying folly was within a mile of him, and then, slewing his gun from left to right, he shot the machines down. They seemed to falter and fall one after another like so many crows.

Once more there was silence.

The attack was repeated twice that day on the same unimaginative lines, but the second assault came from the north. Professor Pye might be dishevelled and wild of eye, but in annihilating those aerial enemies he recovered a kind of malignant exultation.

When would the fools realize that they had to deal with a superman who was their master?

This was the world's Waterloo. Flying cuirassiers charging a little cube of concrete that was invulnerable! He would teach humanity that its salvation would be secured only by surrender.

There followed more than twenty-four hours of silence, and the next night Professor Pye dared to sleep. He was urgently in need of sleep. Wrapped in a great-coat he sat on the tower till two o'clock in the morning. It was too cold here. He dragged the mattress and bed-clothes down into the laboratory. He would allow himself two hours sleep on the laboratory floor.

He slept, but half an hour after the break of day he was awakened by a rush and a roar overhead. Something had passed with the speed of a shell, and set the glass bottles and jars in the laboratory vibrating. For some seconds Professor Pye sat sodden with sleep, wondering whether the thing had happened or whether he had dreamed it, but a distant and diminishing roar warned him of the reality.

In brief, the Italians had brought a couple of flying-boats to Dunkirk, machines built for the Schneider Cup and capable of flying nearly four hundred miles an hour. It was one of these swift machines, which, trusting to its speed, had roared over Sussex and Surrey, and was now making for the Bristol Channel. Professor Pye grasped the significance of the machine's rush across his safety zone. It could enter the lethal zone, traverse its two hundred miles in half an hour, and escape to report.

He was in his pyjamas. He rushed upstairs to the tower. He shivered in the cold morning air. He saw a great yellow sun hanging above the Surrey hills. That screaming hydroplane was more than thirty miles away. In another ten minutes it would be beyond his reach. He ducked down behind his gun, slewed it round, and released the On-force. The hydroplane was over Reading and following the Thames when the force struck it. The machine crashed on to a roof in Friar Street and burst into flames. It started a conflagration that blazed for hours.

Professor Pye stood shivering.

"That fellow might have bombed me."

He realized that with such machines in action against him his margin of safety had been reduced to fifteen minutes. This was serious. It suggested that he would have to sweep the air every quarter of an hour.

But had they located him? Were these machines merely groping for the enemy? Moreover, he could assume that there were not more than half a dozen machines in the world capable of such speed. Let them all come and crash, and the proof of his power would be all the more catastrophic.

But it was cold on the tower. There had been a slight ground frost. He regretted that warm bed; and that morning he mixed brandy with his coffee.

XV

In Paris there was gloom and consternation. Not an aeroplane had returned. The death zone had swallowed them up, and mocked the world with a malignant and ominous silence.

Was humanity helpless?

It was a delegate from Manchester University, a pawky and rather reticent young man with a squint, who brought psychology to bear upon the problem.

Said the Manchester lad: "Granted that there is something inhumanly human behind this devilment—that's to say we have to deal with a man. He is using atomic force or some sort of ray. Let us presume that he has to function, eat, sleep, remain alert. Now, an apparatus or a machine may be more or less infallible—man is not. The flesh can fail, and so can concentration. Let him stew in silence for a week."

The French President nodded.

"You suggest—that silence might unnerve him."

"It might fool him. Imagine a man making war on the world. Silence, solitude, a ghastly and fantastic solitude. He might go potty."

Continental gentlemen had to have "potty" explained to them.

"Mad? But yes, we understand—"

"Surely—the creature cannot be considered sane?"

"He's most damnably sane," said the psychologist, "but he must have sleep. Imagine a man sitting by some apparatus, listening and watching for days and nights. He won't stand it for ever. He'll break down. He'll fall asleep. He might commit suicide."

The shrewd common sense of Manchester was accepted, and the conference at Paris decided to blockade Professor Pye with silence.

For the first twenty-four hours Professor Pye examined this silence and its various and possible implications. His enemies had been profoundly discouraged, or perhaps they were trying to fool him into over-confidence. None the less, this silence worried him; it kept him on the alert—especially so at night. It was so profound and so inhuman. It chained him to the top of the tower. He had connected flexes and ear-phones to his larger installation, and for hours he sat on the tower listening and listening—to silence. Every quarter of an hour he had to sweep the horizon with his atomic gun.

Once more the silence began to frighten him. It was as though nothingness possessed powers of attrition, like dropping water or blowing sand. There was pressure in this silence. It became almost like a heavy hand upon the top of his head, bearing more and more heavily upon his brain. The stillness was both so alive and so dead. He began to long for sound, even for some hostile sound that was human.

The landscape had become a painted scene, the sky a kind of hard blue ceiling across which artificial clouds floated. It seemed to be pressing nearer and nearer. His eyes ached. Almost, he was conscious of his tense and overstrained ear-drums. He had aged; he looked haggard and grey and dishevelled.

Three days and three nights of that silence.

His brain was beginning to manufacture sounds, and sometimes these auditory hallucinations were so real, that he would jump up and look over the parapet. Surely he had heard voices down there? Or he would switch on his gun and sweep the horizon.

He had fed in snatches and slept in snatches. He fought sleep. His desire for sleep was as terrible as the silence. It menaced him like a dark wall of water. He fought it off. It would be fatal for him to sleep for any length of time.

Why had he not thought of this before? He should have been prepared with some mechanism that would keep his gun revolving while he rested.

Why did not those fools flash him a message of surrender?

He was becoming less and less of a superman, God Pye *contra* Mundum, but a little dishevelled ape of a man who was beginning to chatter to himself and to react to imaginary noises.

On the third night he was convinced that he heard a dog barking outside the house. Hands's dog—Jumbo? Had the little beast been near him all the time? But no, he had driven Hands and the dog to Guildford. Nevertheless, he rushed out in a state of strange excitement. He called; he appealed to the ghost dog in a wheedling voice.

"Hallo—doggie! Come here, good dog. Come along, old man. Nice bone for nice doggie."

He whistled and whistled and called, but the silence was like grey rock.

He cursed—"Go to hell, you beast."

He slammed the door and burst into sudden tears.

XVI

Mrs. Hector Hyde's landing at Le Bourget was not fortuitous. The famous airwoman had been engaged in one of her adventurous escapades over Asia, finding other hazards to conquer, when she had picked up an aerial message from Tashkent. This piece of world news had been sufficiently wild and improbable to pique Mrs. Hyde. She had turned the nose of her plane westwards, and landing at Baghdad, had asked to be enlightened.

"What is this absurd rumour?"

Baghdad could assure her that this was no rumour but very terrible reality.

Mrs. Hector Hyde ate, slept for two hours, had her machine refuelled, and took off for Paris. She arrived at Le Bourget late in the afternoon, and asked to be driven at once to the English embassy. Mrs. Hector Hyde, being both a gentlewoman and a world figure, was treated as a person of some significance. In fact she was to be supremely significant. If some nasty little male was—as usual— making a horrid mess of civilization, it was time for a woman to intervene.

The ambassador gave her five minutes. He was due to attend a conference at the Elysée at six. Mrs. Hyde listened to all that he had to tell her, and then asked to be allowed to attend the conference with him.

"I would like to come as a volunteer. I might be of some use—"

She was calmly yet passionately determined to be of use. She had lost things in England, irreplaceable things—relations, friends, a home, dogs who were waiting for her.

"I want to be of use, Sir Hugh. No, there is nothing more to be said."

The ambassador took her with him. She was the only woman in the conference-room, and she sat and listened. Particularly did she listen to the young man from Manchester, Professor Cragg. His name, his appearance, his insurgent hair and strabismic eye might be somewhat uncouth and provincial, but he impressed her.

These very eminent gentlemen, politicians, diplomats, savants sat round a table and conferred; they were dignified, formal, and a little helpless. Professor Cragg was combative, and logically so. He had no oratorical gifts. He was a doer, not a talker.

He argued that the hypothetical enemy in Surrey had been dosed with a week's potent silence. He might be mad or dead, or lulled into a sense of false security. Or he might be preparing further horrors. The psychological moment had arrived for a raid upon Surrey.

"Just one plane, and an attempt to land on the downs and explore them. Yes, a night landing—if possible."

Professor Cragg's was a rational suggestion, but who would undertake this forlorn hope?

"I'd rather like to go myself," said he, "if anybody will fly the plane."

Mrs. Hector Hyde stood up.

"Gentlemen, I ask to be given the duty. There is a full moon tonight. I know that part of the country very well. I was born in Surrey. If Professor Cragg will accept me and my plane—"

Professor Cragg jumped up and gave her an awkward, boyish bow.

"Delighted. Now—we can do something."

Professor Cragg and Mrs. Hyde were driven to Le Bourget. The weather reports were favourable, an anticyclone covered England and the north of France; there was little wind or cloud, but a danger of ground fog at night. Mrs. Hyde inspected her machine in person, and superintended the refuelling. The Professor was fitted out with a bag of bombs and a flying suit. Le Bourget gave them a meal, and Professor Cragg borrowed from the French an automatic pistol and a pair of glasses. They waited for the moon to rise before taking off. The aerodrome gave them a cheer.

Mrs. Hyde had laid her course. She proposed to fly straight across the Channel, strike the South Downs, and crossing the Weald, land on the North Downs. She knew the country from the air. She was sure that she could pick up St. Martha's and the high ground beyond round Newlands Corner. She had danced at that most comfortable and pleasant of hotels at Newlands Corner. As a girl she had explored the Pilgrims' Way, and ridden along the Drove Road. Her plan was to bring her plane down on that broad sweet stretch of rabbit-nibbled turf. It would be outlined for her by the wooded Roughs and the scrub and yews on the hillside. Her face was as calm as the face of the full moon.

XVII

Seven days of silence and of sleeplessness had reduced Professor Pye to a state akin to senile dementia. He chattered to himself; his saliva ran into his beard; hands and head shook with a senile tremor. He was suffering from hallucinations. Imaginary voices threatened him; he was startled by apparitions.

Yet his intelligence retained an edge of sanity. A kind of coldly impersonal Professor Pye could consider and comment upon the figure of a dishevelled and tremulous old gentleman with a dewdrop hanging to his nose. Pye the physicist admonished Pye the man.

"What you need, my friend, is sleep, ten hours' sleep."

Obviously so. The human mechanism that was Pye cried out for sleep. Had it not sat on that tower hour by hour, sweeping the horizon with that gun? Sleep suborned him; it was more than a temptation; it was like the sea coming in. It was irresistible.

Sleep became a tyrant. It said: "No—I shall be satisfied with nothing but completeness. You will take that mattress and pillow and bolster and those bed-clothes and place them on my proper kingly bedstead. No—I refuse to be fobbed off with a shakedown on the floor. See to it that my commands are obeyed."

Professor Pye procrastinated. He climbed to the top of the tower. He saw the face of the full moon staring at him like a vast countenance that had just appeared above the edge of the world. He gibbered at the moon.

"How dare you stare at me like that!"

He turned the atomic gun on the moon.

"Take that, you insolent satellite."

But the moon frightened him. It was like the cold and accusing face of humanity. Yes, he would sleep. He blundered down the stairs, and dragged mattress and bedclothes from the laboratory into his bedroom. He made his bed. He had left all the lights blazing in the laboratory and the blinds up. He was conscious of nothing but the crave for sleep. He closed the door of his bedroom, turned off the lights, and got into bed. He slept like one of the Seven Sleepers of Ephesus.

XVIII

Mrs. Hector Hyde turned her plane to the left about a mile from the wooded crest of the North Downs. They were somewhere over Farley Heath when she spoke to Professor Cragg.

"Do you see those lights?"

Professor Cragg saw them, and realized their significance.

"The only lights in Southern England. If someone is alive there, it means—"

"The enemy."

"That's the inference. And we are still alive. Those lights are windows on the downs."

"I think so. I am going to land near Newlands Corner."

She brought the plane down perfectly on the broad and moon-lit stretch of turf. They climbed out and stood side by side in that world of the dead. There was the most profound silence. Even here the faint odour of death and decay permeated the air. Almost, they spoke in whispers.

"We had better not waste any time."

She shivered slightly.

"No, no—psychoanalysis. Those lights."

Professor Cragg laid a hand on his bag of bombs.

"Yes—that's our—objective. We are humanity's forlorn hope. One can assume that life and electric light advertise—the enemy. If my theory holds—the devil has fallen asleep and left the lights burning."

They followed the downland track under the full moon, nor had they gone thirty yards before they came upon the first dead, a man and a girl with a picnic basket between them. Professor Cragg turned his electric torch on the motionless figures. He said nothing, but quickly switched off the beam of light.

Mrs. Hyde's voice sounded stifled. She had seen the faces of those dead.

"Let's get on."

He understood her. She was compelling herself to control instinctive terror. They passed on, having to step aside or diverge to avoid those dark objects on the grass. The moonlight made the scene more ghastly and macabre, those derelict cars, the tea-tables in the tea-gardens, the odour of death.

Mrs. Hyde spoke.

"And to think I have danced over there."

"Where?"

"The Newlands Corner Hotel. Such a pleasant place."

His voice came like little cold wind.

"Do you know how to use those bombs?"

"Yes. The French showed me."

"You won't hesitate?"

"Is it likely?"

They crossed the main road to Shere, and followed the downs.

There was silence between them. The tension was so acute that time became relative. They might have been walking for an hour or for ten seconds when they emerged from the shadow of a grove of beech trees and on a bluff of the chalk hills saw those lights shining. Mrs. Hyde paused, her hand on her companion's arm.

"Windows."

Professor Cragg looked at the lights.

"I'll go on—alone."

But she would not hear of it."

"No. I don't think I could bear to be left alone here."

"I—understand. We had better not speak."

She nodded.

The track forked in a hollow space below the beech wood, one path ascending, the other descending. Professor Cragg chose the upper path, but on the edge of the plateau a stout fence of netting and barbed wire closed the path. It was Professor Pye's boundary fence erected to keep out hikers and picnic parties, and since Professor Cragg had no wire-cutters and the five-foot fence was unclimbable, they had to retrace their steps and explore the lower path. It brought them out into Professor Pye's private lane, whose rough and flinty surface had been loosened by a spell of dry weather. In fact, Professor Cragg trod on a loose flint, and the stone went rattling down the slope. He stood very still for a moment, inwardly cursing. If the house with the lights could be assumed to be the house of the ogre, then it was more than probable that its ingenious owner had installed some apparatus for the registration and amplifying of sound.

He spoke in a whisper.

"That damned flint may have betrayed us."

But his companion was in no mood for loitering. Hesitation and delay might rupture an overstrained self-control. Professor Cragg saw her face in the moonlight. She pointed upwards, like some pale figure of Fate urging him on. The lane had a narrow grass verge on either side of it, and taking to the grass they pressed up and on. The lane ended in a cindered space outside the gates of the courtyard, and the white gates were closed.

Mrs. Hyde and Professor Cragg stood and looked at each other for a moment. He made a gesture with his right hand. He was telling her to sit down. She shook her head and remained standing, and Professor Cragg, realizing that her courage had to be humoured, sat down on the grass and removed his boots. He left the pistol and the field-glasses at her feet. He advanced on his socked feet to the white gates. Very cautiously he tried the latch. The gates were not locked, and Mrs. Hyde saw him swing one leaf back and disappear.

There was not a sound. In less than a minute she saw him reappear carrying what appeared to be an empty deal box. He moved round the house and along a terrace of grass and weeds under the front windows. She changed her position so as to be able to watch his movements. She saw him place the box under one of the laboratory windows. He unhitched his bag of bombs and lowered it to the ground, and climbing on to the box raised his head with infinite and deliberate caution.

He was looking in at one of the laboratory windows. They were casements, opening outwards, and Professor Cragg raised the casement stay from its iron leg, swung the window back, and put his hands on the sill. She held her breath. She saw the long, gawky figure raise itself and slip through the window. He disappeared.

Silence.

Professor Cragg was prowling like a cat round the laboratory, examining its contents. He came to the laboratory door; it stood ajar. Inch by inch he pulled it open until he could slip through into the corridor. He had pushed up the button of his torch before entering the laboratory, and with the electric torch in his left hand he crept along the corridor. He came to another door which stood ajar. He listened.

A sound of life, a most unmistakable sound, the heavy breathing of someone asleep! Professor Cragg put his hand to that door; so gradual was his pressure that the door hardly seemed to move. Very cautiously he shone his light into the room. The ray rested for a moment on a figure lying on a bed.

Professor Cragg drew back. He stood in the corridor for a moment listening to the sleeper's heavy breathing. There was no break in the rhythm, and Professor Cragg crept step by step back into the laboratory. The bedroom was next to the laboratory, and he had noticed that the window was open and the blind down. He slipped out through the laboratory window, and shifted his box and his bag of bombs along the house. His movements were swift and easy.

He took a bomb from the bag, stood on the box, pushed the blind back with his lighted torch, and gave one glance into the room to make sure. He dropped the torch on the grass, pulled the bomb pin, and lobbing the bomb into the room, crouched down behind the wall. There was a moment's silence, and then—the crash of the explosion. Fragments of broken window glass flew out and fell upon Professor Cragg's head and shoulders.

He bent down and picked up two more bombs, and hurled them one after the other into the room.

A profound silence seemed to surge back like water that had been troubled by an explosion. Mrs. Hyde saw Professor Cragg standing on the box and shining his torch into that room. He gave a leap from the box to clear the broken glass, and came across the grass towards her. His face was very pale, and a stream of blood showed on his forehead.

He spoke.

"There was life—in there. I've effaced it. One had to be ruthless."

She nodded.

He went for his shoes, sat down, put them on, and rejoined her.

"We'll wait five minutes. He may have an understudy. Then—I'll explore."

They waited, motionless, voiceless. Not a sound came from the white house, and with a glance at his companion, Professor Cragg went forward to explore.

"Better stay there. One has to remember—that there may be other devilments—live wires, traps."

She watched him climb in through the same window. The minutes went by in silence, and then she saw a flash of light up above, and heard his voice.

"Eureka!"

She saw him head and shoulders on the tower silhouetted against the moonlit sky.

"There's a damned contraption up here—rather the sort of thing I expected to find. I daren't touch it. It is better that nobody should touch it. I'm coming down."

He rejoined her on the moonlit hill-side, and his face was grim.

"Genius gone mad. In one's imaginative moments one has postulated the case of some anti-social intelligence making war on humanity. My God, but what a war! We little fellows who dabble in mysteries—will have to be watched—in the future."

She looked up at the tower.

"So—your theory was sound."

"Yes, even a super-scientist is human. He had to sleep. Sleep saved us. Well, let's spread the news and prepare the funeral."

"Funeral?"

"Yes, of Professor Pye and his infernal creation."

They made their way along the moonlit hill-side to Newlands Corner. The silence was still profound, but it had lost its ghastly menace. They talked, and the sound of their voices seemed to fill the silence with a vibration of life reborn. The dead were there, but their destroyer was dead with them. The moonlight seemed to play more mysterious in the branches of the old yews and beeches.

Standing beside the motionless plane, Professor Cragg pulled out his watch.

"Another hour—and the dawn will be here. I should like to fly over that place."

She nodded.

And then he glanced at the spread wings of her machine.

"I rather think that this plane of yours ought to be preserved—say—in St. Paul's Cathedral, or a bronze model of it set up on these downs."

She smiled faintly.

"I think I'd rather have some sandwiches and hot coffee. They are in the cockpit. Of course—I never knew—whether—we should need them. I'll fetch the Thermos."

XIX

Mrs. Hector Hyde's plane took off as the sun cleared the horizon, and with the level rays making the machine glow like some golden dragon-fly, it climbed and, gaining height, it made a left-hand turn over the downs. Professor Cragg was leaning over the side and observing the white house below. He could see the white parapet of the tower like a marble plinth surrounding a grave.

He thought: "Yes, better to take no chances. I shall suggest that they drop bombs on that hill-side until nothing is left of Professor Pye and his machine and his discovery. The world is not yet ripe for so much knowledge."

Mrs. Hyde headed south. They saw the shimmer of the sea and then the outline of the French coast. She laid her course for Paris, and at Le Bourget men were watching the sky, and when they saw that aeroplane coming out of the north, an indescribable excitement infected the aerodrome. Those two adventurous souls had dared the death zone and had survived.

When the plane bumped along the landing ground and came to rest a crowd rushed towards it—politicians, diplomats, savants, pilots, aerodrome staff. What had happened? What news did they bring?

Professor Cragg, one leg hanging over the side of the plane's body, waved his airman's helmet.

"We found one live man in Surrey, and he's dead. Satan was sleeping, and we bombed him."

The crowd went mad. Almost, it seemed ready to carry the plane and its crew in triumph round the aerodrome. It shouted and cheered and behaved quite foolishly, only to realize that Mrs. Hyde was still sitting in the pilot's seat, and Professor Cragg standing up as though to address them.

Professor Cragg held up a hand, and there was gradual silence.

"Gentlemen, we are going back. A little breakfast and then—the final ceremony. I want a dozen bombing machines. We will show them their target."

Telephones and wireless stations became busy. Signor Mussolini, who had just arrived from Rome, was one of the elect few who were permitted to go as passengers. The squadron of huge machines roared northwards led by Mrs. Hyde's plane. It was Professor Cragg who dropped the pilot bomb on the white building above the Shere valley. Mrs. Hyde swung her plane clear for the big fellows to come into action. Plane after plane flew low over the house of Professor Pye. The hill-top seemed to spout flame and smoke and debris. In a little while the work was finished. That which had been a building was a crater-field over which little tattered flames flickered. Even the grass and the trees were alight. Professor Pye and his atomic gun—and his notebooks full of cypher—were ashes and particles of shattered metal.

CREATED HE THEM

Alice Eleanor Jones

Alice Eleanor Jones (1916–1981), described as a "scholar-turned-housewife" when this story first appeared in 1955, wrote a handful of science-fiction stories before turning to the more lucrative slick magazines, whereby science fiction lost a potentially huge talent. She had been a teacher at the time she married fellow teacher Homer Nearing, Jr. in 1942. He also sold a series of science-fiction stories in the early 1950s, collected as The Sinister Researches of C.P. Ransom *(1954), and I like to think she contributed ideas for those. Jones continued writing well into the 1960s. With this story we enter a post-nuclear world to consider how the survivors cope.*

ANN CROTHERS LOOKED AT THE CLOCK AND FROWNED AND turned the fire lower under the bacon. She had already poured his coffee; he liked it cooled to a certain degree; but if he did not get up soon it would be too cool and the bacon too crisp and he would be angry and sulk the rest of the day. She had better call him.

She walked to the foot of the stairs, a blond woman nearing thirty, big but not fat, and rather plain, with a tired sad face. She called, "Henry! Are you up?" She had calculated to a decibel how loud her voice must be. If it were too soft he did not hear and maintained that she had not called him, and was angry later; if it were too loud he was angry immediately and stayed in bed longer, to punish her, and then he grew angrier because breakfast was spoiled.

"All *right*! Pipe down, can't you?"

She listened a minute. She thought it was a normal response, but perhaps her voice had been a shade too loud. No, he was getting up. She heard the thump of his feet on the floor. She went back to the kitchen and took out his orange juice and his prunes out of the icebox, and got out his bread but did not begin to toast it yet, and opened a glass of jelly.

She frowned. Grape. He did not like grape, but the co-op had been out of apple, and she had been lucky to get anything. He would not be pleased.

She sat down briefly at the table to wait for him and glanced at the clock. Ten-five. Wearily, she leaned forward and rested her forehead on the back of her hand. She was not feeling well this morning and had eaten no breakfast. She was almost sure she was pregnant again.

She thought of the children. There were only two at home, and they had been bathed and fed long ago and put down in the basement playpen so that the noise they made would not disturb their father. She would have time for a quick look at them before Henry came down. And the house was chilly; she would have to look at the heater.

They were playing quietly with the rag doll she had made, and the battered rubber ball. Lennie, who was two and a half, was far too big for a playpen, but he was a good child, considerate, and allowed himself to be put there for short periods and did not climb out. He seemed to feel a responsibility for his brother. Robbie was fourteen months old and a small terror, but he loved Lennie, and even, Ann thought, tried to mind him.

As Ann poked her head over the bannister, both children turned and gave her radiant smiles. Lennie said, "Hi, Mommy," and Robbie said experimentally, "Ma?"

She went down quickly and gave each of them a hug and said, "You're good boys. You can come upstairs and play soon." She felt their hands. The basement was damp, but the small mended sweaters were warm enough.

She looked at the feeble fire and rattled the grate hopefully and put on more coal. There was plenty of coal in the bin, but it was inferior grade, filled with slate, and did not burn well. It was not an efficient heater, either. It was old, secondhand, but they had been lucky to get it. The useless oil heater stood in the corner.

The children chuckled at the fire, and Robbie reached out his hands toward it. Lennie said gravely, "No, no, bad."

Ann heard Henry coming downstairs, and she raced up the cellar steps and beat him to the kitchen by two seconds. When he came in she was draining the bacon. She put a slice of bread on the long fork and began to toast it over the gas flame. The gas, at least, was fairly dependable, and the water. The electricity was not working again. It seemed such a long time since the electricity had always worked. Well, it was a long time. Years.

Henry sat down at the table and looked peevishly at his orange juice. He was not a tall man, not quite so tall as his wife, and he walked and sat tall, making the most of every inch. He was inclined to be chubby, and he had a roll of fat under his chin and at the back of his neck, and a little bulge at the waist. His face might have been handsome, but the expression spoiled it—discontented, bad-tempered. He said, "You didn't strain the orange juice."

"Yes, I strained it." She was intent on the toast.

He drank the orange juice without enjoyment and said, "I have a touch of liver this morning. Can't think what it could be." His face brightened. "I told you that sauce was too greasy. That was it."

She did not answer. She brought over his plate with the bacon on it and the toast, nicely browned, and put margarine on the toast for him.

He was eating the prunes. He stopped and looked at the bacon. "No eggs?"

"They were all out."

His face flushed a little. "Then why'd you cook bacon? You know I can't eat bacon without eggs." He was working himself up into a passion. "If I weren't such an easygoing man—! And the prunes are hard—you didn't cook them long enough—and the coffee's cold, and the toast's burnt, and where's the apple jelly?"

They didn't have any.

He laughed scornfully. "I bet they didn't. I bet you fooled around the house and didn't even get there till everything was gone." He flung down his fork. "This garbage!—why should you care, you don't have to eat it!"

She looked at him. "Shall I make you something else?"

He laughed again. "You'd ruin it. Never mind." He slammed out of the kitchen and went upstairs to sulk in the bathroom for an hour.

Ann sat down at the table. All that bacon, and it was hard to get. Well, the children would like it. She ought to clear the table and wash the dishes, but she sat still and took out a cigarette. She ought to save it, her ration was only three a day, but she lit it.

The children were getting a little noisier. Perhaps she could take them out for a while, till Henry went to work. It was cold but clear; she could bundle them up.

The cigarette was making her lightheaded, and she stubbed it out and put the butt in the box she kept over the sink. She said softly, "I hate him. I wish he would die."

She dressed the children—their snowsuits were faded and patched from much use, but they were clean and warm—and put them in the battered carriage, looping her old string shopping bag over the handle, and took them out. They were delighted with themselves and with her. They loved the outdoors. Robbie bounced and drooled and made noises, and Lennie sat quiet, his little face smiling and content.

Ann wheeled them slowly down the walk, detouring around the broken places. It was a fine day, crisp, much too cold for September, but the seasons were not entirely reliable any more. There were no other baby carriages out; there were no children at all; the street was very quiet. There were no cars. Only the highest officials had cars, and no high officials lived in this neighbourhood.

The children were enchanted by the street. Shabby as it was, with the broken houses as neatly mended as they could be, and the broken paving that the patches never caught up with, it was beautiful to them. Lennie said, "Hi, Mommy," and Robbie bounced.

The women were beginning to come, as they always came, timidly out of the drab houses, to look at the children, and Ann walked straighter and tried not to smile. It was not kind to smile, but sometimes she could not help it. Suddenly she was not tired any more, and her clothes were not shabby, and her face was not plain.

The first woman said, "Please stop a minute," and Ann stopped, and the women gathered around the carriage silently and looked. Their faces were hungry and seeking, and a few had tears in their eyes.

The first woman asked, "Do they stay well?"

Ann said, "Pretty well. They both had colds last week," and murmurs of commiseration went around the circle.

Another woman said, "I noticed you didn't come out, and I wondered. I almost knocked at your door to enquire, but then—" She stopped and blushed violently, and the others considerately looked away from her, ignoring the blunder. One did not call on one's neighbours; one lived to oneself.

The first woman said wistfully, "If I could hold them—either of them—I have dates; my cousin sent them all the way from California."

Ann blushed, too. She disliked this part of it very much, but things were so hard to get now, and Henry was difficult about what he liked to eat, though he denied that. He would say, "I'd eat anything, if you could only learn to cook it right, but you can't." Henry liked dates. Ann said, "Well…"

Another woman said eagerly, "I have eggs. I could spare you three." One for each of the boys and one for Henry.

"Oranges—for the children."

"And I have butter—imagine, butter!"

"Sugar—all children like sugar. Best grade—no sand in it."

"And I have tea." Henry does not like tea. But you shall hold the children anyway.

Somebody said, "Cigarettes," and somebody else whispered, "I even have *sleeping pills!*"

The children were passed around and fondled and caressed. Robbie enjoyed it and flirted with everybody, under his long eyelashes, but Lennie regarded the entire transaction with distaste.

When the children began to grow restless, Ann put them back into the carriage and walked on. Her shopping bag was full.

The women went slowly back into their houses, all but one, a stranger. She must have moved into the neighbourhood recently, perhaps from one of the spreading waste places. They were coming in, the people, as if they had been called, moving in closer, a little closer every year.

The woman was tall and older than Ann, with a worn plain face. She kept pace with the carriage and looked at the children and said, "Forgive me, I know it is bad form, but are they—do you have more?"

Ann said proudly, "I have had seven."

The woman looked at her and whispered, "Seven! And were they all—surely they were not *all*—"

Ann said more proudly still, "All. Every one."

The woman looked as if she might cry and said, "But seven! And the rest, are they—"

Ann's face clouded. "Yes, at the Centre. One of my boys and all my girls. When Lennie goes, Robbie will miss him. Lennie missed Kate so, until he forgot her."

The woman said in a broken voice, "I had three, and none of them was—*none!*" She thrust something into Ann's shopping bag and said, "For the children," and walked quickly away.

Ann looked, and it was a Hershey bar. The co-op had not had chocolate for over two years. Neither of the boys had ever tasted it.

She brought the children home after a while and gave them their lunch—Henry's bacon crumbled into two scrambled eggs, and bread and butter and milk. She had been lucky at the co-op yesterday; they had had milk. She made herself a cup of coffee, feeling extravagant, and ate a piece of toast, and smoked the butt of this morning's cigarette.

For dessert she gave them each an orange; the rest she saved for Henry. She got out the Hershey bar and gave them all of it; Henry should not have their chocolate! The Hershey bar was hard and pale, as stale chocolate gets, and she had to make sawing motions with the knife to divide it evenly. The boys were enchanted. Robbie chewed his half and swallowed it quickly, but Lennie sucked blissfully and made it last, and then took pity on his brother, and let Robbie suck, too. Ann did not interfere. Germs, little hearts, are the least of what I fear for you.

While the children took their naps, she straightened the house a little and tinkered with the heater and cleaned all the kerosene lamps. She had time to take a bath, and enjoyed it, though the laundry soap she had to use was harsh against her skin. She even washed her hair, pretty hair, long and fine, and put on one of the few dresses that was not mended.

The children slept longer than usual. The fresh air had done them good. Just at dusk the electric lights came on for the first time in three days, and she woke them up to see them—they loved the electric lights. She gave them each a piece of bread and butter and took them with her to the basement and put them in the playpen. She was able to run a full load of clothes through the old washing machine before the current went off again. The children loved the washing machine and watched it, fascinated by the whirling clothes in the little window.

Afterward she took them upstairs again and tried to use the vacuum cleaner, but the machine was old and balky and by the time she had coaxed it to work the current was gone.

She gave the children their supper and played with them awhile and put them to bed. Henry was still at the laboratory. He left late in the morning, but sometimes he had to stay late at night. The children were asleep before he came home, and Ann was glad. Sometimes they got on his nerves and he swore at them.

She turned the oven low to keep dinner hot and went into the living room. She sat beside the lamp and mended Robbie's shirt and Lennie's overalls. She turned on the battery radio to the one station that was broadcasting these days, the one at the Centre. The news report was the usual thing. The Director was in good health and bearing the burden of his duties with fortitude. Conditions throughout the country were normal. Crops had not been quite so good as hoped, but there was no cause for alarm. Quotas in light and heavy industry were good—Ann smiled wryly—but could be improved if every worker did his duty. Road repairs were picking up—Ann wondered when they would get around to the street again—and electrical service was normal, except for a few scattered areas where there might be small temporary difficulties. The lamp had begun to smoke again, and Ann turned it lower. The stock market had closed irregular, with rails down an average of two points and stocks off three.

And now—the newscaster's voice grew solemn—there was news of grave import. The Director had asked him to talk seriously to all citizens about the dangers of rumourmongering. Did they not realize what harm could be done by it? For example, the rumour that the Western Reservoir was contaminated. That was entirely false, of course, and the malicious and irresponsible persons who had started it would be severely dealt with.

The wastelands were not spreading, either. Some other malicious and irresponsible persons had started that rumour, and would be dealt with. The wastelands were under control. They were *not* spreading, repeat, *not*. Certain areas were being evacuated, it was true, but the measure was only temporary.

Calling them in, are you, calling them in!

The weather was normal. The seasons were definitely not changing, and here were the statistics to prove it. In 1961... and in '62... and that was *before*, so you see...

The newscaster's voice changed, growing less grave. And now for news of the children. Ann put down her mending and listened, not breathing. They always closed with news of the children, and it was always reassuring. If any child were ever unhappy, or were taken ill, or died, nobody knew it. One was never told anything, and of course one never saw the children again. It would upset them, one quite understood that.

The children, the newscaster said, were all well and happy. They had good beds and warm clothes and the best food and plenty of it. They even had cod-liver oil twice a week whether they needed it or not. They had toys and games, carefully supervised according to their age groups, and they were being educated by the best teachers. The children were all well and happy, repeat, *well and happy*. Ann hoped it was true.

They played the national anthem and went off the air, and just then Henry came in. He looked pale and tired—he did work hard—and his greeting was, "I suppose dinner's spoiled."

She looked up. "No, I don't think so."

She served it and they ate silently except for Henry's complaints about the food and his liver. He looked at the dates and said, "They're small. You let them stick you with anything," but she thought he enjoyed them because he ate them all.

Afterward he grew almost mellow. He lit a cigarette and told her about his day, while she washed the dishes. Henry's job at the laboratory was a responsible one, and Ann was sure he did it well. Henry was not stupid. But Henry could not get along with anybody. He said that he himself was very easy to get along with, but they were all against him. Today he had had a dispute with one of his superiors and reported that he had told the old ———— where to go.

He said, with gloomy relish, "They'll probably fire me, and we'll all be out in the street. Then you'll find out what it's like to live on Subsistence. You won't be able to throw my money around the way you do now."

Ann rinsed out the dish towel and hung it over the rack to dry. She said, "They won't fire you. They never do."

He laughed. "I'm good and they know it. I do twice as much work as anybody else."

Ann thought that was probably true. She turned away from the sink and said, "Henry, I think I'm pregnant."

He looked at her and frowned. "Are you sure?"

I said I *think*. But I'm practically sure.

He said, "Oh, God, now you'll be sick all the time, and there's no living with you when you're sick."

Ann sat down at the table and lit a cigarette. "Maybe I won't be sick."

He said darkly, "You always are. Sweet prospect!"

Ann said, "We'll get another bonus, Henry."

He brightened a little. "Say, we will, at that. I'll buy some more stock."

Ann said, "Henry, we need so many things—"

He was immediately angry. "I said I'll buy stock! Somebody in this house has to think of the future. We can't all hide our heads in the sand and hope for the best."

She stood up, trembling. It was not a new argument. "What future? Our children—children like ours are taken away from us when they're three years old and given to the state to rear. When we're old the state will take care of us. Nobody lives any more, except—but nobody starves. And that stock—it all goes down. Don't talk to me about the future, Henry Crothers! I want my future now."

He laughed unpleasantly. "What do you want? A car?"

"I want a new washing machine and a vacuum cleaner, when the quotas come—the electricity isn't so bad. I want a new chair for the living room. I want to fix up the boy's room, paint, and—"

He said brutally, "They're too little to notice. By the time they get old enough—"

She sat down again, sobbing a little. Her cigarette burned forgotten in the ashtray, and Henry thriftily stubbed it out. She said, "I know, the Centre takes them. The Centre takes children like ours."

"And the Centre's good to them. They give them more than we could. Don't you go talking against the Centre." Though a malcontent in his personal life, Henry was a staunch government man.

Ann said, "I'm not, Henry, I'm—"

He said disgustedly, "Being a woman again. Tears! Oh, God, why do women always turn them on?"

She made herself stop crying. Anger was beginning to rise in her, and that helped a good deal. "I didn't mean to start an argument.

I was just telling you what we need. We do need things, Henry. Clothes—"

He looked at her. "You mean for you? Clothes would do you a lot of good, wouldn't they?"

She was stung. "I don't mean maternity clothes. I won't be needing them for—"

He laughed. "I don't mean maternity clothes either. Have you looked at yourself in a mirror lately? God, you're a big horse! I always liked little women."

She said tightly, "And I always liked tall men."

He half rose, and she thought he was going to hit her. She sat still, trembling with a fierce exhilaration, her eyes bright, colour in her cheeks, a little smile on her mouth. She said softly, "I'll hit you back, I'm bigger than you are. I'll kill you!"

Suddenly Henry sat down and began to laugh. When he laughed he was quite handsome. He said in a deep chuckling voice, "You're almost pretty when you get mad enough. Your hair's pretty tonight, you must have washed it." His eyes were beginning to shine, and he reached across the table and put his hand on hers. "Ann... old girl..."

She drew her hand away. "I'm tired. I'm going to bed."

He said good-humoredly, "Sure. I'll be right up."

She looked at him. "I said I'm tired."

"And I said I'd be right up."

If I had something in my hands I'd kill you. "I don't want to."

He scowled, and his mouth grew petulant again, and he was no longer handsome. "But *I* want to."

She stood up. All at once she felt as tired as she had told Henry she was, as tired as she had been for ten years.

I cannot kill you, Henry, or myself. I cannot even wish us dead. In this desolate, dying, bombed-out world, with its creeping wastelands and its freakish seasons, with its limping economy and its arrogant Centre in the country that takes our children—children like ours; the others it destroys—we have to live, and we have to live together.

Because by some twist of providence, or radiation, or genes, we are among the tiny percentage of the people in this world who can have normal children. We hate each other, but we breed true.

She said, "Come up, Henry." I can take a sleeping pill afterward.

Come up, Henry, we have to live. Till we are all called in, or our children, or our children's children. Till there is nowhere else to go.

THERE WILL COME SOFT RAINS

Ray Bradbury

Ray Bradbury (1920–2012) was one of the greats of science fiction but though his roots were firmly set in the pulp magazines of the 1930s and 1940s his writing skills took him way beyond the confines of the science-fiction magazines to become one of the best known and most widely published authors in the field. He was the true poet of the spaceways. He incorporated very little hard science into his stories, preferring instead to capture the attitudes and emotions of people trying to survive in ever demanding societies. His best known work is The Martian Chronicles *(1950), which includes the following story, but closely rivalling it is* Fahrenheit 451 *(1953), a product of the McCarthy era in American politics, reflecting the fear of destroying knowledge and the truth.*

What is remarkable about the following story is that Bradbury manages to evoke an explosion of human emotion without there being a single human around.

I N THE LIVING ROOM THE VOICE-CLOCK SANG, *TICK-TOCK,*
seven o'clock, time to get up, time to get up, seven o'clock! as if it were
afraid that nobody would. The morning house lay empty. The clock
ticked on, repeating and repeating its sounds into the emptiness.
Seven-nine, breakfast time, seven-nine!

In the kitchen the breakfast stove gave a hissing sigh and ejected
from its warm interior eight pieces of perfectly browned toast,
eight eggs sunnyside up, sixteen slices of bacon, two coffees, and
two cool glasses of milk.

"Today is August 4, 2026," said a second voice from the kitchen
ceiling, "in the city of Allendale, California." It repeated the date
three times for memory's sake. "Today is Mr. Featherstone's birth-
day. Today is the anniversary of Tilita's marriage. Insurance is pay-
able, as are the water, gas, and light bills."

Somewhere in the walls, relays clicked, memory tapes glided
under electric eyes.

Eight-one, tick-tock, eight-one o'clock, off to school, off to work, run,
run, eight-one! But no doors slammed, no carpets took the soft tread
of rubber heels. It was raining outside. The weather box on the
front door sang quietly: "Rain, rain, go away; rubbers, raincoats
for today..." And the rain tapped on the empty house, echoing.

Outside, the garage chimed and lifted its door to reveal the waiting car. After a long wait the door swung down again.

At eight-thirty the eggs were shrivelled and the toast was like
stone. An aluminium wedge scraped them into the sink, where hot
water whirled them down a metal throat which digested and flushed

them away to the distant sea. The dirty dishes were dropped into a hot washer and emerged twinkling dry.

Nine-fifteen, sang the clock, *time to clean*.

Out of warrens in the wall, tiny robot mice darted. The rooms were acrawl with the small cleaning animals, all rubber and metal. They thudded against chairs, whirling their moustached runners, kneading the rug nap, sucking gently at hidden dust. Then, like mysterious invaders, they popped into their burrows. Their pink electric eyes faded. The house was clean.

Ten o'clock. The sun came out from behind the rain. The house stood alone in a city of rubble and ashes. This was the one house left standing. At night the ruined city gave off a radioactive glow which could be seen for miles.

Ten-fifteen. The garden sprinklers whirled up in golden founts, filling the soft morning air with scatterings of brightness. The water pelted windowpanes, running down the charred west side where the house had been burned evenly free of its white paint. The entire west face of the house was black, save for five places. Here the silhouette in paint of a man mowing a lawn. Here, as in a photograph, a woman bent to pick flowers. Still farther over, their images burned on wood in one titanic instant, a small boy, hands flung into the air; higher up, the image of a thrown ball, and opposite him a girl, hands raised to catch a ball which never came down.

The five spots of paint—the man, the woman, the children, the ball—remained. The rest was a thin charcoaled layer.

The gentle sprinkler rain filled the garden with falling light.

Until this day, how well the house had kept its peace. How carefully it had inquired, "Who goes there? What's the password?" and, getting no answer from lonely foxes and whining cats, it had shut up its windows and drawn shades in an old-maidenly preoccupation with self-protection which bordered on a mechanical paranoia.

It quivered at each sound, the house did. If a sparrow brushed a window, the shade snapped up. The bird, startled, flew off! No, not even a bird must touch the house!

The house was an altar with ten thousand attendants, big, small, servicing, attending, in choirs. But the gods had gone away, and the ritual of the religion continued senselessly, uselessly.

Twelve noon.

A dog whined, shivering, on the front porch.

The front door recognized the dog voice and opened. The dog, once huge and fleshy, but now gone to bone and covered with sores, moved in and through the house, tracking mud. Behind it whirred angry mice, angry at having to pick up mud, angry at inconvenience.

For not a leaf fragment blew under the door but what the wall panels flipped open and the copper scrap rats flashed swiftly out. The offending dust, hair, or paper, seized in miniature steel jaws, was raced back to the burrows. There, down tubes which fed into the cellar, it was dropped into the sighing vent of an incinerator which sat like evil Baal in a dark corner.

The dog ran upstairs, hysterically yelping to each door, at last realizing, as the house realized, that only silence was here.

It sniffed the air and scratched the kitchen door. Behind the door, the stove was making pancakes which filled the house with a rich baked odour and the scent of maple syrup.

The dog frothed at the mouth, lying at the door, sniffing, its eyes turned to fire. It ran wildly in circles, biting at its tail, spun in a frenzy, and died. It lay in the parlour for an hour.

Two o'clock, sang a voice.

Delicately sensing decay at last, the regiments of mice hummed out as softly as brown-grey leaves in an electrical wind.

Two-fifteen.

The dog was gone.

In the cellar, the incinerator glowed suddenly and a whirl of sparks leaped up the chimney.

Two thirty-five.

Bridge tables sprouted from patio walls. Playing cards fluttered onto pads in a shower of pips. Martinis manifested on an oaken bench with egg-salad sandwiches. Music played.

But the tables were silent and the cards untouched.

At four o'clock the tables folded like great butterflies back through the panelled walls.

Four-thirty.

The nursery walls glowed.

Animals took shape: yellow giraffes, blue lions, pink antelopes, lilac panthers cavorting in crystal substance. The walls were glass. They looked out upon colour and fantasy. Hidden films clocked through well-oiled sprockets, and the walls lived. The nursery floor was woven to resemble a crisp, cereal meadow. Over this ran aluminium roaches and iron crickets, and in the hot still air butterflies of delicate red tissue wavered among the sharp aroma of animal spoors! There was the sound like a great matted yellow hive of bees within a dark bellows, the lazy bumble of a purring lion. And there was the patter of okapi feet and the murmur of a fresh jungle rain, like other hoofs, falling upon the summer-starched grass. Now the walls dissolved into distances of parched weed, mile on mile, and warm endless sky. The animals drew away into thorn brakes and water holes.

It was the children's hour.

★

Five o'clock. The bath filled with clear hot water.

Six, seven, eight o'clock. The dinner dishes manipulated like magic tricks, and in the study a *click*. In the metal stand opposite the hearth where a fire now blazed up warmly, a cigar popped out, half an inch of soft grey ash on it, smoking, waiting.

Nine o'clock. The beds warmed their hidden circuits, for nights were cool here.

Nine-five. A voice spoke from the study ceiling:

"Mrs. McClellan, which poem would you like this evening?"

The house was silent.

The voice said at last, "Since you express no preference, I shall select a poem at random." Quiet music rose to back the voice. "Sara Teasdale. As I recall, your favourite…

> *"There will come soft rains and the smell of the ground,*
> *And swallows circling with their shimmering sound;*
>
> *And frogs in the pools singing at night,*
> *And wild plum trees in tremulous white;*
>
> *Robins will wear their feathery fire,*
> *Whistling their whims on a low fence-wire;*
>
> *And not one will know of the war, not one*
> *Will care at last when it is done.*
>
> *Not one would mind, neither bird nor tree,*
> *If mankind perished utterly;*
>
> *And Spring herself, when she woke at dawn*
> *Would scarcely know that we were gone."*

The fire burned on the stone hearth and the cigar fell away into a mound of quiet ash on its tray. The empty chairs faced each other between the silent walls, and the music played.

At ten o'clock the house began to die.

The wind blew. A falling tree bough crashed through the kitchen window. Cleaning solvent, bottled, shattered over the stove. The room was ablaze in an instant!

"Fire!" screamed a voice. The house lights flashed, water pumps shot water from the ceilings. But the solvent spread on the linoleum, licking, eating, under the kitchen door, while the voices took it up in chorus: "Fire, fire, fire!"

The house tried to save itself. Doors sprang tightly shut, but the windows were broken by the heat and the wind blew and sucked upon the fire.

The house gave ground as the fire in ten billion angry sparks moved with flaming ease from room to room and then up the stairs. While scurrying water rats squeaked from the walls, pistoled their water, and ran for more. And the wall sprays let down showers of mechanical rain.

But too late. Somewhere, sighing, a pump shrugged to a stop. The quenching rain ceased. The reserve water supply which had filled baths and washed dishes for many quiet days was gone.

The fire crackled up the stairs. It fed upon Picassos and Matisses in the upper halls, like delicacies, baking off the oily flesh, tenderly crisping the canvases into black shavings.

Now the fire lay in beds, stood in windows, changed the colours of drapes!

And then, reinforcements.

From attic trapdoors, blind robot faces peered down with faucet mouths gushing green chemical.

The fire backed off, as even an elephant must at the sight of a dead snake. Now there were twenty snakes whipping over the floor, killing the fire with a clear cold venom of green froth.

But the fire was clever. It had sent flame outside the house, up through the attic to the pumps there. An explosion! The attic brain which directed the pumps was shattered into bronze shrapnel on the beams.

The fire rushed back into every closet and felt of the clothes hung there.

The house shuddered, oak bone on bone, its bared skeleton cringing from the heat, its wire, its nerves revealed as if a surgeon had torn the skin off to let the red veins and capillaries quiver in the scalded air. Help, help! Fire! Run, run! Heat snapped mirrors like the first brittle winter ice. And the voices wailed Fire, fire, run, run, like a tragic nursery rhyme, a dozen voices, high, low, like children dying in a forest, alone, alone. And the voices fading as the wires popped their sheathings like hot chestnuts. One, two, three, four, five voices died.

In the nursery the jungle burned. Blue lions roared, purple giraffes bounded off. The panthers ran in circles, changing colour, and ten million animals, running before the fire, vanished off toward a distant steaming river...

Ten more voices died. In the last instant under the fire avalanche, other choruses, oblivious, could be heard announcing the time, playing music, cutting the lawn by remote-control mower, or setting an umbrella frantically out and in, the slamming and opening front door, a thousand things happening, like a clock shop when each clock strikes the hour insanely before or after the other, a scene of maniac confusion, yet unity; singing, screaming, a few last cleaning mice darting bravely out to carry the horrid ashes away! And one voice, with sublime disregard for the situation, read poetry aloud in the fiery study, until all the film spools burned, until all the wires withered and the circuits cracked.

The fire burst the house and let it slam flat down, puffing out skirts of spark and smoke.

In the kitchen, an instant before the rain of fire and timber, the stove could be seen making breakfasts at a psychopathic rate, ten dozen eggs, six loaves of toast, twenty dozen bacon strips, which, eaten by fire, started the stove working again, hysterically hissing!

The crash. The attic smashing into kitchen and parlour. The parlour into cellar, cellar into sub-cellar. Deep freeze, armchair, film tapes, circuits, beds, and all like skeletons thrown in a cluttered mound deep under.

Smoke and silence. A great quantity of smoke.

Dawn showed faintly in the east. Among the ruins, one wall stood alone. Within the wall, a last voice said, over and over again and again, even as the sun rose to shine upon the heaped rubble and steam:

"Today is August 5, 2026, today is August 5, 2026, today is…"

COPYRIGHT ACKNOWLEDGEMENTS
AND STORY SOURCES

All the stories in this anthology are in the public domain unless otherwise noted. Every effort has been made to trace copyright holders and the publisher apologizes for any errors or omissions and would be pleased to be notified of any corrections to be incorporated in reprints or future editions. The following gives the first publication details for each story and the sources used. They are listed in alphabetical order of author.

"Within an Ace of the End of the World" by Robert Barr, first published in *The Windsor Magazine*, December 1900.

"There Will Come Soft Rains" by Ray Bradbury, first published in *Collier's Weekly*, 6 May 1950. Reprinted by permission of the author's estate.

"Two by Two" by John Brunner, first published in *New Worlds*, May 1956 and collected in *No Future in It* (1965) as "The Windows of Heaven". Reprinted by permission of the author's estate.

"The Madness of Professor Pye" by Warwick Deeping first published in *The Passing Show*, 14 April to 5 May, 1934 and collected in *Two in a Train* (1935). Reprinted by permission of the author's estate.

"London's Danger" by C.J. Cutcliffe Hyne, first published in *Pearson's Magazine*, February 1896.

"Created He Them" by Alice Eleanor Jones, first published in *The Magazine of Fantasy and Science Fiction*, June 1955. Reprinted by permission of the author's estate.

"The Last American" by John Ames Mitchell first published in 1889 by
    F.A. Stokes, New York.

"The End of the World" by Simon Newcomb first published in *McClure's
    Magazine*, May 1903 and in *The London Magazine*, September 1905.

"Days of Darkness" by Owen Oliver, first published in *The London
    Magazine*, April 1927.

"Finis" by Frank Lillie Pollock, first published in *The Argosy*, June 1906.

"The Freezing of London" by Herbert C. Ridout, first published in *The
    Red Magazine*, March 1909.

"The End of the World" by Helen Sutherland first published in *Truth*,
    26 November 1930.

'It's a hazardous experiment,' they all said, 'putting in new and untried machinery.'

Caution – beware the menace of the machine: a man is murdered by an automaton built for playing chess; a computer system designed to arbitrate justice develops a taste for iron-fisted, fatal rulings; an AI wreaks havoc on society after removing all censorship from an early form of the internet.

Assembled with pieces by SF giants such as Isaac Asimov and Brian W Aldiss as well as the less familiar but no less influential input of earlier science fiction pioneers, this new collection of classic tales contains telling lessons for humankind's gradual march towards life alongside the thinking machine.

The fact that humanity is not alone in the universe has long preoccupied our thoughts.

In this compelling new collection of short stories from SF's classic age our visions of 'other' are shown in a myriad of forms – beings from other worlds, corrupted lifeforms from our own planet and entities from unimaginable dimensions.

Amongst these tales, the humble ant becomes humanity's greatest foe, a sailor awakes in a hellish landscape terrified by a monstrous creature from the deep, an extra-terrestrial apocalypse devastates our world but also brings us together, and our race becomes the unwitting agent of another species' survival. Be prepared to face your greatest fears and relinquish your hold on reality as you confront the menace of the monster.

A CLASSIC NOVEL BY
CHARLES ERIC MAINE

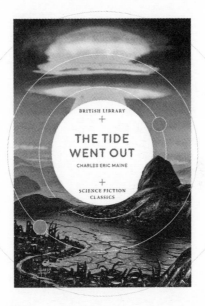

When London journalist Philip Wade learns that his article on nuclear weapons testing has been censored by the British government, his interest turns to the attempted cover-up. Wade's investigation leads to a mysterious job offer in a newly-formed government department, and here the truth of the oncoming catastrophe is revealed. The country is rife with uncertainty and distrust – then the water levels start to drop.

Originally published in 1958, this gripping apocalyptic novel poses pertinent questions about censorship and the potential for violence in the face of dwindling resources. How much of the truth is too much? Who can you *really* trust? And what happens when the water runs out?